UNBELIEVERS

Trevor L. Smith

Usherance, Sacramento, CA
www.usherance.com
First Edition: December 2012
ISBN 978-0-9888383-0-7
Editor: Frances Portillo
Cover Design: Trevor L. Smith

Like us on Facebook:
www.facebook.com/usherance

Follow Usherance on Twitter
www.twitter.com/usherance

Follow Trevor L. Smith on Twitter:
www.twitter.com/iTrevorSmith

Sacramento, CA

This book, from now to eternity, is dedicated
to the little angels and guardians of
Sandy Hook Elementary School in Newtown, Connecticut.
My heroes, my heart. 12/14/12

~

*"There is no greater love than to lay down
one's life for one's friends."*
John 15:13

*"The greatest darkness will always bow before
even the faintest of lights."*
Trevor L. Smith

Based on True Future Events

 **Prologue**

"Certainly, the time is coming when people who murder you will think they are serving God." John 16:2

THE sounds of the ocean plays from an archaic battery operated radio held together with electrical tape and strands of purple yarn. The strum of an acoustic guitar accompanied the crashing of waves and it reminded Tage of his past and how beautiful the world was before that day.

What do you remember? Think back to the most surreal and euphoric moments of your life. Who was there? What were you doing?

Did every sense in your body erupt with the pleasures of those moments; memories forever etched and embedded in your psyche, snapshots of life to be withdrawn and viewed to carry you through any valleys of desolation and every ocean of despair.

"Though I walk through the valley of the shadow of death, I will fear no evil," wrote the Psalmist, David.

But there was no going through the valley of the shadow of death any longer. To live there, or die to be more accurate, was now life's reality.

~

The drone of the rickety truck's engine, which transported him and two others, further calmed his restlessness and he drifted into a light sleep. A sleep that allowed his mind to play. Waves smacked against the unbending rocks and the seagulls singing their morning song ushered him into a fleeting moment of comfort, a feeling as elusive as a butterfly evading a determined child. He felt as if he were there; a sense of the day being new with the crisp, damp, morning air on his clean shaven face. His chest expanded as he drew a massive breath and smelled the salt of the ocean.

The emerging sun wrapped him in its tantalizing embrace, and the breeze carrying the plans and dreams whispered by countless who have walked those shores, brushed against him as he took in the surroundings of a life no longer in existence. He instantly became aware that he was so small and yet at the same time special in that place. He had purpose.

Yes, Purpose.

There was life... and it was meant to be lived.

Yes, it was definitely a reflection of something much bigger than him.

Much bigger than anything he thought possible.

Tage was jolted awake when his head banged against the grimy window supporting his worn out body. His eyes fluttered open and he stared briefly out the glass stained with dirt and toxic resin, catching glimpses of the ominous glow of campfires against the backdrop of a charred night sky. The flickering lights brought him a sense of wellbeing and were a reminder of years gone by. His heavy eyelids dipped and rose at half-mast as he scanned the horizon with uninterested floating eyes.

The distant blazes triggered old memories of summer camping trips. Camping used to be a form of recreation in a time when such activities brought families and friends closer together; the pitching of tents that refused to stand erect and fishing in the early mornings and dead of night. It was a wonderful time whether you caught anything or returned empty handed. The stories told of the ones that got away held just as much value as the net with a heavy haul.

He remembered the guitar being played by his father who knew only a few basic chords and even fewer songs. The corner of his mouth broke and began to rise when he thought about him, serving only to tease the smile that wanted to surface but never did.

His father could strum a song a thousand times and each time he'd play it the same, completely wrong. They always had to ask him what he was playing because it never sounded like anything anyone had ever heard before. Nevertheless, they sang, they laughed, and they lived. They roasted marshmallows and cooked S'mores over an open flame, always managing to end up with more collected in the burning embers of the fire pit than in their ravenous mouths.

They danced, all of them, even complete strangers that happened upon their site, drawn in by the festivities like those under the hypnotic spell of a Pied Piper.

The star studded beauty of night tied everything together with sheer perfection.

It was magical. It was as it should be. It was a memory.

The smell of whatever was being cooked in the desolate foothills seeped into the cab of the truck as they traveled. The stench crept past the rags stuffed into the vents. Tage couldn't help but wonder what was on the menu; squirrel, rabbit, possum or human. Most likely it was the latter.

It made no difference to him either way; he had conditioned himself not to care. He wasn't always that way, being brought up in Bogalusa Louisiana, where everyone was considered family, whether you knew them or not... or at least until proven otherwise.

Now, it was just better not to extend the same hospitalities of yesterday.

It wasn't natural for him to feel the way he did. It ate away at the core of his being, which forced him to once again justify his callused position. There was no point in caring, he reasoned, because whoever was eating out there in the valley was dead already; some knew it and no longer wished to prolong the inevitable, others had no idea the suffering that would be visited upon them in their final moments of life.

Campers who annoyingly insisted on surviving became proficient at wiping away all evidence of having been anywhere. They became ghosts, drifters, always on the move in their hollowed vanquished existence. Just as quickly as their fires were lit, they were extinguished, because hunters were always watching with an insatiable thirst for spilled blood.

These hunters were the enforcers of law in their society. Those in times past who were called upon to serve and protect, to right the wrong, those who were the knights in shining armor, the heroes whose sole existence was to rescue the damsel in distress, were now the legalized villains who would burn or skin you alive, collect severed limbs as trophies, or engage in recreation using certain parts of your anatomy to place bets during a friendly card game.

4

It didn't matter what side of the law you were on, everything hinged upon your view of society and your acceptance of one man, Alexander Demetri, "the savior of the world".

If everything did rise and fall on leadership, which was often touted by the educated masses, how great the evil must be that has befallen mankind. Today, a serial killer who had the right world view, even a monster who preyed upon children, would end up with nothing more than community service and a voucher for sixteen weeks of counseling, give or take a few weeks, as punishment for his crimes. Whereas, an elementary school teacher, happily living just above the poverty level because she loves her job; investing countless hours on and off campus teaching reading, writing, and arithmetic, helping to instill character, and working to build a foundation for children to grow and become good productive members of society. If it were found out or even rumored that she had the wrong world view, she would be slowly and publically tortured to death, after first being forced to watch her own family die, due to her influential position as an educator.

Tage's body rhythmically swayed with each dip, as the truck slowly plodded along a deserted road in the middle of nowhere. His eyes grew increasingly heavy. Several minutes had passed since he first spotted the fires outside the truck's window and he was certain that those gathering around the outlying bonfires would not live to see another day.

Why care? Soon they will be as dead as whatever they're cooking, roasting over an open fire like a chestnut during the holiday season.

The radio he cradled loosely in his hands fell to his feet as he surrendered to a deep haunting sleep, and without delay, memories buried in shallow graves immediately seized their opportunity to surface. Birds perched in a flourish of green trees whisked themselves away, frightened by the shriek of a civil defense siren. Images began to assault his mind and senses as he drifted deeper into unrest. The sound of deafening gunfire resonated. His eardrums felt as though they would rupture. Bombs laid waste to cities and people; their bodies, or the clearly identifiable parts, flew forcefully into the air, along with visions of contorted faces frozen forever in time. Police attempted to contain rioting in the streets, but were overrun by ferocious mobs that no longer respected or responded to law and order.

Was it race? A verdict rendered that the masses saw as injustice? Or people "occupying" something to make a statement?

Whatever the cause, or lack thereof, people died.

Tage's eyes tightened as he feebly attempted to stall the battering of rapidly changing pictures of swirling chaos and destruction that brutally assailed the cinema of his mind. The accompanying odor of decomposing bodies and the pungent aroma of seared and rotting flesh were unbearable. The imagery revealed the contrast of life as he knew it; a world filled with violence, death and destruction, greed, and hate, but never completely absent of love or hope.

Tage begged himself to wake, pleaded with himself not to continue this downward spiral, but it was too late.

A sharp pain welled in his chest as every conceivable emotion coursed through him. He remembered the day of the vanishings, hundreds of millions of people disappearing into thin air; men, women and children from all over the world, including all the unborn babies in their mother's wombs, gone.

Some spoke of this day, but their cries fell upon deaf ears or were drowned out by the barrage of laughter of those finding humor in utter nonsense. No one liked being the punch line of a tasteless joke, yet there he was. He often wondered if those who warned of that dreadful day, those departed, were laughing at him now. He was certain that sooner rather than later, when he finally decided to answer death's call, he would find out the answer to that nagging question. Tage did not fear death and it no longer stalked him. Its presence was always felt as he lingered in the murky shadows of sadness.

He was lost, weary, and every fiber of his being longed to bring closure to his torturous existence.

Would he be so selfish or gutless...

...to surrender his life uncontested?

Never! She needed him...

Chapter 1

THE high-pitched squeal of faulty brakes and the grinding of metal on metal forced Tage Craddock's eyes to peel. The rumble of a sputtering engine echoed as the clunker of a truck crept through an alley with its lights off.

It was an unexplainable wonder how the rust-colored 1950 Ford F-1 still ran at all. There was nothing restored, remodeled, or repainted, the bucket looked as though it had just crawled out and escaped an angry field; held against its will for the past sixty years.

The iron beast drudged deep into a filth ridden cul-de-sac and came to rest concealed between two overflowing waste containers. Tage's reflection struggled to stare back at him through tiny columns caused by streaks of slicing moisture that burrowed through the tainted glass.

"What a difference a day makes," he thought to himself.

Dark weary circles accentuated his sunken eyes, his cheeks were hollow, and his skin was paper white. The only color on his bony face was borrowed from the stubbles of a sorry excuse for a beard that had taken him nearly a month for him to grow, so he wasn't complaining.

Tage had never been a man of many words, his face said it all, and what it was saying right then as he locked eyes with his own gaze, was certainly better left unsaid. What used to be bright blue eyes, the windows of his soul reflecting a vibrant life, was now just a paled and dimmed reminder of devastation and loss.

In a way, Tage was a representation of what was good in the world; he was someone who believed that hard work paid off, and that there was value in honesty.

He was raised believing that your word was your bond, a handshake meant something, and love and faith were not just words flippantly tossed about, but must be proven by action. Something more than just an occasional post on Facebook.

Most of what that southern gentleman believed he lived.

Most of it.

Tiny flashes of light emitting from the cab of the truck shattered the pall of darkness. Frank Taylor, a tall slender man in his fifties with silver closely cropped hair, a square jaw, and a constant scowl seemingly tattooed on his hardened face, attempted to light a bent cigarette with a faulty lighter, which looked like a Tic Tac container. His thumb flicked hard and fast on the flint wheel as if it was caught up in a thumb-a-war battle. Sparks spewed from the top of the replicated breath mint bottle, but there was no fire. No flame. His lungs were desperate for repair and tar sticking to them like saltwater taffy was just what the doctor ordered.

He violently shook the lighter close by his ear, tightly clamped between his thumb and index finger, listening to the slosh of liquid butane inside. He tried to spark it again and then resorted to slamming the lighter against the dash. Tage immediately reached out to stop him, amazed by his blatant disregard for other people's property. Tage held his breath knowing that the highly pressurized and flammable contents of the lighter could explode, taking digits with it. He saw it with his own eyes when he was a kid, and that scar ran deep. Frank would never be able to give someone a high five again, more like a high two if things went south.

None of that mattered to Frank, who scoffed at the hiss of gas now leaking through a crack in the lighter's outer casing.

He was bitterly forced to find fulfillment in the spit soaked toothpick he already had tucked away in the corner of his mouth. His nerves were getting the best of him and the jitters licking at him elevated everyone's anxiety level. Frank tried to calm himself by slapping the toothpick back and forth in his mouth with his tongue.

Frank used to be a businessman, a commodities broker who was very good at what he did. And by good, one should not make the mistake of believing the reference reflected his ethics or integrity. No, not Frank. In fact, it was common practice for him to embellish or minimize, manipulate or mislead, fudge a few numbers and even flat out lie for the sake of the greater good.

He was always in control, calculated.

He knew exactly what he wanted, how to get it, and he did not know the meaning of the words settle or compromise. There was no such thing as a win-win situation with him; he had to win, which means someone had to lose. Frank was always good for a laugh, but not anymore. It was difficult to even look at him altogether, because to view him was to risk having your heart ache over the brokenness of a once powerful and successful man, who was now only a sour rotting shell of what he used to be; hiding behind his own personal

11

demons, a feeble exertion to find some sense of normalcy, fooling no one but his oblivious self.

Walter Perkins sat behind the wheel of the truck. His breathing was shallow and his eyes looked intently into the dark uninviting alley. His marred wrinkled hands had a white-knuckle grip on the helm, one that would choke the life out of anything caught in their grasp. To say that he was a little scared would be like saying that Americans were a little upset about the hijacked airliners being crashed into the World Trade Center in New York.

Walter's eyes swung towards Tage, who allowed a half crooked smile to grace his face, giving Walter the permission he needed to breath. He sighed and released the steering wheel from his strangling hold. Tage wished that Walter didn't have to be there, but his extensive knowledge of construction and the city's infrastructure could mean the difference between success and failure, life or death; not just for them, but for others who were counting on them.

Walter had been a foreman and super for thirty-nine years and has worked on and supervised the building of many of the structures in downtown Sacramento, when the world was a different place. No one would ever guess that this city, now filled with derelict and dilapidated war ravaged buildings was once the proud capitol of California. The city and the world were different than they used to be, no longer holding the beauty they once had. Colors were lost in the darkness, vibrancy didn't exist, and contrast had given way to muted shades, as if ash and soot covered the face of the earth and the entire world could now only be viewed through a filtered lens of dusty gray.

Any glimpses of its former self were only clouded by a prevailing evil, giving the world a long-deserted appearance; like a ghost town centuries in the making.

The words, good and moral, were relics from the past. Words that were as dead as those who would attempt to speak them. The old ways have been put away. Anything or anyone that was a reminder of the way things used to be were tortured and killed, and anyone desiring to live in freedom was that reminder.

Tage found himself staring out the window; hopelessly he tried to read his own expressionless face. His unblinking eyes, starving for moisture, began to burn. His eyelids clamped down, and he soon was forbidding their release; he refused to be robbed of that moment, so his eyes tightened.

Frank and Walter begin to converse, but muted gibberish was all Tage heard. He reached into the pocket of his tattered black jacket and retrieved a tarnished silver pocket watch, which he caressed in his hands before opening the cover and his eager eyes.

The piece was beautifully crafted with gold hands and Roman numerals; a sight to behold, but clearly forced to come of age too quickly. It too had endured a difficult existence. The white enamel face was painted with a scene of two men plowing in a field. One man was looking back, and the plow was being pulled by three horses. Tage's face remained vacant and unreadable, though his heart began to soar. His cracked lips edged upward into a grin as if a string attached to the corners of his mouth were being tugged from above. Emotions conflicted as he gazed at a picture glued to the inside cover of the watch, which was veiled in darkness. Tage slipped deeper into the closest thing he knew to a dream.

Frank, curious, leaned towards him attempting to catch a glimpse at the object of his stare, but before his view could become clear, Tage snapped the lid closed and hastily shoved the watch back into his pocket.

Tage's jagged glare slammed shut any doors for questions.

"Just wanted to know the time, sport. No need to get your pull-ups in a bunch," Frank snickered.

Walter stared into the darkness in a state of disbelief.

Quietly he responded to Frank's inquiry. "It's just after twelve."

Frank took a swig from a flask pulled out from his grubby coat pocket. The frigid weather failed to stop beads of sweat from coursing down his face. What was thought to be jitters were actually withdrawals. Frank used the inside of his arms to wipe the moisture from his hairline and face. He cracked his knuckles, trying to stop his hands from shaking, but the only thing that would serve that purpose was a fresh flow of homemade gin washing through his system. Well, that and a smoke.

He gawked at the blackened sky and Walter followed his gaze.

"Only twelve o'clock in the afternoon and it looks like the dead of night," Walter announced.

"And a third of the day did not shine," Frank muttered.

To say that Frank was a bit of a freak was an understatement, and the last thing anyone there needed was a drunken prophet.

"You remember what to do on this one, right?" Walter asked.

Frank knew that he was talking to him, but he had other things on his mind. So he slammed back more booze and gestured an offer to Tage as if he already knew the answer.

Tage shrugged him off with annoyance, causing Frank to laugh so deep and breathy it came out as a cross between a smoker's cough and a dry heave. Being in his presence for any length of time was like being locked in a room taking the test of your life, next to someone that tapped their pencil's eraser on the desk, smacked chewing gum, and had a stabbing high-pitched whistle coming from their nose that sliced the air every time they exhaled.

14

"Frank!" Walter chided.

"What! Yeah, yeah, I know what to do," Frank snapped.

He then thought for a moment, tilted his head and paused. "I'm 'bout to blast some fools." He broke into a laugh that sounded like a sputtering lawn mower. Spit flew out of his gaping mouth and peppered the dashboard.

Walter, already on edge and looking like death incarnate, appealed to Frank. He asked him to pace himself concerning his liquor intake. Frank craned his head yet again, pondered his words, and defiantly choked back the remaining contents of the flask.

As he guzzled, he held his index finger in the air as if to say, "Just a moment. I'll be right with you."

He sucked the liquid courage from the flask like he was firing up a stogie, and he didn't stop until the container was bone dry.

Frank then tossed the empty flask to Walter, threw his hands innocently into the air, and with a shrug of his shoulders said, "No more drinking. I promise."

If looks could kill, Tage would be found guilty of murder by reason of insanity and still sentenced to die because of the murderous gaze he gave Frank.

As Tage turned away, his eyes caught a flash of metal inside Frank's coat; it was the unmistakable shimmer of a nickel plated revolver. Tage's muscles tensed and he grit his teeth. Walter, the voice of reason, caught wind of the quickly deteriorating situation and chimed in.

"The lookouts are supposed to carry the guns, Frank. You know that."

In a drunken stupor, Frank mockingly snapped to attention.

"This is my gun. There are many like it, but this one is mine. My gun is my best friend. It is my life. I must master it as I must master my life," Frank belted. Tage shook his head, his jaw tight with anger. The alcohol had once again taken the control Frank was more than willing to give up. It was now an unfortunate matter of weathering the storm.

Frank wasn't typically an angry or abusive drunk. He was more like the guy at a party who'd get punched hard in the face for getting on someone's last nerve; and when he came to, everyone would tell him that he fell down the stairs. Frank was that guy.

"Is anyone hungry in here besides me?" Frank spoke out of the blue, casually glancing back and forth between the two men. "I'm ready. Come on let's rock 'n' roll," he commanded. "Hoorah!"

Walter and Tage exchanged apprehensive looks. Tage suggested to Walter that they leave him behind, discreetly flashing a fist at Walter, who chuckled, understanding the implication. Walter felt safer with everyone together. Frank was definitely a loose cannon but he was a cannon nonetheless.

"Don't talk about Frank as if he wasn't sitting right here." Frank said, pointing his bony little finger at them.

It was almost comical, Frank having just referred to himself in the third person. Maybe Frank was still good for a laugh.

"Come on, Vamanos. Let's go!" Frank barked, motioning towards the door.

The heavy metal doors squealed open, creaking as though they were in agony. The choking smell of the city and the darkness that could be felt, instantly flooded the cab. Tage's stomach began to churn and his skin crawled as he took his first hesitant step outside. The night air used to be so sweet, now the fetid and jabbing stench of the heavens assaulted their internal organs with every drawn breath.

16

Tage's eyes were immediately drawn to a woman; at least he thought it was a woman, who had squirmed out from underneath a pile of weathered boxes. She was writhing in filth on the ground, clawing at herself as if something was embedded under her skin. The plagued woman flicked out her blackened tongue and it looked like a mangled party favor. The twisted expression on her face caused a painful knot to rise up in his throat. She cried out in anguish and her piercing howl hit him like a wall of ice.

These sluggish creatures of the night typically had yellow eyes, broken teeth, blood stained mouths and cadaverous complexions. Many were deformed and had missing limbs resulting from a mysterious outbreak of mutating diseases that started three years prior. But make no mistake, these things were not to be pitied or trifled with. Those that ventured too close to what they called bottom feeders would have their tongues eaten and their throats ripped out before they could formulate words in a futile effort to scream out for help. Even with missing limbs, these tortured souls were not in the least bit helpless. They were often well fed, and that alone said it all. Bottom feeders were the least of their concerns at that point, because they were a blessing compared to their counterparts with properly functioning limbs. The walking dead? Sorry, but that was a joke. The able bodied creatures that had not been ravaged by disease, RAN. In a heartbeat they could outrun their would-be victims, even though they themselves didn't have a beating heart. They could think, reason and feel. They didn't necessarily have the motor skills to hot-wire a car and take a joyride, but those who thought hiding in a locked room or jumping a chain link fence would keep them self, found out the hard way that it didn't. These were the undead who were driven by an undying appetite and by self preservation.

17

Evil spirits were a plague on the planet, and because of this, more and more possessed people were surfacing. The only useful purpose they served was being made sport of by those who would place wages on how long they would survive games involving their torture. They were worse off than the rodents and vermin they dwelled with, but not nearly as valuable.

Most of those who were possessed remained out of sight, living, feeding and gathering away from the general public; which was now a comical term to use, considering society as a whole had become nothing more than a demented game of survival, where the winners were the ones who died the fastest.

Like a colony of mass producing roaches, when the bottom feeders' homes became too infested, more were seen out in the open and in the light, on those rare days where the bipolar sun decided to reveal itself to a shattered world it deemed unfit.

Tage tried to imagine who and what this grotesque woman once was, but couldn't even settle his mind on whether this thing before him was eighteen or eighty years old.

Was she married?

Did she have a family?

What did she dream of being when she was a little girl playing with carefully carried dolls and having tea parties with her imaginary friends who knew her better than her own parents?

Bitterness grew like a tumor in his mind. He was saddened by this woman, but he could not deny that the mere sight of this thing with a total of five fingers to share between both hands sickened his stomach.

"You need me to hold your hand, junior?" Frank cracked.

Tage shook free of his daze, and the three of them strode in the direction of the main street. Tage was not normally one to complain, but his joints ached with each step, and the burning sensation that started in his legs now shot throughout the rest of his weakened body. The three men were all malnourished and emaciated; all looking like they should be holding signs that read, "Will work for food," while pacing up and down the center isle of a freeway exit ramp.

Tage hadn't eaten in so long that his body no longer craved food. During the first few days, his thoughts became muddled and it was difficult to concentrate. Now, nearly two weeks without anything aside from a cup of broth that barely had more nutritional value than tap water, Tage's mind was sharp. Sharp like his closest childhood friend's, Jordan Smith, who he was always proud to say was chosen to attend the Junior National Young Leaders Conference in Washington DC when she was in the sixth grade.

He thought it was funny when he came to the realization that even as an adult, he still wasn't as smart as she was in elementary school. He and his best friend went from kindergarten through their sophomore year in high school together, but lost contact when her family moved to the Philippines to do missionary work with her Grandmother, Donisha Worsham. Jordan, who he knew with certainty was in a better place, would be happy to know that his mind worked just fine. No, it was the fatigued muscles he had a problem with. They felt like they were on fire.

The trio gave themselves a quick once over and found a measure of comfort knowing that their frayed clothing blended well with their surroundings. Frank glanced at the plagued woman now convulsing on the ground. Many of her sores had burst open and now oozed greenish puss onto the pavement. He had no sympathy. No compassion. He felt as though suffering humanity was receiving her just reward.

Frank stared at the woman for a moment with raised eyebrows, then reached into his pants pocket, dug out a wad of wrinkled bills and tossed it at her as if it were going to do her some good.

"Frank! Come on, man." Tage chided.

"What? This is the closest I've come to real entertainment in a long time," Frank responded at once, as he took a few slow but steady steps toward the plagued woman.

She looked blindly past him, twitching on the ground and making a clicking sound with unidentifiable parts of her body. She was sounding off like a Geiger counter.

Her head tilted to different angles so she could better listen to the clomp of Frank's approaching boots.

"Hey, miss thang. You got a light?" Frank said, maliciously amused.

He pulled the bent cigarette from his coat pocket.

"What are you doing, Frank? We don't have time for this?" Tage harshly whispered.

"We always got time for a smoke, boy, now shut it!" Frank snapped.

"He's going to get himself killed." Walter quietly said to Tage.

"Sometimes I wish we'd be so lucky."

Tage's word hadn't lingered in the air long enough for them to grow cold, and he was already wishing he could have taken them back.

Frank stepped to within three feet of the plagued woman. Her gurgled chattering grew louder and faster. Tage and Walter tried to coax Frank away from the woman who couldn't see the meal now within two feet of her, but could smell and already taste the fresh meat.

"Come on, Suzy Q. You got a light for me?" Frank murmured.

He took another healthy step forward, lowering himself and extended his hand holding the bent cigarette. The closer he got, the more he massaged the toothpick in his mouth with his tongue.

Tage and Walter knew Frank had passed the point of no return, and before they could draw their next breath, the Plagued Woman's clicking suddenly stopped.

Frank's eyes darted to Walter and quickly swiveled back to the woman who suddenly lunged at him with the power and speed of a trap-jaw ant. Frank's eyes went wide.

"Oh..." he blurted.

Before Frank could even contract a muscle to jump back, the Plagued Woman had already snatched the cigarette out of his hand and had it in her mouth, grinding its contents.

"...crap," he finally finished.

Frank, fell back, slack jawed, and quickly scurried over to the others.

He righted himself, and slapped his knee as he laughed.

"Did you see that? I mean, what in the boneyard was that?" He said, red-faced with excitement. "My heart is beating so dawg-gone-fast... Gentlemen, we are NOT doing that again," Frank said, bouncing from the adrenaline now crashing through his system.

"Walter, why don't you give my little darlin' a kiss?" Frank tipsily said.

He pretended to grab Walter, making him foolishly flinch.

"Pull yourself together, Frank. We've got work to do," Tage heatedly said.

"I'm just playin'. Lighten up. That's your guys' problem right there; you just don't know how to have fun." Frank pointed at the woman and said, "That's the kind of stuff that lets you know you're still alive."

The woman's mouth opened and closed as if she was gasping for air. She wasn't speaking, not that they could tell, but indiscernible sounds were coming from somewhere on her as if distorted voices were shifting within her, scanning vocal frequencies like one would flip through static filled radio stations.

After Walter caught his breath and the rapid thumping of his jolted heart slowed, he went over some last minute instructions before they ventured onto the main road.

"This place only has two scanners. I can take care of the first one from the outside the building, but the second one has an internal feed at the register—"

"I vote we just go in and shoot everybody," Frank quipped.

In a flash Tage snatched him by his collar and attempted to throw him against the side of a building, but found himself with his gaunt face pressed hard against the concrete wall instead, with the tip of Frank's S&W .44 mag pressed even harder against the back of his head.

"It's nice to see there's a man in you after all, slick." Frank sneered.

His breath reeked of alcohol; it was leaking through his pores.

"Let me go!" Tage barked.

"What's the magic word?" Frank said playfully, his mouth smacking loudly on the bowed toothpick. The amplified sound in Tage's ear was like the screech of long fingernails clawing down an endless chalkboard.

Tage thrust back against Frank, with no regard for the gun.

"Get off me, Frank!"

22

"Or what! You gonna call me names and hurt my feelings?" Frank cackled so hard he snorted. "I can't believe you've lived this long through all this," he said as he released Tage.

Tage straightened his clothes and headed for the main road with Walter, instantly feeling better about the words he had spoken moments ago about Frank getting killed.

Frank was in no particular rush. He placed his gun in his waistband at the small of his back and followed, annoyed by their irritation with him having a little fun.

As he strutted away, the plagued woman tracked him with her ears. She opened her mouth impossibly wide and the inside looked like a thin layer of moldy cheese still clinging to the grater. A hauntingly shrill voice spoke through her. It was a woman's voice fused with the whirring of a table saw cutting through wood.

"You got a light?" She said and continued to repeat over and over again, as her head tilted and swiveled. She looked as though she were searching for the source, unaware that the words were emanating from her.

Frank glanced back at the woman before he rounded the corner, thinking he was certain that had heard a familiar voice, the distinctive high-pitched tone of his third wife, who was killed in a pileup she caused when she was driving under the influence. He was immediately unnerved, but shook off the uneasiness and moved on.

Chapter 2

ONLY a handful of private cars traveled the roads, so it was always a fairly safe bet to assume that every set of headlights seen would belong to a patrol car. The few people they encountered as they marched towards their destination walked just as quickly as they did, anxious to get off the street. Those courageous enough to glance in their general direction had eyes that were immensely dark and lifeless. The look of oppression was evident and the reek of death floated in the wind throughout the entire city.

The three men could sense the presence of the evil that lived within the darkness surrounding them. Tage felt things brush against him, even physically bump him, only to turn and see nothing around him that could have knocked him off course. It was not like this for him in the woods where he lived, only in the city, and in certain company.

On occasion, out of the corner of his eyes, he caught glimpses of a shadowy silhouette, but whatever it was he spotted, it would disappear just before his sights narrowed or fixed on it. These were the dark forces that played with your hair and whispered in your ear at night as you wafted into sleep; they stole your breath as they watched you, like a frightened child who snuck silently into your room and crept to the head of the bed, only to stand staring wide eyed, watching you in the darkness as you breathed. Without so much as a peep coming from them, you'd somehow sense their presence and woke with a pounding heart, scolding the child for their stealthy entrance, unaware that something sinister had entered the room before they did and was the very reason they were unable to speak; the same darkness that woke them was the same evil that pulled the covers from your bed and ran their fingers along your body, opened doors you knew you had closed, moved things around in your room, and invaded your dreams; the eyeless faces that watched you through the cracks in your doors.

Years ago, while Tage was looting a store, he heard the blood curdling screams of a woman a couple aisles over.

He immediately abandoned his cart and rushed to the woman's aid, only to see her being dragged viciously by her hair towards the back of the store by an unseen force. He could see where the spirit had her brown curly locks within its grasp, but there was nothing to fight against; though he swung and kicked with all his strength, he only beat the air. He grabbed the woman's leg and pulled with all his might, crying out for help, feeling the deathly chill of whatever entity wanted her. He could feel the hot malodorous breath of something breathing on him and his neck suddenly got wet when what he thought was a large prickly tongue tasted his flesh.

The woman, whose greenish gold eyes he would never forget, was dragged behind the plastic hanging curtains and into the meat locker. All he could hold onto was one of her shoes, a scuffed black and white Van with the name, Candice B., written on it in faded purple permanent marker. He beat against the door until Candice's wails ceased, mid scream.

As they walked, Tage felt as though the smothering darkness was trying to enter him, intimately searching him for a point of entry like a noxious gas trickling in through a bedroom vent. Nothing seemed to be bothering Walter aside from the obvious, and Frank seemed to be enjoying whatever ride he was on. Neon signs flashed on the darkened street, most of them were missing letters, but all of them blinked "closed." Only a handful of stores would open when it was dark because few employed people crazy or desperate enough to work at this hour, even if it was only around one in the afternoon. The somewhat civilized citizens wisely stocked up on food and other essentials, as much they were allowed by the government, when the sun had nothing better to do than shine. Because 99.9999% of the time, only cops, bottom feeders, cannibals and criminals, dared walk the streets when there was no light coming from the heavens. Tage and his partners were a testament to the accuracy of that statistic. They were the highest form of criminal.

Walter plodded alongside Tage, whose thoughts once again were misplaced. As he looked around, he was amazed and disgusted at how much the city, and probably the world for all he knew, has rotted and decayed since he had last walked these streets over a year ago. Everything and everyone, including himself, had been brutally robbed of what life was supposed to be; plundered to the point where a forced smile or positive expression would indicate to the powers that be, the god of this world, that they had not been broken down enough.

The right to life, love, and the pursuit of happiness was a pipe dream. It no longer existed.

As they continued to make their way down the trash laden streets, a fight broke out between two men. One of the men smashed the other man's head through a car window. The victim jerked on the ground holding his neck, which poured blood, and the other, coolly continued on his way as if nothing had happened.

No one helped. No one cared.

There didn't have to be a reason for such encounters, because life was the reason. The man, who lay on the ground awaiting death, was better off than many of the people who remained.

Tage and Walter walked briskly with their heads down. Frank, falling behind, took in his surroundings with a sense of reckless abandon. The shackles of his chained mind were broken. The 120 proof spirits he indulged back in the truck spoke to him like an oracle and he was now on a crusade; Frank's eye-opening revelation was that he was born into a country celebrated as the land of the free and the home of the brave, a country which he had sworn to defend from all enemies both foreign and domestic. No longer was he going to tuck tail and bury himself in the sand, undermining the freedoms that his brothers in arms had died to preserve. Frank sang. He danced. He was liberated.

A black-n-white veered onto the street they were traveling and cruised straight for them. Walter's heart stopped as he drew a sharp breath and he halted dead in his tracks, instinctively looking for an alternate route. He attempted to alter course but Tage grabbed his forearm and pulled him along. He was surprised by how strong that wiry old man was.

"It's okay, just keep moving. Head down. Don't look." Tage

gruffly said, finding no moisture in his barren throat and mouth.

Walter's heart pounded like a jackhammer.

Tage questioned whether he himself was being foolish as Walter yielded in trusting obedience.

Walter fearfully confessed, "My heart is going to beat right out of my chest."

"I know. I can feel it."

Walter let out a nervous chuckle.

Tage feebly attempted to distract him as the police car drew closer, now within range of being able to closely examine them. Tage already knew the answer, but he asked Walter how long he'd been married. Walter searched his scattered and presently preoccupied mind; the pressure had seemingly caused his brain to stall.

"Thirty six… No, wait. Thirty seven years next month."

"You know, that's five years longer than I've been alive." Tage responded. "You're old, Walter."

A wave of sudden calm washed over Walter, but he knew better than to smile as the Officer passed alongside them. Interestingly enough, the patrolman paid no attention to them, his eyes were fixed on something...

Or more likely someone behind them.

Tage glanced back and spotted Frank about ten yards behind, waving stupidly in the direction of the patrol car. Tage quickly turned back around, his heart rose to his throat. They had to decide quickly about distancing themselves. Frank stood at attention and saluted the approaching patrolman, acting as though he were a long lost battle buddy. The Officer flipped on his vehicle mounted spotlight, turned it on Frank and stopped the car.

"Evenin', Officer." Frank enthusiastically yelled, loud enough for the cop to hear through his closed window.

Once Tage heard the single chirp of the police siren, he realized that the beginning of the end could be drawing near.

Walter and Tage stopped, feigning as though they were not even taking notice of what was taking place behind them. They discussed running as an option, but rapidly concluded that once other cops were called in, their chances of survival were slim to none; Frosty had a better chance of making it out of hell unscathed than they did trying to outrun the law. They had no choice but to stand together, regardless of who brought the fight to their doorstep. Tage had been in his fair share of schoolyard brawls, but he was not often faced with doing the unthinkable. He was brought up to add value to life, not take it. But he knew without question he would do whatever needed to be done if push came to shove.

The officer exited the vehicle and positioned himself behind the open door. He threw a probing glance towards Tage and Walter, eyed them suspiciously and then wheeled his eyes back on Frank.

Frank and the officer stared each other down; the officer looked hardened and stone faced, and Frank gawked mockingly in return. You could almost hear the famous western showdown whistle from The Good, the Bad and the Ugly being played by the wind.

Never mind the gun, the officer stepped out from behind his vehicle and slipped his baton from his duty belt. His bowed legs strode towards the sidewalk and Frank nearly laughed at the seasoned looking officer. It was clear that the bowlegged officer had no intention on calling anything in, because what he was about do would be off the record and personal. Tage and Walter slowly begin taking steps toward Frank, realizing that whatever was about to happen, would happen fast. Suddenly the bowlegged officer stopped, halting his advance. Orders from a dispatcher on his radio were belted out; a 10-35 officer needs assistance call came forth. With eyes still narrowed on Frank, he jerked his paddle mic from his lapel and responded with his call sign. Without hesitation, the he quickly reversed course, jumped into his vehicle and tore down the street, lights flashing and siren blaring.

Tage and Walter, tensed and dripping sweat, let out a collective sigh. Their bodies were numb and tingling with fiery anticipation.

Frank casually walked up to and passed them with not so much as a break in his stride.

"Don't just stand there, gentlemen, come on." He said in a frustrated tone. Frank was ready for a fight, but that afternoon there seemed to be no takers.

Tage and Walter traded looks and followed after him cautiously.

After what seemed like hours of walking, they had finally arrived at their destination, a building that should have long been condemned, with a sign out front saying, Nu-Way Market.

The corner store was only six blocks from where they parked the truck, but babysitting Frank, needless to say, was exhausting.

Tage discreetly walked the perimeter of the building, his body had began to stiffen, the cold felt like it was working its way into his bones. As he passed the front of the store he stopped to tie the laces on his left foot that he had purposely undone. He peered inside the glass door, and from what he could see, there did not appear to be any customers inside. His bones creaked as he rose to his feet. A slight nod of his head signaled to Walter that it was time for him to go to work.

Tage and Frank posted themselves at the back corners of the brick building. Walter stood poised in front of an electrical box located between his two sentries. Tage's elevated heart rate kept him alert, his head was on a swivel and his eyes darted, taking in everything. Frank's attention was on his busted lighter. The shafts of light that sparked every time he tried to ignite it pulsed like an unwelcome beacon.

Walter's jaws clamped tightly on a small flashlight, and his hands quickly worked on cutting, disconnecting, and switching a bunch of wires tangled inside of a circuit board. The arthritis in his hands were aggravated by the frosty air; his hands and body were shaking harder than Milli Vanilli when the tone-deaf charlatans from the 80's had to actually sing for the first time instead of lip-syncing to someone else's vocals.

Frank's mind was all over the place. He looked as though he was having a heated argument with himself. Over what? That's a question for the ages. Ritalin was the first thing that came to mind when Tage saw him poke at a dead cat, try to peek through a broken window, try to pry open a locked door, count milk crates, and play hopscotch.

If Frank had been paying attention, maybe he would not have been startled by the sound of bottle breaking nearby, but that wasn't the case. Frank hit the deck so fast, he couldn't have done it faster if someone yelled grenade. He went down with the quickness, but he couldn't pull his gun out to save his life.

Frank lowered his head and expelled a deep breath. He slowly climbed to his feet after spotting a man about 30 yards away, barely dressed, who was groping around in the shadows on his hands and knees. Frank's first thought was that he was thankful that the half naked man's only item of clothing was a pair of shredded tan colored khakis that covered everything that needed to be covered.

The plagued man, another bottom feeder, had thick cuts over 90% of his body and looked as though he had been scourged repeatedly with a whip. He growled at the air and clawed himself. He then felt around the cold wet ground, picked up a piece of broken glass, and began cutting into his own flesh.

Frank watched intently and whispered, "…and their torment shall be like the torment of a scorpion."

Out from nowhere, a six foot two, three hundred fifty pound grizzly of a man, with brown crusted teeth, pale green skin and sores all over his body. He... or it, depending on who you talked to, grabbed Frank from behind and locked him in a vicious bear hug.

Frank struggled to break free, his scrawny legs dangled in the air. The grizzly tried to sink his teeth into Frank's neck, but Frank's thrashing prevented him from latching on.

Tage raced toward him, not quite sure what he could do, but he was determined to do something. He ripped off a piece of wood that hung from a partially boarded up window. Walter stopped what he was doing in order to join the fray, but Tage yelled for him to continue.

Frank kicked his legs back attempting to cave in the grizzly's knees, but without success. Frank felt as though his ribs were on the verge of snapping, being crushed in the creature's monstrous grip, like the coils of a python tightening around its prey. All the blood from his body felt like it was headed up north and he was sure that his head was going to pop like an adolescent's pimple. Tage swung mightily with the board and smacks the grizzly in the back of the head. The clap echoed in the alley but the blow only seemed to irritate him.

Frank kicked against the wall like he was doing a leg press and the grizzly stumbled back and slammed against the building behind them, but Frank was still trapped in the man's hungry clutches. The grizzly bore down on Frank's shoulder with his choppers and tried to clamp his jaws shut, but Tage jabbed the thing in the face with the end of the plank before he could draw blood. The grizzly's head flipped back like a Pez dispenser. Tage rocked his arms back and thrust them forward again, shoving the end of the board into its Adam's apple. The crunch sent chills down Tage's spine, but it didn't quite have the effect he was going for. The blow only served to snap the man's head back to where it was before. Frank's eyes grew red and began to bulge. He could no longer draw air. Frank was weakening, but he continued his efforts to break the death hold. He grabbed the man's forearms and noticed a, "Don't Worry. Be Happy," tattoo on the man's right arm. He tried to pry the man's arms apart, but the skin on his left forearm rolled back like an accordion. All Frank and Tage could now see of the grizzly's left arm was raw pink meat.

Frank threw his head back and thumped him square in the face, busting his nose. The crack of the snapped cartilage knotted Tage's stomach.

The man maintained his crippling hold. Tage repeatedly struck the man with the board, but he still didn't release.

"Use the other side!" Frank squelched.

Tage quickly scanned the board and for the first time noticed three large nails protruding out the opposite end of the timber. Tage wondered how Frank managed to see that.

"Do it!" Frank silently mouthed.

Tage hesitated for a moment, understanding that some serious damage was about to be done.

"Now!" He ordered.

With a hefty swing, Tage struck the burly man in the back of his calf, not once, but twice. The grizzly buckled, but didn't cave. Tage then smashed the grizzly in the back of his head. The board snapped in half, and the half with the six inch rusted nails jutting out from it, buried themselves into his dome. The beastly man released his strangling hold enough for Frank to free himself and then dropped to his knees, sobbing like a lost child in a crowded mall. The grizzly ripped the dangling board out from his melon. No blood as you would expect. In a flash, Frank had his gun pulled out, the hammer was cocked, and he shoved the muzzle forcefully into the crying man's mouth, popping out three of his teeth upon entry.

Tage plead with Frank not to pull the trigger, but everything in Frank wanted to liquefy his vile assailant's brain. He wiped his slimy hand, coated in grizzly's body fluids, on his jacket. Walter finished rewiring the circuit board and rushed up beside Tage.

"If you pull that trigger, Frank, we're done. Every cop in the area will be on us in a matter minutes."

Frank considered Tage's words. The jury was still out, but he was beginning to think it was worth it; you know, being able to splatter the grizzly.

Frank didn't have much respect for Tage, he downright hated him to be more exact, but he knew without question he was right.

Frank looked around, the grizzly's crying turned to whimpers. Frank spotted his toothpick which had flown out of his mouth after the initial grab. He slowly withdrew his gun from the grizzly's mouth, but kept it trained on him.

"I'm, I'm, I'm sorry," the grizzly stuttered.

"Not yet, you're not," was Frank's chilled response, still toying with idea in his head about splitting his skull.

"I'm sorry, sorry, sorry. I'm, I'm hungry." Frank looked him over with repulsion.

"You don't look hungry, big boy… How many people have you eaten anyway, fat Freddy?"

"Freddy? Freddy? Is that my name?" The grizzly asked, reeling on the ground, like a frightened child."

"Let it go, Frank, we've got work to do." Walter said, wanting to clear the area.

Their overly extended stops, being anyway for too long, chewed away at his insides.

"You know, I'm not in the business of taking prisoners." Frank said in a grim tone.

"You're not at war anymore, Frank." Tage responded.

"… And that's the reason I don't like you," Frank blurted, shifting his eyes to Tage. He had hoped to see some type of measured response, but Tage only scoffed, which set Frank ablaze with suppressed Rage.

"You see? You see! Right there. Right there. Right there." His voice roared with chorus of rising anger.

He wheeled the gun towards Tage and jabbed the air with it as if he were poking him in the chest with the muzzle. Tage flinched back.

"You better believe I'm still at war. You are too. We all are. You're just too stupid to see it, sport."

He calmed himself and turned his attention back to grizzly.

"You can be as diplomatic as you want, and protest all you want, but until you're willing to fight, until you're willing to cross over into enemy territory, you can always expect to lose."

Frank then forced the sniveling grizzly shakily to his feet. He pushed the limping giant away from the others.

"Don't do it, Frank," said Tage.

Frank shoved the grizzly onward without mercy. A decision has been made. Completely destroying the brain of these creatures was the only way to put them down.

"Don't shoot him, Frank." Walter said sternly.

"I'm NOT going to shoot him, skipper," he fired back with a much more respectful tone toward Walter, who served nearly 20 years in the Navy.

Frank marched him another fifteen yards out and stopped the grizzly.

He glanced at his anxious partners...

And with a smirk...

He smashed his duct-taped boot into the grizzly's overflowing belly with a stomp kick, hurling his massive body backwards. Before he came to a grinding halt, skidding across the pavement, the plagued man, with fresh flowing cuts all over his body, seized him and smothered him with his seeping body, muffling the grizzly's cries. The plagued man flashed the chiseled spear-like teeth in his mouth and tore into the man, who bucked on the ground like someone who was pinned down and being tickled mercilessly at a slumber party. The plagued man reared his head. Blood poured from his lips. He turned to Frank and hissed as if to communicate to him that he should move along, there was nothing to see.

Frank didn't have to be told twice.

"Enjoy your meal," he quipped as he walked away smiling, still trying to wipe off whatever body fluids remained on his hand from the grizzly.

The plagued man opened his jaws wide before he dove back in to feed.

"You gotta light?" The words spilled out of the plagued man's mouth with the same distinct female voice Frank had heard earlier.

Frank felt as though his blood had been transfused with lead, and the icy surface of his existence gave way; pulling him down, drowning him in a bottomless frozen abyss. He shut his eyes and released the last bit of air that hadn't already been knocked out of him.

Tage and Walter traded looks of confusion; their minds spun as if they were asked a question in Chinese and had to respond in Russian.

They heard the same lucid voice, were freaked by the phrase, but didn't make the connection that had Frank's bones chattering.

Frank's gnawing suspicions about Jenni, his third wife, the true love of his life, had been confirmed. Slowly his eyes peeled, and he walked on, crushed, slumped shoulders and eyes trained on the pavement, feeling as though he had been gone over with a steam roller. He plodded along, to the sound of frenzied feeding in the background.

Frank rejoined the others, deflated, unable to make eye contact. Walter scanned the area, arms folded, eyes the size of dinner plates, trying to avoid looking at Frank's new pet feed.

"We can't do this. There's no way we're going to pull this off," Walter Said.

Tage sternly reminded him that they had no choice.

Frank looked on with indifference, still fighting to surface, still searching for a reason.

Walter squeezed his forehead and his fingers began to message his temples. He drew a long deep breath and his sweaty hand darted from his head, to his mouth, and wrapped its tour with his hand stroking his light colored beard that was as thick as wheat. Reluctantly, he nodded his agreement.

They all had to come to grips with knowing that no matter how apprehensive they felt, or how slight their chances were for success, they were going inside that store.

Walter desperately tried to smother the growing flame of panic spreading through his mind like a grease fire. The fear that gripped him caused a tremor in his calloused hands that he could not control, but he elected not to place his hands in his pockets or fold his arms upon entering the store because he didn't want to arouse any undue suspicions. He didn't know what to expect, but he hoped that lady luck would grace him with her mysterious presence.

Religiously, at least twice a week for many years, Walter would hit the casinos; Vegas, Atlantic City, the Tunica Resorts in Mississippi, depending on where he lived, and made yearly trips to Macau, France, and Germany. Such frequency understandably would imply that he was either an addict, risk taker or thrill seeker, or that the glamour, escapism, or social aspect of the casino life was his draw; or that Walter was just plain lucky and that he would be a fool not to play. In any event, that was not the case. He was not the lucky one, nor did he believe in it. He used to have more money than he knew what to do with, and was from the camp that believed that if you wanted something you worked for it; luck was simply a crutch spoken and sported by those seduced by reality shows, those who sat by applauding others pursuing the passions of their heart, unaware that their own dream, which was on life support, was dying a slow and agonizing death.

No, more often than not, Walter found himself sitting in the casino or hotel lobby reading something off the NY Times Best Sellers' List, playing cribbage or golf on his iPad, or quickly wiping the spittle from the corner of his mouth after being awakened by a worried receptionist, because of his excessively loud snoring or frightful gasps that sounded like he was being deprived of oxygen due to his sleep apnea.

It was his wife, the seasoned gambler, who studied books on how to beat the house and read articles on how to determine when a machine was about to hit; she was the one who sweet talked the Lucky Seven slots, and massaged the glass of the Cash Vaults in order to coax out the prized jackpot. Walter was not allowed anywhere in her vicinity when she played. If he was a "cooler", those employed to derail hot streaks in the casino simply by their presence, Walter's gifting of bad luck would have kept him gainfully employed in the early days of mafia run casinos.

Walter's bet today, as he pushed open the glass door to the store, struggling to slow his heart rate and breathing, was that whoever was found inside, would equate his trembling hands and quaking body to Parkinson's disease.

Walter hated being elected to take point. He wanted to draw straws or Ro Sham Bo for the honors, but the argument was he was the least threatening in terms of appearance, so unfortunately it was valid. Frank was feenin' to shoot someone, so him volunteering to go first was immediately shot down. As expected, the store was as filthy on the inside as it was on the outside. The place was shut up like a tomb. There was no form of circulation flowing through the building, so by the time Walter stopped to grab a maroon colored carrying basket from a stack of carriers near the front door, his nose hairs felt as though they were being singed and his eyes were burning from what smelled and tasted like ammonia and rotten walnuts. There were about twenty air fresheners hanging throughout the store, which made Walter suddenly crave fruit salad. Industrial sized fly traps hung from the four corners of the room stretched like demented fruit roll-ups. Flies hovered and squirmed atop the layer of dead insects stuck to the poisonous adhesive like black waves, anxiously awaiting their turn to die. The corner market looked and felt like the first apartment most guys could afford on their own; the month-to-month place, in the worst part of town, with no deposit, rental history, or credit check required, where a chalk outline of a murder victim would not be cleaned up, but just covered with a rug. Though the establishment was in dire need of a deep cleaning and repairs, it had everything from bagels to motor oil, medicine to pop rocks.

Walter, with his disheveled gray hair and infectious smile, greeted the brawny red-neck cashier, Robert Timothy, who had to be a direct descendant of Sasquatch; big, hairy, and dumb. Robert nodded guardedly and spit chew into a flower covered Dixie cup, most of which spewed over the edge. The black film coated his hand and dripped onto his Boot Barn clearance rack cowboy boots. He wiped his fingers on his Wrangler jeans and watched the trio closely as the filed in. His eyes floated up above the entrance door, to a corroded old metal box with a cluster of dents all over it. The box must have been mistaken for a piñata a time or two, but as beat up as it was, it emitted a steady green light.

If it were any other color, the three men would have already been seen for what they were. Walter successfully disabled the sensor located near the store's entrance, which would scan and read an electronic implant of every person that entered.

That "mark", a term developed by so called religious fanatics, was the digital implant found in the wrist of every citizen, signifying their unity with the new world order, and essentially contained every piece of information about a person that could possibly be known; name, physical description, address, marital status, income, account information, work, credit, medical, or criminal history, and education, everything down to your known family members and friends, the movies you have, like to watch, and what they thought about them, websites they frequented, the music they listened to, their temperament, hobbies, and anything they owned, bought or sold. That information and more was instantly sent to a centralized government agency that tracked and disseminated collected data to various local agencies for every citizen in the entire world.

Being caught without an implant was an automatic death sentence in one way or another. The implants became mandatory for every citizen of the world under orders from Alexander Demetri. What was once called Radio Frequency Identification, technology developed to keep track of merchandise in a warehouse, packages being shipped, or to follow the work flow in a production process, became useful in the late 90's to keep track of pets, with chips being implanted under the skin of animals. In the early 2000's a club in Baja began implanting their patrons with an RFID chip about the size of a long grain of rice. Upon entering the club, the price of admission was drafted directly from a person's bank account by a sensor that read their individualized chip. A drink from the bar was paid for once an eager hand took possession of a glass. Hospital patients were chipped for the purpose of communicating vital information to doctors in case of incapacitation, and it became common place in society for children to be implanted due to the steep rise in child abductions. The world as a whole saw tremendous value in implanting, and based on conditioning, Demetri's argument for worldwide marking seemed rational, logical and sound.

It just made sense.

Walter, Tage and Frank each grabbed a basket and strolled to different areas of the store. Tage shopped the aisles, filling his basket with essentials; bread, milk, eggs, and whatever fruit he could find that wasn't moldy or being consumed from the inside out by bugs; his health teacher would have been proud because he was all about the four food groups. Walter's prior training kicked in and his nerves began to settle as he scanned the aisles. "Be prepared. Be prepared," he repeated in his mind, being a former Eagle Scout and one of the 1.2 million adult Boy's Scout Leaders back in his younger years. He snatched up medical supplies, batteries, and other household items; taking only items that looked as though they hadn't already been used or lay broken inside the packaging.

Frank blew through the store like a wild Tasmanian devil with road kill in its sight. Within moments, he was hightailing it for the cash register with a bag of chips, a six-pack of warm Pepsi, a cold beer, and a pre-made deli sandwich that he had already taken bites from.

Tage met up with Walter, concerned about Frank's deviation from their plan. That was only the first of many stops, and if they were going to acquire enough food and supplies throughout the course of the day, they couldn't afford to make mistakes.

Breadcrumbs and a smatter of mayonnaise stuck to the corners of Frank's mouth. The bread was hard, the roast beef was tough, and the lettuce and tomatoes were wilted and soft, but his entire body declared the enjoyment of that most welcome feast as he chewed feverishly; his jaws grinding and mouth wide open. Frank placed his faded blue basket on the counter. Robert glanced at Tage and Walter, who immediately silenced their quiet discussion and stared at him as though they were deer caught in the heart stopping and immobilizing beams of a vehicle's headlights. Walter's nerves gave way to fear.

"There is no way we can pull this off," he stammered, barely able to get the words out. "He knows we don't belong here."

"Walter, look at me." Tage quietly demanded.

Walter halfheartedly looked into Tage's face and drew much needed confidence from him. Without speaking a word, Tage threw a box of band-aids into Walter's basket.

"I'll finish getting the rest of my stuff," Walter said.

Tage nodded.

Walter felt as though every dirty secret in his life was playing out before Robert, and a flood of relief washed over him as Robert, seeing nothing out of the ordinary, lazily shifted his eyes back to the customer standing before him.

Walter took a slow deep breath and started to walk off.

"Wait." Tage spoke with a harsh whispered tone as if they were in enemy territory and Walter was about to step on a trip wire.

Walter turned his attention back to Tage, whose tunnel vision eyes stared past him. Walter curiously followed his gaze, and then drew a sharp breath when his eyes locked on freshly stocked packages hanging from a long metal rod jutting out from display fixture, packages containing a syringe and vial.

Walter, who was closest to the product, grabbed one, and then snatched up another. He spun around, eyes dancing in disbelief, "Since when... I thought these things were illegal."

"Never mind that, grab a couple more."

"What! Let's take 'em all."

"No. We might give ourselves away. Just two more. It might be a trap." The crushing reality of Tage's words punched Walter in the gut with the force of a UFC fighter.

Fear once again crouched at Walter's door, accompanied by the shame of his brief celebratory attitude moments ago. Disheartened, he dragged himself away, taking only one extra package of the medicine labeled Nathancleovoxalyne, an antidote named after the world renowned physicist who designed it, Nathan Carey.

The best that Tage could hope for under the current circumstances was to try and keep Walter busy and his mind off Frank, which was not an easy task.

Robert slammed down a bottle of bourbon and gold label Scotch on the counter. He stared with a snarl on his fat face, glaring at Frank as though he had asked him to explain the technical difference between a dime and ten cents. The first bottle Robert retrieved for Frank, a 10 ounce bottle of Grey Goose vodka, was in Frank's mouth and already halfway gone.

"You can't do that, Sir." Robert said, in a quiet rage, that only those who knew Frank could understand.

Frank stopped his drinking, "What! Why? This is America still, ain't it?"

"Yeah, but you can't—" Frank hushed him with his raised palm, suddenly finding entertainment in the food particles that floated around in his liquor.

Robert studied him for a moment, and then asked. "Together?" Frank shrugged at Robert and contorted his face as if he had just spoken to him in a Pig Latin.

45

Robert responded by speaking unhurried and deliberate, as if Frank was a little slow... Special.

"Are you to-ge-ther?"

Frank finally got it. "Oh, yeah, yeah. We are, but I'm going to pray for my stuffing right now."

Frank laughed at his drunken self, catching wind of his pray vs. pay mix-up, he clasped his palms together and bent over in hysterics. His knee then shot up towards his chest and he leaned back tightly holding his stomach, riding a wave of gut wrenching air depleted laughter.

Tage walked up beside Frank forcing a smile as fake as the I.D. he got caught with in a bar when he was 18.

"I apologize for my friend here. He's ahh... an idiot." Tage, unable to think of anything else to say, hoped that his remark would ease the situation that was unraveling quickly.

Robert just stared, uninterested, and spit more of the stuff that looked like brake fluid into his cup. A thin track of the chewing tobacco lined his shaggy beard, but he made no effort to remove it.

"Why don't you let me take care of this for you, Frank?" Tage said, as he placed his hand on his shoulder.

Frank shot upright, looking as though someone had just slapped him on his sunburned back.

"Get your hands on me! Touch me again and I'll kill you." Frank barked, lips shaking with anger and his hardened eyes stabbing into Tage's.

Everything and everyone in the room froze and fell silent.

Even Robert was reluctant to move a muscle.

If there was a cricket anywhere in the area, it would have been belting a hearty tune because of the eerie stillness of the room.

Tage shrugged off Frank's outburst and slowly, carefully, backed away and went back to slipping things into his carrier. He felt Walter's eyes trying to meet with his, but he avoided the contact.

Frank laid a bunch of twenty dollar bills on the edge of the counter closest to him. Robert, annoyed, examined the bills. He seized one of the old crumpled bills and held it up to the light, eyeing it suspiciously. He flipped the bill around, scratched its surface, and checked for colored threads inside the note. Frank slowly began to reach towards his back where his gun was kept. He shifted his eyes towards Walter and winked at him with a cynical grin that told him he needed to prepare himself. Tage was obviously not privy to such a warning from Frank, but he saw all he needed to see on Walter's face, which was pouring sweat. All the terrified and heated blood in his body was summoned to his head and his red face looked like a plate of corned beef and cabbage.

The silent message he shot back to Frank, encoded within his thinly concealed fear, was for Frank to get control of himself; but that was not what he wanted to hear. Frank turned back towards Robert as he continued to pour over the spread out bills. Frank's finger touched the handle of his revolver, and he drew a slow pleasurable breath as a delightful tingle coursed through his body.

"What? You still recycle here, don't you?" Frank said with a smirk, definitely feeling like he knew something Robert didn't, as he massaged his gun with his fingers.

"Yeah, we do, but I ain't seen bills like this in a long time. They'll only get'ya 'bout forty cents on the dollar."

Tage and Walter released their held breath and Frank pried his hand from his weapon.

Long before the vanishings, the most dominant and influential nations, those leading in the areas of political, economic, and nuclear power, worked jointly to create a more permanent solution to stabilizing the world's economy; a unified currency. Within two weeks of the chaos that ensued after the disappearances, Alexander Demetri successfully united all nations of the world and a single world currency bearing his image was produced and placed into circulation. Old currency could still be spent, but held little value. Once collected, the bills or coins were systematically destroyed.

It was rare to see money of any kind that was not issued by the one world government. And with the implementation of the global implant that everyone was required to have by law, very few bothered carrying around purses, wallets, or cash, because money could be easily drafted or credited directly from or to an account with just a simple scan of ones wrist.

Tage and Walter went back to acting naturally unnatural, and began filling the remaining space in their baskets. Robert sifted through the bills Frank gave him and placed them in the cash register that was barely holding together. Frank took another hearty bite of his sandwich, paying no attention to the crumbs falling to the already dirty floor.

"Where's the head?" asked Frank.

Robert pointed to a hallway.

"First door on the left."

Frank mumbled to himself as he turned. "I wish we had a stinkin' toilet. I'm sick of squattin' in bushes. Havin' twigs poke me where nobody should be gettin' poked." He shouted to Walter, "I'm gonna take a leak before we hit the road."

Frank, now feeling an overpowering urge to relieve himself, walked briskly towards the restroom. Robert double checked his register display.

"Hey, thirty more cents," he yelled at Frank, who had already started unbuckling his pants.

"I got it," Walter said as he sheepishly made his way towards the front with a full basket, but Frank hurriedly whipped by him and pulled out a five dollar bill from his dangling pants.

"Here you go, Jefe," Frank said.

Without thinking Frank reached across the counter and handed the bill to Robert instead of placing it on the counter and letting Robert retrieve the money. In doing so, his hand was scanned by the register's sensor. The green light next to the cash register suddenly flashed red and the register shut down.

Robert, confused for a moment, pounded his fist on the register, muttering obscenities under his voice.

The beating of the register directed all eyes to the front.

From the moment of Robert's realization, everything began to play out in slow motion before Tage's eyes. A single heartbeat thumped his chest, and the blood pumping through his veins gridlocked. Robert's eyes darted and connected with Frank's, whose reflexes have been dulled by his ill-advised over consumption of booze.

Frank reached for his gun, his anxious fingers going for steel.

He laid hold of the handle, his mind screamed the words of one of his heroes, Martin Luther King Jr. "Free at last, free at last, thank God almighty, we're free at last." He yanked the gun from its resting place, but was no match for the unhinged country boy behind the register. Just as the gun cleared his jacket, Robert swept a sawed-off shotgun into his arms like a country line dance partner, cocked the hand cannon, and shot. Boom!

The blast caught Frank center mass and blew a hole in his chest.

Frank's trigger finger jerked, causing him to pop off rounds mid flight.

Tage's heart finally beat for a second time, thump-thump.

Frank launched back into a display of chips, dead before his body hit the ground.

Walter, who stood only a few feet from Frank, looked on, petrified, his eyes bulged with terror.

"Wal-ter!" The word poured from Tage's mouth like Blackstrap molasses.

He tried to run towards Walter, who just stood there looking as dumb as a can of paint. Tage felt as though he were enveloped in the shutters of fractured time. Thump-thump, Tage's heart beat for a third time. His eyes captured every scrap of detail.

His feet felt as though they were glued to the greasy tile surface, making movement difficult, his advance sluggish. No matter how hard he tried to move his legs, he felt as though he were running in a doughboy pool filled with Skippy peanut butter and he was getting nowhere fast.

"Who's next? Keep 'em comin'," Robert hollered, as he quickly wiped his face with a confederate flag bandana and shoved it in his back pocket.

"Wait. Please." Walter pleaded as he wisely made a dash for cover.

"Please, don't shoot. We have money. We just want to buy some—"

Robert Timothy narrowed in on the sound of Walter's voice.

Boom!

The shot missed, blowing a hole in the candy rack instead of taking off Walter's head. Tage's heart hit him again, this time, smacking him with such force, and thrusting so much blood through his system that everything suddenly began to speed up.

Robert, strangely giddy with excitement, closed in on Walter who cowered next to a bunch of tampon packages and other feminine products. Tage yelled for Walter to run.

"Oh God," Walter said, making the mistake of glancing at Frank's body whose electrical impulses were still firing and the gas and air releasing from his body eerily made it look like the deader than dead Frank was trying to do crunches.

Walter shot his eyes heavenward.

"Walter, run! Get out of here."

Walter raised himself from a hunched position and shuffled toward the doors. Robert crept up from the backside of Walter's position and got a bead on him. Tage's heartbeat was thunderous. He followed Robert's line of sight to Walter and immediately bolted towards the gunman, whose muscles tensed, preparing to pull the trigger. Robert braced himself; the tip of his finger lightly caressed the trigger as he wondered what his den would look like with a human head mounted on the wall.

Tage pulled up to within a few inches of Robert, his legs driving like pistons. Tage rose up into the air and planted both of his feet into Robert's portly chest. Robert was violently propelled back by the impact, but he still managed to fire off a round. Walter shrieked as the blast peppered his Vastus Medialis Obliquus, shattered his Femur and the orphaned particles unable to find lodging, were kicked out through his Semimembranosus; in laymen's terms, Robert shot Walter in his right butt cheek.

His leg was swept out from underneath him and he collapsed, quietly and strangely silent to the floor. Robert slammed against the wall and collapsed into a massive heap. A concussive wave of fat rolled through his body.

Tage fell heavily to the floor, planted his hands wrong, banged his head on the tile, but still jumped up and swiftly righted himself. His head was spinning and he flailed for balance as tiny flashes of light danced before his eyes. He felt as though he had just gotten off the teacup ride at Disneyland; how he hated that ride with a passion. He stumbled over to Walter, who looked as though he were in shock, which would have been understandable.

What plagued Tage's mind, what terrified him, was the thought of Walter going into cardiac arrest. He had been complaining of chest pains lately. Putting a cork in a hole to stop some bleeding was one thing, but the probability of Dr. Craddock ND (Not-a-doctor), fixing or restarting a man's ticker was about as likely as a man being comfortable poolside in hell because he applied sunscreen. Walter just laid there; he made no noise, wouldn't move a muscle, and seemed perfectly content with starring at the cockroaches playing who's your daddy underneath the product shelves.

Without deliberation or mercy, Tage scooped Walter up and stumbled towards the exit. Tage's body slammed against the door, but instead of busting out into freedom, his body lurched back, springing forcefully off the unyielding closed glass. He quickly checked for some type of locking mechanism, but there was none to be found. He threw his hands up. What gives? He took a quick step back and kicked on the glass with the heel of his foot, but the reinforced pane refused to break.

Robert began to stir. Tage, enraged, unleashed a flurry of kicks on the glass, while still trying to keep Walter on his feet, but the glass remained intact.

Robert shook himself awake, his face tensed at the light. It didn't matter that he saw three of each of them; he was going to shoot them all, starting with the ones in the middle. He reached back and felt a pitcher's mound taking up real estate on his throbbing head. Tage spotted a fire extinguisher mounted on the wall behind the counter. He broke free from Walter and slid over the top of the counter, knocking Frank's basket, food, and whiskey bottles to the floor. He ripped the extinguisher from the metal forks securing it and jumped back over the counter. Walter, holding tight to his bleeding leg, spotted Robert crawling slowly in the direction of his shotgun. Tage took the weighty silver canister and ran at the door like he was throwing a shot put in the Olympic games. The extinguisher sailed out of his hands and smashed through the door, spraying pieces of shattered glass.

Tage kicked out the remaining teeth of glass jutting from the door's frame, as Robert laid hold of his shotgun. Robert once again took aim on Walter, who slowly limped towards the exit. Tage snatched Walter and frantically rushed through the door just as Robert pulled the trigger. The shotgun blast wiped out a bundle of defenseless magazines and a cloud of shredded pages rained down and settled on the ground.

Chapter 3

TAGE'S head was in a fog, and his vision blurred. Ghostly streaks of light trailed with each turn of his head. The streets were still empty of travelers, but full of despair. Everything seemed so surreal, dreamlike. "Think, Tage, think!" He demanded of himself. He couldn't believe what just happened, but now was not the time for a recap. Walter's howl brought clarity to the moment. Tage's eyes darted down and he saw Walter's pant leg soaked through with blood. He broke off into a run, half-carrying half-dragging Walter in tow.

As they barreled down the street, they could hear the screaming of sirens quickly approaching. Flashing lights began descending on them from every direction. Panic gripped them, knowing that neither of them were prepared for where they now found themselves. This was new, uncharted and unwanted territory. The only alternate plan to success was failure, and failure was not simply returning home empty handed, it was not returning home at all. Death. Frank was the only one that successfully executed plan B thus far and Tage was not overly fond of the idea of following in his footsteps.

"We've got to get out of sight, fast," Tage declared.

Still holding onto Walter, Tage rushed toward the nearest set of doors. He checked the door knob and tried to spin it with his hand. It was locked. He reaches for another. No good. He began banging on the door, hoping that a sympathetic citizen would come to their aid, but no one dared answer. His well-intentioned efforts to kick doors in, served only to waste precious time. Every door he tried wouldn't budge. Tage felt nauseated. He was drenched, looking as though he had been standing in the rain. Steam began to rise from his hot sweat soaked head as it clashed with the wintry air. One old woman with patchy gray hair and missing teeth, stood right before them on the other side of her door. Tage and Walter begged her for help and offered her all the cash in their pockets, but she stared at them without expression or concern, trying to put a dent in a red apple that slipped repeatedly on her gums.

"I don't want to die." Walter admitted. "What kind of animal could kill so quickly, giving no thought—"

"Come on," Tage interrupted.

Walter held tight to Tage as they pressed on, still looking, hoping for a way out. Walter's mind couldn't come to terms with the loss of Frank. Dying like a rabid dog was warranted by some, but Frank was not one of them. Frank certainly had his issues, like a walking contradiction, but he was not deserving of such a fate. Walter believed that Frank had been warped and twisted by the life he was left with, which drove him to drink to escape the anguish of it all. His life should not have ended like that. Not like that.

Tage and Walter made their way down 32nd Street.

The closest patrol car could be heard from the next street over and they knew the dragnet around them was tightening like the security detail around the President after a terrorist threat. Walter groaned as his drooping eyes lifted.

"Where are we going? The truck is in the other direction," he said. "Got to respect the man," Tage thought to himself. Walter took a shotgun blast to the leg, was bleeding profusely, and he still had the gumption to imply that Tage didn't know what he was doing.

"There's no time. We'll be dead before we get your old truck started... No offense," Tage responded.

"None taken," Walter spoke out through gritted teeth.

They reached the end of the street and it split off into two narrower streets running east and west; both ran a couple hundred yards with no breaks. It was a straight shot. They had to make it to the end or they would be trapped.

Before going any further, they stopped to take care of Walter's leg. Tage grabbed the sleeve of Walter's shirt and tore off a strip; it was easy to do considering it already had rips in the material. He fastened the torn ribbon of clothing above the wound on Walter's leg, in an effort to slow or better yet stop the bleeding. Walter threw his head back and his entire body shook like an arcade game that cheated a kid out of his quarter.

A patrol car zipped passed them and Tage's body instantly seized up, his heart climbing into his throat. He paused, frozen in the moment, watching and listening as Walter bit into his arm, moaning, struggling to remain quiet. Tage held his breath, unwilling to move, hopeful that the cop car he just saw didn't turn back around.

Tage quietly climbed onto an electrical box that was close to the wall at the end of the t-intersection. The box was producing a low hum from what was most likely an electrical transformer inside. He moved delicately, superstitiously, almost believing that the slightest bump or creak would somehow sound off louder than the sirens that warbled around them. The hum and vibration of the electrical current traveling inside the metal unit he was kneeling on, tickled his hands and feet. The warmth too, breathed some much needed life back into his body. He raised himself and warily lifted his head up over the wall, holding his breath for good measure. His eyes took in the sights, surveying the area, but he saw nothing but darkness; empty glorious darkness.

Tage couldn't believe they caught a break, which provided evidence to the belief that the "beggars can't be choosers" philosophy was flawed. He was a beggar in every sense of the word, but he would never resign himself to death as society would have it because of his social standing. He turned back around, almost smiling, relieved.

He extended his hand. "Come on, Walter."

Walter stared at it for a moment, and then dropped his head, battling with the unrelenting urge to give up.

Tage wasn't in a talkative mood, so he latched onto Walter's clothes and pulled. Walter mustered his remaining strength and feebly tried to climb up onto the box, but his eyes began to dip and his body went limp. He grunted like a mule deer, his chest rose and fell in rapid succession, exchanging air like clothes that didn't fit. Tage struggled to lift his dead weight.

A police cruiser, backing up, came to a screeching halt at the end of the street. No doubt it was the same one that had passed a few moments ago. "Why else would it be backing up," Tage thought; as if that made any difference or would have any bearing on the outcome of their grave situation.

When the spotlight of the patrol car was suddenly flipped on, the alley was lit up like the butt of a lovesick firefly.

"Let's go. Now!" Tage demanded.

Walter struggled weakly for a moment and then suddenly re-signed himself to his fate. The cruiser peeled back slightly further, enough to turn down their street, and raced straight for them, full throttle.

"I made a promise to Aubrey, to YOUR wife, that I would get you home, Walter," Tage reasoned. "Don't make me break that promise."

The take-down lights on the patrol car switched on, flooding the entire street with forced daylight. If there was something, anything, that needed to be seen, it was seen.

"I can't. You go. I want you to go." Walter spoke with sincerity, but his words were devoid of truth.

"Don't give me none of that save yourself crap." Tage interrupt-ed. "We can fight or we can run, and I cast my vote for the latter, but either way we're doing it together. Now get up here, skipper." Tage spit out his words faster than the cruiser approached.

"Move it!"

Walter's eyes shot open and he gave everything he had. He made it further up than he had before, but it still wasn't enough.

Tage's eyes swung up. He tried to determine if he had enough time to jump down and help Walter up, but Walter grabbed him and pulled him down street-level before he concluded that it wasn't a good idea.

The sound of speeding tires and the belting siren drew closer. Trash cans and empty crates were blown out the way by the swiftly moving car. The flashing red and blue lights were beautiful against the darkened sky, but at the same time a dreadful reminder of what would be, if captured.

The government showed no mercy. Any opposition to societal unity meant death. In the days before the vanishings, there was evil in the world, but now, today, evil was life and good was the rare fool hearted exception to the rule. Soon after the disappearances, all the world governments united and became one world government, and the one man, Alexander Demetri, who seemed to be able to make sense out of all the mayhem was given the reigns to lead. Almost everyone, including Tage and Walter were mesmerized by the greatness of that man. How could a single individual literally rebuild their world? For the first time in the history of mankind, there was no war. Peace was all they knew. Everyone was provided for. Every person valued. Homelessness was a thing of the past and all manner of diseases were cured.

There was no violence, no fear; tolerance, inclusion and acceptance were preached from every known and established church. For all everyone knew, hatred was only a nightmare that the world had awakened from, a figment of their collective imaginations, and all physical evidence of its existence was wiped out so there would be no reminders of what used to be. It was often quoted that those who'd ignore or forget history were doomed to repeat it, but all that mattered to the world was Demetri and "his-story."

There was a captivating and compelling and obsessive believability about him; as if he spoke to everyone in the voices and spirit of those they were hardwired to respond to. Demetri became what people wanted and needed to see and hear. In a gathering that was wall-to-wall, standing room only, Demetri could address a sea of people; and each person felt as though they were the only one there, and that it was not Demetri speaking, but the essence of all that was good in their life; a tender mom or compassionate grandfather, a patient teacher or friend who was closer than a brother. He was a spiritual guide that told them everything their itching ears wanted to hear.

The world's mantra became, "peace and safety." There was one government, one currency, one faith, one religion, one way, and Alexander Demetri was at the center of it all. He knew the way and they followed.

With very little resistance... the world followed.

They were believers.

An uncomfortable jolt spread through his body when he landed on the asphalt next to Walter, and the warm tingle in his limbs from the electrical current gave way to pain. He hoisted Walter up faster than his damaged body wanted to go. Once he was up, Tage climbed up on the box behind him. The patrol car skidded to a stop a few yards behind them and the door quickly flew open.

Tage, with his mental fingers crossed, instinctively heaved Walter over the concrete divide. Walter dropped on the other side with a cringing thud. The muffled cracking, as Walter's body descended, gave hope that at the very least his fall was slowed. An open trash bin would have been too much to hope for, so his guess was some crates or boxes of some sort.

"Freeze," yelled Officer Bell, a gangly looking man with no command presence or power; one who wouldn't be a threat to a third grader stealing candy without his uniform, badge and gun.

Tage placed his hands on the wall to jump over, but before his muscles could even twitch to climb, Bell shot at him.

Blam!

Walter's eyes went wide and he took his cue to hobble for the hills. Tage covered himself, and then promptly scanned his body looking for a bullet lodged he was too shocked to feel. Finding nothing, he locked eyes with Bell, whose knowing smirk was indicative of an imminent surrender. Tage's surrender.

In a flash, Tage suddenly launched himself off the box and bolted down the street heading east.

Fragments of concrete from the wall sprayed as bullets narrowly missed his fleeting frame. He never imagined he could run so fast. He ran from Johnny Newbury's dog when he was a kid and he got caught; now he was outrunning bullets. Tage never doubted that Jesus walked on water, especially now, feeling as though he was running on nothing but air.

Tage quickly cleared Bell's line of sight, and the surprised officer jumped into his vehicle and accelerated in pursuit. Before Bell was able to round the corner, Tage had already scaled another section of wall and threw himself over.

Hungry eyes followed Walter from the shadows as he limped along, searching, eager to reunite with his companion. He winced with each pull of his deadened leg. He was not sure whether Tage was dead or alive, but he searched nonetheless. The streets were wet and the temperature continued to fall. Frost bellowed from his lips with each breath. He knew what was out there, and at the moment, the police were the least of his concerns. He was being followed by scavengers even more frightening than the invalid bottom feeders. The ones who stalk, those like the grizzly, who could move and move quickly, were lurking from within the shadows. They had a taste and a nose for blood and Walter's blood was aged to perfection and pouring down his wilted leg, and they were honing in on the delectable scent.

Long before the vanishings, people began to acquire a taste for the delicacies of human flesh. Theories were plentiful as to what brought this about; mental disorders, cult practices and rituals, drug and alcohol abuse, and the rise and financial success of books, television shows, and movies about vampires, zombies, and were-wolves. There was no escaping the impact and influence of the un-dead, and gradually, with the world becoming desensitized by what it deemed entertainment, people turned themselves over to their reprobate minds. Cities around the world even sponsored events called Zombie Walks, where tens of thousands of your average everyday citizens would dress up as the blood thirsty and flesh eating undead, carrying props like bloody limbs and organs.

Every boy growing up has heard a parent or guardian say emphatically, "It's all fun until someone gets hurt."

Well, the Zombie Walks were all fun until people actually started eating other people.

Walter, enveloped by fear, tried not to think about the homeless man in Miami who was the same age as him, who had his face eaten off in broad daylight while he was still alive. His attacker, on his hands and knees like an animal, reportedly dined on him for eighteen minutes and onlookers were unable to do anything against the deeply spiritual naked man that devoured him.

Was this part of the "Zombie Apocalypse" that was so often talked about on the news, internet chat rooms and forums?

Walter tried unsuccessfully to block out the imagery of a man in his early twenties being beheaded on a greyhound bus by the stranger who sat next to him, who then proceeded to dismember him and chomp on his limbs. The attacker believed that he was the second coming of Christ and that he was protecting himself and others by killing the "alien" next to him.

Fatigue was setting in, but Walter knew he could not stop to rest. His mind swirled, unwillingly forced to summon up the news report of a gay adult film star who ate his boyfriend. He thought about the college student in Maryland that devoured his roommates heart and part of his brain, the Swedish Professor who munched on his wife's lips, the cannibal who killed his victims with a crossbow and feasted on their cooked and raw organs, and the chef who turned his victims into meatballs and sausages.

Right before the disappearances, what some referred to as the rapture of the church, a mother beheaded her three week old son and consumed parts of the newborn's brain and bit off three of his toes. Walter was sickened by the grizzly images wreaking havoc on his mind, intensely fueled by the sounds of loud moans and gaining footsteps. He quickened his pace, his head snapping in every direction at the slightest thump or bang. He tried to trick himself into believing that the heinous stories he recalled about people mutilating and eating other people were not true, that they were just stories, make believe, or just… entertainment. He shuddered at thought of that word, entertainment. He knew better. He saw the pictures, watched the trials, read the news reports about some of the attackers being killed at the scene and others who were sentenced to consecutive life sentences. There was no undoing what was permanently branded in his mind. It was real. It happened. And like countless others on the planet, he talked about it for a day or two, contemplating what was happening to the world, but then promptly moved on to more pressing matters, retaining the information only to be used to spice up any dull conversations.

Now he found himself wishing that he didn't know what he did, that he could give due credit to some writer, director, or actor for their excellence in tapping into the most disturbing part of the human psyche; but sadly enough, these were only a handful of actual cases that flooded the news headlines before the vanishings.

Now, killing and eating people were not even newsworthy; it was life as they knew it; an everyday occurrence and a legitimate means of survival in that hell on earth.

To be plagued with such thoughts was of no benefit to Walter. He began to talk to God, in the only way he knew how as he limped along the way; as one friend would talk to another. His time spent conversing with God, pouring out his heart, asking for strength, coming to grips with his fear, and praying for his loved ones, caused his heart and mind to quiet as he roamed through the streets, wounded, and surrounded by utter darkness.

He began to think about his wife, Aubrey. Together, they've seen the good and the bad of life, but it was the good times that came rushing into his head. A terrifying image suddenly hijacked his mind. An image, far more frightening than anything his mind had conjured exploded into his thoughts; the sight of himself dressed down in his high school PE uniform with his yellow tank top, purple shorts, and glasses that covered most of his face; he almost laughed thinking how utterly cruel life could be at times.

It was a mystery as to why he went back to their days together in high school. His marching band, chess club, and debate team accolades, by comparison, should never have gotten the attention of the beautiful cheer captain and freshman class president, but it did. He recalled the day he asked her to wear his class ring, and almost smiled at the thought of knowing that she still had it.

No doubt she would have been voted prom queen at their senior ball, but things beyond her control, namely him, played into the voting and she wasn't even considered.

She kept reminding him that she won everything she needed or wanted to win the day. She was his moon and he was her sun. They shared everything; they watched and played sports together, loved going to the movies, and loved dancing even more. They were a team from the start. There had always been a comfort in knowing no matter what, their love would take them through whatever lay ahead. Though everything around them could collapse, together, they would remain a tower of strength. Thinking of his wife gave him the strength he needed to press onward. He was prepared to take on anyone or anything, if it meant seeing his Aubrey once again.

Tage carefully worked his way through the maze of streets desperately looking for Walter. Police activity seemed to have quieted, but he continued to move only within the shadowy darkness. Though he moved carefully, the slow moving and thoughtless bottom feeders, whose only remaining instincts were that of survival and feeding, did not give him much concern; he was too fast for them, unless of course he stumbled into within arm's reach of one of them, because once that's happened, Blitzkrieg. The only reason they would halt their savage feeding frenzy was if they felt threatened by an uninvited guest who showed for dinner.

It suddenly dawned on Tage how comfortable he has gotten with the darkness. He never liked being alone, especially at night. How vivid were the nightmares he still carried from his childhood, waking up in cold sweats with his heart pounding out of his chest. He remembered hiding under the blankets fearfully scanning the room with his eyes, looking for the comfort that's supposed to come with realizing that it was only his imagination after all. Of course, he was convinced otherwise by the clothes that hung on the closet door; they would become monsters, and he was still convinced that something terrible lived underneath his boyhood bed. He never put his hand down over the edge because he just knew something lurking below would surely lay hold of him and drag him, kicking and screaming, to his death.

Sometimes he would just lie partially on his side, blankets wrapping him in a mummified stupor, paralyzed with fear, unable to move anything but his eyes. Frantically he would try screaming at the top of his lungs for his mom and dad, who he knew would come to his rescue, but the only sound that would escape his lips, was the bellowing howl of silence. Help never came, so he was left alone to be tortured by his crippling imagination. He'd give anything for an exchange of his past fears, for the fears that were now his reality.

Tage's fingers were stiff from the cold and he no longer felt his toes.

He avoided the streets with trash barrels burning, because the fires more often than not were used only to lure in a most welcome meal, and he had no intention of running into anyone like the grizzly they had encountered earlier. He scoured the area searching for Walter, and then decided to head back towards the truck in hopes of finding him there. He spotted a dimly lit park nearby with a handful of work lamps surrounded by pools of darkness. The surrounding trees reminded him of the home he was desperate to return to.

There was no place like home.

No place.

Home... Was that too much to ask for?

Tage checked the vacant street, counted to three to summon his courage, and bolted; it was now or never. He hit top speed in a matter of seconds, racing straight into the darkness.

He made it across safely, running full speed ahead, and was suddenly smacked in the face with a stench that instantly made his face and other things pucker.

He pumped his breaks, but his unresponsive feet slowed too late, way too late.

He faltered over the edge of a man-made canyon in the park; a gorge filled with human remains, tangled and weaved together in a collage of spare parts. He had heard the stories about mass graves, but had never had the misfortune of seeing one up close, until now.

Anyone not coming under submission to the government were taken to slave camps, and once their usefulness was exhausted, they were exterminated. All were given numbers, just like those given by the Nazis in the hellish concentration camps during World War II. Instead of showers or ovens, many would be driven like cattle to the guillotines.

Tage began ruthlessly clawing his way back up before his body was even done spiraling downward. He was engulfed in an unimaginable nightmare. He gripped, stepped, and clung onto decaying bodies in an effort to scrape his way out. There must have been hundreds, thousands of bodies filling that hole. Some, freshly killed; bodies burned, diseased, decapitated, shot. His lungs fought against every forced breath. His body adamantly rejected the air filled with such a putrid odor that it stuck inside his gullet. He desperately tried to seal his mouth and nose with his hands, but with each breath he had to take, he could literally taste the death, along with the flies that somehow managed to make their way into the back of his throat.

"How could a thick layer of flies exist in this frigid environment?" He wondered, as he fiendishly spit them from his mouth, or swallowed those that were too far back. Maybe they have taken up residence inside the soft warm bodies themselves or perhaps they too have learned to adapt and change their genetic makeup in order to survive. He scaled the mound of corpses as quickly as he could, slipping repeatedly on moist skin and bone, and wads of misplaced flesh.

As soon as he made it topside, he dragged himself against whatever patches of grass and dirt he could find, attempting to remove anything on him that could be removed. He lay still for a moment, sickened, vomit rising up into his throat. He coughed so hard that his ribs felt as though they were going to snap, like wishbones yanked for good pleasure. When his contracting stomach settled and the nausea subsided, he wondered if Frank's body was in there. He had cultivated a love hate relationship with Frank for the past three years; Frank loved to hate him, so he was puzzled as to why he would be thinking of him and his quotes from the "Good Book." Tage remembered Frank telling him about his upbringing, he was raised in a Christian home, but didn't want anything to do with God. He was turned off by all the perceived rules and regulations; the whole, "you can do this, but you can't do that," mentality. Frank's parents, who vanished along with the others, were the type that continued to give, even when they didn't have, and Frank resented them for that. There were things he felt that he needed, wanted, things that he couldn't have because his family never lived above getting by. That was the main reason he joined the military, enlisting before his senior year of high school, and choosing an MOS that would ship him as far away from home as possible.

On the day he was sworn in, it suddenly donned on him, what others tried to get through his mule head; he wanted nothing to do with the church because of the perceived rules and regulations and he was now becoming a soldier in the United States military who must live and abide by rules and regulations.

Frank often wondered why people, even complete strangers were so important to his mom and dad, and no answer Frank's parents provided when asked made any sense to him. Tage on the other hand, just couldn't understand Frank's problem, every time he made mention of his family, it sounded to all who gave ear to him that they were good people; they loved and cared for each other, they loved and cared for Frank and his brother, who also vanished, and they loved and cared for people others would rightfully turn away from. They were happy even though material possession and assets came few and far between. They went through difficult times like anyone else, but seemed to have an inner peace that was not based on their situation or circumstances.

Frank's parents were church goers, so were Tage's, and they were all decent enough people, but Tage, his folks, and Frank saw life differently than Frank's parents did. Frank got dragged to church every Sunday and Wednesday. Tage went more often than not, but his parents allowed him to make up his own mind about what he wanted and how much he wanted to commit of himself. Frank and his brother would go to Sunday school, were sent to Christian camps, and had to memorize a bunch of scriptures from the Bible. Tage speculated that the reason why Frank drank so much was that it was his attempt to kill the pain of being left behind. Without question, the reality of hell was embedded in him for as long as he could remember. He used to say that "The world we live in is the only heaven a sinner will ever know and the only hell a Christian will ever know." No matter what your belief, or lack thereof, that was definitely food for thought.

Tage honestly hoped that Frank had made heaven his home, but Frank was not the One who had the final say in those matters. God was supposed to be merciful and forgiving, right? At least that's what he heard preached on the rare occasion that he found himself actually listening instead of doodling or passing notes. Tage didn't know for sure or understand much of what was said in church when he attended, and the thought of God's mercy and grace caused emotions to boil on the inside, creating a knot in his gut as suppressed anger began to surface. Tage didn't think he could imagine anything worse than where he was now, but not making it home to be with his daughter again, would certainly be his own personal hell and this hope deferred was making his heart sick. He felt as though life was draining from his pores. His longing to be reunited with his daughter had begun working itself through his body and tore up his insides. He threw the crippling thoughts from his mind with a forbidding shake of his head, cleared the bile in his mouth, pulled himself up and marched on, staying hidden among the trees that encircled the craters of death.

Chapter 4

THE frost of a forceful wind blew through the foothills, a forest thick with dead or dying trees, intermixed with different varieties of extinguished vegetation and plant life. Leaves that struggled to stay green were a rarity, proud among their brown and black counterparts.

The ground was hard and the terrain, treacherous. A lone figure laid beside a hollowed out log, nearly buried in a scrap of brush. Antonio Derosa concealed himself and kept a watchful eye on the surrounding area. The cold made its way through his pricey Forzeiri black leather coat, causing him to shiver. He tried to tell himself to be still, but it was an unreasonable request. His name-brand hat, pants, and gloves helped a little, but too little he thought considering how much they cost. His pale and torn clothing were once sharp with color and character, but now only covered with earth toned shades of dirt.

Antonio would never have guessed in a million years that this was what his life would become. He lived in the lap of luxury. He never had need of anything, his parents made sure of that. Antonio was self motivated; meaning, you would never find him motivated by anything other than what would directly benefit him. He was a nice enough guy for the most part, a little eccentric, but you can't fully blame him for his personal views and self-centeredness. His parents wanted their children to have anything their hearts desired, deserving or not, and they worked extremely hard to see that happen. It was a shame they didn't pass along their work ethic, because now, he just drifted aimlessly through life, or what was left of it.

Antonio was in his early thirties, but the delicate man was not aging well. He resented life for the simplest of things; his hands were not as soft as they used to be, he had three calluses on each of them that he loathed, and it was nearly impossible for him to keep dirt out of his neatly trimmed nails. His fiery hazel eyes still complimented his healthy head of black hair, so he was still grateful for that, and for his thick unibrow and mustache he constantly brushed with his fingers. It was amazing to think that the jet-setter who dined at the finest restaurants on the planet, dated celebrities, and entertained dignitaries, was now laying prostrate in the muck, hungry for a sip of broth after an eight hour watch. His parents started looking for answers after the vanishings; answers to questions their wealth could not buy. When the celebratory cries of peace and safety began to wane in the world, when officials close to Alexander Demetri, began to question, began to turn up dead, his parents turned to an exiled family member who spoke to them about God and about faith. It was not long after that when Antonio's parents became Christians and were killed in a raid against an underground movement which threatened to reveal Demetri for who he really was. Antonio was not ready to buy into whatever his family began peddling and neither was his brother, Paul. It turned out that he was the snitch that informed the government of his parents turning to Christ and their association with an underground church.

Paul betrayed them for the promise of a continued life of luxury, but the fine print didn't disclose how long that life would be. He was killed in the penthouse of swanky hotel cradling a bottle of champagne, the same night his parents were butchered. Antonio should have been dead too, but he was dancing the night away that evening and never made it home. He heard what happened and ran as far as money could take him, and then some.

The sky was dark and gloomy even though it was still early afternoon. There was a thick fog rolling over the mountainside. The moon looked blood red and its throw of light beamed through the branches of the trees. The sun was AWOL. Nowhere to be found. The stars were falling from the sky, beautiful to look upon, but at the same time hauntingly unnatural. Antonio looked over decomposing wildlife as he surveyed the area. The smell of rotting corpses permeating the air was repulsive. The whole atmosphere was despairing, like living with a plastic bag over their heads; the layer of plastic acting as a valve covering their nose and mouth, sealed tightly with the moisture created by their hot final breaths.

Animals were a useless source of food anywhere outside the city limits, which were controlled by the government. Eating anything caught or killed out there brought about an agonizing death to the consumer.

A third of all crops in world had been destroyed by floods, earthquakes and other natural disasters, locusts, and fiery hail storms; making it difficult for anyone to believe this was not some form of judgment.

The remaining crops outside of the governments control were poisoned, so only those who were implanted would have access to uncontaminated food and water. Demetri had made it seemingly impossible for people to live off the land, but life always found a way. Things grew, slowly, discreetly, but they grew. Planes used to fly overhead, dumping poison on the earth and into the sea, killing off anything that wasn't dead already, but there hadn't been a flyby in their area in so long they no longer were forced to wear masks. Nothing man-made seemed to fly anymore in that war torn world.

Antonio, staring, mind wandering, was startled by the cracking of twigs and pine needles behind him. He whirled around, heart racing, and caught Tai in his sights. He pushed his captive breath out with a deep sigh of relief, his heart felt like a racquetball being smashed against his chest cavity.

"What are you doing? You flippin' scared me, man."

"I was workin' on my creepin' skills, bruh."

Tai was a stocky dark-skinned Hawaiian, with jet black curly hair, wire-rimmed glasses and sarcasm coded in his DNA. He tried to bundle himself in a small pink blanket with colored flowers on the inside, far too small for his thick build. If there was ever a party, he surely would have been the life of it.

"Man, I'm freezing," Tai Said. "I bet you I can milk a cow and get ice cream." He clenched his jaws together to keep his teeth from rattling.

Antonio turned his attention back to his duties and Tai eyed his coat like a piece of meat.

"Brotha, I'll give you a dolla' for that jacket."

"If you have a dollar, I'm the one that gave it to you."

"Come on, man. Look around. Worms are sticking out the ground like sticks."

"Shhh. Quiet. Quiet!" Antonio snapped in a hushed voice.

Tai settled down, instantly becoming nervous and alert.

Antonio looked intently into the woods. "I thought I heard something out there."

"What are you looking-" Antonio shot up his hand, cutting Tai off with a gesture.

"Whatever, I'm going back inside. I've had enough of your paranoia." Tai started to walk away.

"I did hear something," Antonio said sternly.

"Yeah, me too... It was the sound of nothing. The same nothing you heard yesterday and the night before that." Tai strolled away, grumbling, "last week you even saw three whole nothings in one night."

"Hey!" Antonio said sharply. "Aren't you here to relieve me?"

Tai shot back a questioning look, "I got you, bruh. Believe that." He then continued off into the darkness, leaving Antonio alone to try and make sense out of what just happened.

A rundown ranger's shack long forgotten, was nestled near the backside of a mountain, hidden from view by towering pines and foliage. The mountain appeared to be solid rock that appeared as though it was carved out by human hands, but was the result of a volcanic eruption thousands of years ago. The lofty trees were thick in that area of the woods.

The shack was one large room with no plumbing or electricity. Three out of the five windows were still in place, but were permanently stained and nearly impossible to see through. The other two were covered to prevent the excess of unwanted odors from freely entering. Lean-tos, emergency shelters and sheds made out of tarps, ponchos, and tree branches surrounded the front part of the shack and were filled with camping gear, blankets, lamps, water jugs, and other necessities.

The grounds were well kept, organized, and the area camouflaged to aid in the defense against intruders, especially eyes from the sky. Raked piles of leaves had been scattered around the trunks of the trees as compost. The many fallen trees in the area provided fuel for fires, when it was safe for such luxuries. A blazing fire raged from a large pit. Engulfed in the flames were the carcasses of birds, squirrels, and other small animals that had to be burned for sanitation.

The carcasses carried diseases that were deadly to humans. The smoke rose and spiraled into the air like a donut twist, then dissipated in the thickness of the trees. That was one of the few places in the wild that had been left untouched by natural calamity and the government's efforts to destroy it were mediocre at best. The aroma of anything pleasant cooking inside the shack was drowned out by the indescribably awful stench of dead rotting animals roasting outside.

Tai, within view of the cabin, heard Brandy, a six-year-old German shepherd and Collie mix, barking loudly inside. As Tai drew closer, he picked up on an escalating argument taking place inside the usually peaceful dwelling place.

"Quiet, Brandy," Hollie yelled in frustration.

The dog yelped, and suddenly became quiet.

"No! I'm not doing it, Gina. I have to draw the line somewhere, and it's drawn, okay."

Gina, Hollie's wife fired back. "What's the big deal?"

"You're making it into a big deal. I'm not doing it. End of discussion."

Tai continued to plod along, thinking that Hollie's booming voice had caused all conversation to cease.

"This discussion is not over until I want to stop talking about it. That's how it works."

"Whatever, Gina," was all Hollie could manage to say at that point.

Hollie was a man in his forties with salt and pepper hair and a matching mustache and goatee. He was a steelworker by trade and built solid. Inside the kitchen area of the single room shack he was putting the finishing touches on a pot of soup cooking on a wood burning stove. A shotgun was mounted above him for easy access.

The stove was an antique and was used in the caboose of a train until it was relocated to its current home. It had a built-in oven on one side, and a compartment on the other side for stoking wood. The top was oblong, had an area for cooking, and a portion that could be used for heating up the coffee pot, which was on twenty-four-seven.

While Hollie was stirring the soup, the light from the candles and battery operated lamps reflected against the florescent pink polish covering his nails. Jazz music played from a small portable satellite radio. Gina, Hollie's better half, snickered at the sight of her strapping man. She was beautiful inside and out; personable, fun-loving and laid back. She would give you the shirt off her back, but without a doubt could be an instrument of wrath and destruction when it came to protecting those she loved. She had midnight black hair, and fair, pale, Irish skin. Audrey, Walter's wife, sat on a park bench at a table along with Gina and Sal, a six-year-old light skinned black girl, with two braids tied with a trio of brightly colored yarn. She was painting another one of her artistic masterpieces.

"Honey, that's not fair to me and it's not fair to Sal. Look what it's doing to her."

Hollie glanced in Sal's direction, who continued painting, pretending not to notice his finger nails.

Deep dimples surfaced on her face as she bit her lip, trying not to laugh.

"Tell him you're sad." Gina whispered to Sal.

"But I'm not sad," she quietly responded.

"Tell him anyway. I'm trying to teach you something." Gina said with a wink.

"I'm sad, Uncle Hollie." Sal spoke in a would-be whiny voice, trying to sound heartbroken.

"See honey, she's all broken up," Gina said, pointing to exhibit A.

"Yeah, I can see that," scoffed Hollie. "You want to paint my fingernails, Fine! I can live with that, but there is no way you are going to pluck—"

"Tweeze," Sal interjected, as Hollie shook his head, confused.

"Tweeze, Dad. We don't pluck, we tweeze," Gina corrected.

"I don't care what you call it, there's no way I'm going to let you do either one of those things to my eyebrows."

The suppressed laughter around the table was finally released.

Even Hollie joined in with a stifled laugh as he continued with his food prep.

Sal was born before her time; a thirty year old, second grader, who seemed to have more wisdom and intellect than those placed in her life to educate her. Her words, knowledge, and reasoning were remarkable. The works of her hand, through artistic expression, incredible. Sal was fascinated by every aspect of life, and always found a light no matter the darkness, which had inspired her creativity. She painted on whatever she could get her hands on, newspaper, scrap wood and even walls.

Sal's giggles, pranks and childlike humor were what brought everyone back to the reality that she was not even seven years old.

Hollie bounced around the stove, smelling, tasting, and spicing. Distracted, Sal struggled to concentrate on the picture she has begun of an angel, painted with meticulous detail. Her eyes lifted and she caught a glimpse of Hollie.

"I love your nails, Uncle Hollie," she finally let out, and then covered her mouth and giggled.

"And I love you, sweetheart. How's that picture coming along?" Sal lifted the colorful picture with pride.

Everyone gathered were amazed at Sal's gifting. She was fascinated by butterflies and angels, and this picture she said, was her daddy's guardian angel.

The walls of the shack were without insulation so the stove had to have a roaring fire for any sense of warmth to be maintained. Four sleeping pallets lined the wall near the main entrance. There was a cluster of heavy tools stashed in the corner of the front room; axes, sledgehammers, rakes, shovels and a pitchfork. A wooden beam fitted into metal holders secured the heavy wooden door. Blankets hung from the ceiling inside the shack, which separated the main area into rooms, which allowed for some sense of privacy. Mattresses lay on the floor piled with blankets and sleeping bags, sweats and long underwear. Each one in the house had a bug-out bag already packed in case of an emergency escape was needed. Hollie invested in survival supplies long before the disappearances. He was secretly relieved that his paranoia paid off; the ridicule he was subjected to by those who saw little to no value in investing hard earned and limited resources into disaster preparedness was insufferable at times. But no amount of preparation could prepare you for the times they now lived in. They had pots, pans, utensils, a water purifier, and gallon containers that previously were filled with food pouches. The water purifier didn't work in the bodies of water surrounding the camp because of the poison and blood in the water, but they found a cave that led to a mineral spring. Without that hidden water source there would have been no chance of survival out there.

The food and medical supplies have run dangerously low and needed to be replenished, which meant a trip into the city, a trip that many rightfully deemed a suicide mission.

There was an old storage room on the outside wall at the back of the shack that was used to house one person, jokingly referred to as the Chokey, a place where misbehaving kids were placed by Headmistress Trunchbull in the children's novel, Matilda. Usually this room was kept available for someone passing through the woods and was only in need of a place to safely stay for a single night.

Hollie passed by one of the grimy windows and peered out.

"Mom, can you get the door? It's Tai."

Gina headed for the door. Brandy, her loyal sidekick, named after Gina's drink of choice back in her boozing days, strolled by her side.

Gina found Brandy three weeks after the disappearances. Alone and frightened, Brandy cowered under a pile of rubble. The puppy was famished, nothing but skin and bone, hair matted from stained blood and dirt. Gina nursed Brandy back to health and he has been a member of the family from that moment on. Gina removed the wooden beam from the metal holders.

Tai entered, and before he could set foot inside, he began danc-ing to the music, whipping his hair back and forth, gyrating, and doing every tired, old and out-of-date move that came to his no rhythm having mind, much to Sal's amusement.

"Oh, that's my jam right there." He didn't have a clue as to what was playing on the radio, but none of that mattered with Tai. Life was meant to be lived and he lived it.

"What are you doing back here? Aren't you suppose to relieve Antonio?" Hollie demanded.

"Was that today?" Tai stated in a surprised tone.

Tai had nothing on his wrist, but he flicked his arm up as though he were looking at an imaginary watch.

Hollie stared at Tai, straight faced.

"I'm just playin'," Tai said, laughing.

"You shouldn't be here, Tai. You need to leave."

"Man, do you know how cold it is out there? Last night a snow-man knocked on the door and asked me if he could come in and sit by the fire." Everyone laughed but Hollie.

"Okay. I can take a hint. I'm going."

Tai shimmied back towards the door.

Hollie stopped him. "Wait a minute. Take this with you." He then grabbed a large coffee mug and filled it halfway with the soup he'd been preparing.

Tai's face lit up child getting his student of the month award.

Hollie hands him the broth.

"That's for you, Antonio, and Erika."

Tai's countenance fell in stinging disappointment.

"Make sure they get some," Hollie concluded.

"Can't we at least get separate cups?"

"First, stop breaking my cups or losing 'em in the woods, then I'll think about trusting you with more cups."

Tai stood there glaring at the partially filled cup, and Hollie stared at him staring at the cups.

"Why are you still here?" Hollie finally asked. "I promise you, you're not going to starve, okay."

"If it ever gets to the point where we have to start eating people... You first, Hollie. Believe that. I'm eatin' you first," Tai said as Gina laughed and pushed him out the door.

Sal jumped up from the table excited, "Can I go too, Uncle Hollie? Please." She batted her eyelashes at Hollie, a nearly angelic look on her face.

"I don't know, honey. Things can be a little dangerous out there." Hollie was glowing. Looking into her eyes he smiled.

"You do realize that you've been saying the same thing for the last four months, don't you, and you let her go every time." Tai stated matter-of-factly.

"Please." Sal's green eyes dug straight into Hollie's soul.

Brandy was now wagging his tail in excitement as he was waiting for an answer too.

"Brandy, lay down." Hollie commanded.

Brandy followed orders. He returned to Gina's side and plopped.

Hollie caved. "Okay, sweetie, you can go for a few minutes, after you grab something to eat."

Sal, delighted, had already bolted for the door. "I'll eat when I get back."

She suddenly stopped, backtracked, gave Hollie a smothering hug, and Gina a kiss before dashing out the door, dragging Tai by the hand.

Once the door was secured, Hollie sat down at the table and Gina poured him a meager amount of the potage. She served up some for Audrey and for herself as well. Hollie then nervously bowed his head. Gina and Audrey followed suit. He cleared his throat and his body became hot with nervous anxiety. With a grateful and sincere heart, he prayed to the best of his ability. It took him a moment to work up the courage; the formulation of words didn't seem to come easy when it came to this.

"Uh, thank You for this food, bless it and let it nourish our bodies, and… please protect those out there in harm's way; those we know…" Gina placed her hand upon Audrey's, who peeked up at her and smiled. "And we pray also for those we don't know. Amen."

Gina flashed a dopey ear-to-ear grin. "You go, boy. That was good. I'm so proud of you, Dad."

Hollie gushed, but felt as though he butchered yet another prayer.

Chapter 5

WALTER, barely able to stand any longer, plodded along doubled over, weak and exhausted. He peered down into the filthy alley and spotted his truck, untouched, right where they left it. He staggered down the alleyway, fumbling in his pockets for his keys. Pain coursed through his body with each step. Desperate to return to Audrey, he refused to allow his suffering to stop him. He unlocked the vehicle door and slid behind the wheel. In his wildest dreams, he would have never imagined that this day would turn out as it had. He feebly tried to pump the gas with his injured right leg and every nerve in his body screamed out in protest. He crossed his left leg over and completed the task.

He turned the ignition switch and the engine began to rumble as he pressed the gas pedal with his good leg. The engine groaned and then sputtered to a stop. "Come on, girl. Start," he muttered as he repeated the failed process. A patrol car turned down the alley behind him and pulled forward. Walter spotted the approaching cruiser in his rear view mirror. He made another attempt to start the truck, but to no avail. He lowered his head on the steering wheel; having no clue as to what to do, but fully aware of what was about to happen. He resigned himself, accepting defeat.

"If only I had listened to you," he whispered.

Early one morning years ago, Audrey was jolted awake, panicked, and barely able to breathe. Sweat poured down her face, though their room was plenty cold from the morning air blowing through the windows they left open, even during the winter. She couldn't even speak until she took in some water and paced the floor. Frantically she tried to make sense out of what she had just saw or experienced, even felt, judging from the look on her face. She was terrified. In the dream, she and Walter were running from judgment, running from the wrath of God. Walter didn't let her get too far into her story before trying to comfort her, or more like blow her off; not only because he was tired, but he was offended by what she was implying. Why would they be running from God? If sides had to be chosen, they were on the side of good. Walter refused to listen to any more and he argued with her about their goodness, especially in comparison with others in the world, even those they surrounded themselves with. They helped many charitable organizations by donating money, food and clothing, and never missed a Christmas or Easter service in all the years they've been married. He was raised on this tradition and determined to continue the practice in his family.

Audrey insisted on finishing. Walter could see in her frightened face and heard in her quivering voice that she needed to speak and he needed to shut up and listen. She continued on, her whole body telling the story of how fire was falling from the heavens and how they found shelter inside of another couple's home. Walter's knee began to bounce, and he was biting his lip, trying hard to keep his mouth shut. Oddly enough, he was particularly ticked off because he couldn't understand why they would not stay in their own home; after all, he built it, and it was head and shoulders above any other dwelling place in the entire community, in terms of safety as well. By this time Audrey was spitting mad. She told him that they left the home where they were held up, but the couple insisted on staying. Then only moments after they stepped out, the home was destroyed by a massive fire ball. Walter knew it was not the time or place to chuckle or say, "I told you so", but it did cross his mind.

They were helpless. All they could do was watch the ensuing destruction from under a bridge with a handful of other friends living in the same close-knit community.

She felt God was talking to her, telling her to alter course, to go back and find her first love, to remember that little girl that used to go Sunday school, the one who knew the Truth. By this time, Walter was sound asleep, and Audrey was left alone to wrestle with her own thoughts. In the days following her dream, they had lengthy discussions about spirituality, church and religion, and considering how close they were to retiring, living among the financial elite, they concluded that they had more important things going on.

They didn't want to be sidetracked by spiritual matters. If need be, they would take care of it later when things slowed down. After all, they felt they had all the time in the world to pursue new ventures.

The patrol car pulled to within only a few feet from the truck's rusted chrome bumper. Walter slouched over the wheel, whispering a few words of prayer. He tried to fire up the truck yet again, and suddenly it roared to life. Walter, elated and shocked by what had just happened, exhaled sharply. He righted himself and quickly glanced over his shoulder to see the position of the police car behind him.

He cranked the shifter in gear, and he stomped hard on the gas.

The truck lurched forward a few yards and then abruptly died.

Another patrol car swept in from the front, its presence stripped away even the slightest chance of an escape. Walter exhaled painfully, shaking his head, "I should have listened to Audrey back then, and to You, God… But, I have no regrets because I know you now, and that's all that matters." He half-smiled, as he quietly said, "I will see you soon, my love," and then he laid his head back against the headrest. He shuts his eyes, listening to the rhythmic and pounding echo of the approaching officers' boots against the street.

~

It was disheartening to see the moon appearing so tortured, its deep crimson hue was a far cry from what used to be a majestic expression of light. Still it hung, defeated, but proud. A constant and bloody reminder of what used to be. The painful chill of the elements tightened its grip, yet Tai playfully chased Sal along the perimeter of the campsite. Erika Bertolino, an intensely focused and guarded woman in her early thirties, kept watch; her constantly shifting blue green eyes stared intently out into the darkness as the wind tossed her long curly brown hair. Life experiences and her grandparents who raised her, taught her to always protect herself, her heart, and those important in her life. She had never known her dad and her mother chose drugs over her own children, so everything she valued in life came from her grandparents who fled Italy to the United States to escape life within the Italian mob.

She seldom allowed people to come into her world, thus explaining the reason for its smallness, but when she did, they were afforded the pleasure of seeing this funny, talkative sparkle of life for who she really was.

This area around the campsite was the only place that allowed an unobstructed view of the sky; a huge clearing of fallen trees with what looked like giant crop circles in the center. Erika allowed herself a moment to star gaze, never getting used to peering up into the heavens and seeing what looked as though a portion of the sky had been erased, completely extinguished of everything, as if someone with a cosmic eraser scratched away its existence. A third of the sky was dead and contained nothing but the deepest of black; just a vast cavern of darkness. Even shooting stars careening across the night sky appeared to be forbidden to enter the nonentity of that expanse.

Tai took a sip of his soup. His eyes closed, savoring the flavorful liquid. He offered the cup to Erika.

"No, thanks. I'll pass," she said, still staring into the sky.

He continued to press. "It's not just spit at the bottom of the cup, see," Tai responded as he showed her the contents of the mug.

"I'm good. You look like you could use it a lot more than me."

"Was that a crack about my weight?" Tai fired back, playing things up for Sal, who was enjoying the exchange of dialogue.

"You look tired, that's all. The energy could do you some good."

Sal blurted out. "My dad says you're just big boned."

Erika leaned down and whispered into Sal's ear. "I think that's something that supposed to stay between you and your dad."

Sal's eyes widen, and so does her innocent smile. She quickly turned to Tai. "Never mind."

Erika and Sal exchanged smiles.

"I'll show you never mind."

Tai playfully reached for Sal. She scurried behind Erika, laughing as she barely escaped from his grasp.

Her eyes suddenly fixed on the moonlit outline of a haunting figure in the trees across the clearing. She screamed and buried her face into Erika's back. She wrapped her arms tightly around Erika, holding on for dear life.

"Hey, he was just playing, sweetie, he didn't mean to scare you."

Tai moved in slowly, nonthreatening. "I'm sorry, girl. You know I'd never do anything to hurt you."

Every muscle in Sal's body was clinched. With a broken voice she confessed. "I saw something in the trees over there."

Erika and Tai's eyes swung out across the field, but saw nothing.

Sal released one of her trembling hands and they trailed her pointed finger to the trees directly opposite them.

"Over there, something moved." She said faintly, hoping that whatever was out there, would not hear her muffled words.

Tai carefully pried Sal away. "You saw something in the—" Tai choked on his words as something darted from one tree to another. Erika knelt down to Sal's level and looked her directly in the eyes.

Tai squatted, keeping a watchful eye on the trees. His heart hammered like a battering ram trying to cave in his chest.

"Sal, I want you to listen to me, okay." Erika said frankly.

Sal's eyes darted. She fearfully continued to scan.

Erika used her hands to turn Sal's face back on her. It took a moment for the fright to subside enough for Sal to give Erika her full attention.

"Sal, Tai is scared."

Tai scoffed.

"I need you to be a big girl, and take him back to the house, okay."

Tai shook his head and puffed his chest. "Tai ain't scared of nothing, woman, you better recognize the skills, son."

Erika shoots him a quick look and he finally understood what Erika was doing.

"I want you to take him home okay, as fast as you can."

"I know what you're trying to do, but okay. I appreciate it." Sal admitted.

Erika, tensed, released a quick laugh.

"Go on then. Hurry."

Erika gave Sal a gentle shove to get her moving.

Sal snatched Tai by the hand and they took off running. Tai glanced back at Erika, worried and unsure. After the pair covered a little distance, he flipped on a flashlight. The beam danced gracefully in the blackness until it was swallowed by the trees.

Erika whipped out a banged up .45 automatic from her pocket.

She popped the clip, checked the ammo, smacked it back in with the palm of her hand and chambered a round.

She slowly made her way around the clearing, her face tight and flushed red, driven steadily by the concentrated exhilaration now injected in her veins. She weaved a path through the trees, maintaining cover, unaware that she was being watched.

~

Tage navigated the urban terrain without incident. Police activity on the streets had become nonexistent and it suddenly became all too clear as to why. Somehow he had managed to get himself within a perimeter. He was unclear as to how; maybe he took a route to his current location that even law enforcement would not take without adequate backup. He surveyed the area and questioned his ability to safely backtrack, suddenly finding himself surrounded by officers on every street corner. There appeared to be no chance of him making it out, so he decided to climb.

He spidered his way to the top of a two story building overlooking the alley where their truck was parked. Loud voices could be heard below. The chatter on the police radios chirped away incessantly. Tage crouched down and quietly scooted to the edge of the roof, strangely aware of a sudden and drastic drop in temperature. He felt as though he could realistically kick a hole in the air.

His hands were stiff from the cold, and pressing them against the icy roof was painful. He covered his mouth to prevent the bellow of heated breath from announcing his presence, as he carefully crept to the ledge of the building. His entire body felt an immediate but fleeting moment of invigoration because of the warmth lingering on his fingertips. Leaned with his back pressed against the cold ridge of the roof, he drew another purposeful breath as he cupped his balmy hands in front of his mouth and slowly exhaled. His eyes fell, wanting to savor, to listen to his body hum its joyful response to the temperate air from his lungs traveling from his moist hands to every cell in his shivering body. He forced his unwilling eyes to open and then placed his reluctant hands upon the frosty rain gutter, which shot an icy jolt through his system.

He peered over the low hanging wall and his eyes were instantly drawn to Walter, barefoot and stripped of his clothing, except for a ripped T-shirt and poorly fitting blood-stained boxers.

Walter trembled, plunged into the frigid depths of the frosty elements and of mortal fear, but mostly it was fear that caused him to shudder. Headlights accentuated his frail broken frame, and illuminated the three Officers who encircled him, toying with their prey. A brown sack had been placed over his head and drawn tight around his neck. Tage noticed that the officers were gracious enough to allow his improvised tourniquet to remain in place on his leg, which looked like a piece of tenderized red meat; no doubt simply to prolong his life and his suffering. Officer Mitchell, an overweight man by anyone's standards, held onto one of Walter's arms as Officer Stevens, black with freckly skin, and Officer Bell, the lanky officer that shot at him earlier, looked on, amused.

Helplessly, Tage watched as Bell delivered a crushing blow to Walter's stomach, doubling him over hard and fast, the wind forcefully knocked out of his aged body. Walter tried to suck in air, but his lungs refused him. Tage sat back in utter disbelief, his eyes shifted and his mind was unable to still itself. He struggled to find his breath. He scanned the rooftop and saw only a handful of useless items permanently affixed to the structure from which he perched. He lamented at the thought of seeing his friend in the merciless hands of the police. He hated them for what they were doing and what they represented, he hated Walter for being captured, and he hated himself for being rendered powerless. He felt trapped by his inability to intervene.

"Why did you come back here?" Tage wondered, pointlessly; They both knew there was no other way.

Walter's moaning and the officers' laughter forced him to look once again. Surely he could not allow Walter to die alone.

"I'm here, Walter," he muttered, hoping that Walter could sense, somehow know, that he was not alone.

Walter managed to straighten himself. He stood tall, refusing to submit; his act of defiance.

There was an acute awareness of the demonic presence seen

in the distorted faces of the three cops. Their movements were suddenly jerky, almost puppet like, as if their bodies were being controlled by an outside force and their limbs were attached to concealed strings. Mitchell's face went from being its normal chubby self to drooping and slouched on one side, hanging as though his skeletal mass, his insides, had somehow diminished and his skin was now too big for his oversized frame.

Tage slammed his eyes shut, hoping that once he released them all would appear as it should, but it was apparently too much to ask. All their teeth appeared broken and decayed. Their nails were jagged and dark, and their eyes were lifeless and black as oil. Stevens' face had shifted and his skin looked as though it was dying to peel back and separate from his flesh, to burst at the seams because the fabric of his body was being stretched to the point of tearing. Bell looked like someone who had been savagely beaten to death with a heavy blunt instrument; his body was bruised and discolored, enormous veins webbed through every inch of his cadaver-like body. Tage could not make sense out of what he was seeing. He wondered what kind of world he had stepped into when he left the sanctity of his home. But long before that, what shifted in the hearts and minds of men to where they gladly voted in policies, bills and laws, which took away their rights and freedoms. Everything from education, gun control, and healthcare, all aspects of individualized life freely handed over and given to government control.

In a flash, all three men returned to their former selves; even their coal black eyes shifted back to what they once were.

They taunted and jeered, haggling and placing bets about Walter's longevity.

"Double or nothing," shouted Mitchell.

96

Stevens tried to talk him out of the wager because he had already lost a substantial amount of money and it wasn't his day.

"Come on, double or nothing. You know I'm good for it," Mitchell demanded.

Bell tried to convince him to cut his losses, but Mitchell was extremely persuasive and it was still early. He successfully pressed the issue to his favor. The madness would continue because there was money to be won.

The playful banter was sickening.

A chill snaked down Tage's spine as Mitchell stabilized Walter. Stevens and Bell circled him like sharks to mask the angle of their destructive intent. Walter knew it was coming, but what, and from where, he had no idea.

Suddenly, Bell threw a wild haymaker of a punch into Walter's face. His head snapped back as if it was on a hinge, his feet were scooped up and he landed hard on the cold wet pavement.

Stevens knelt beside Walter, his knee pressed into the upper portion of his chest bordering his neck.

"Who hit you?" He commanded with an icy pitch.

Walter, disoriented, turned away, refusing to answer. He gasped for air; his shallow, labored breathing could be heard from under the hood.

"Hey! Answer me. Did I hit you?"

Mitchell, fed up, grabbed Walter and yanked him up like a rag doll.

He flicked out a large folding knife.

"I suggest you answer the question or we'll start playing this game with my knife." Mitchell threatened with a smirk as he dug the tip of his blade into Walter's chest. He cut downward and produced a thick rill of free flowing blood.

Officer Mitchell turned to Stevens and motioned for him to question Walter again.

"Did I hit you?" Stevens says.

Walter remained still for a moment, and then slowly nodded his head. Stevens and Bell erupted with laughter. Mitchell kicked away the closest piece of garbage he could find. Not good enough. He took Walter and hurled him into the air. He slammed against a building and collapsed to the pavement, motionless.

Tage slunk to the ground, overcome by the paralyzing shock which seized him. His chest heaved and through grinding teeth he choked back the growl which attempted to escape his throat. Growing up, he was taught never to lose his head, to always keep a clear mind. Mistakes were most often made in the heat of madness. He had to calm himself. He retrieved his pocket watch, opened it, and stared into the eyes of his wife, Shannon. Her long blond hair was wrapped into a bun when the picture was taken, and her bright blue eyes left Tage breathless every time he looked into them. There was so much that he loved about her, so much he wished he could talk to her about now. If only to have her just listen and grin as only she could do.

No matter how overwhelmed he was, a peace would settle over him, because she always looked as if she knew something about the situation that he didn't. She effortlessly brought a wellness to his being. That's what her expression and her eyes said every time he lost himself in them. There was a simplicity about her that was so complex. She never felt that she had much to offer anyone, but so many family members and friends would be hopeless without her. Tage longed to hear the sound of her low raspy voice, to once again smell her scent on his clothes and feel the warmth of her touch. He smiled at the thought of being stung with her icy gaze, a look that would cause his heart to stop and his stomach to tie in knots.

With her, he knew that everything would always be okay. There was always a way, it just needed to be found. That was the magic of their love, her love. She was and continued to be that in his life.

The wind sliced through Tage's clothes, and the biting chill was a constant reminder of her fire and her fighting spirit that few could contend with, including him; it's what made them perfect for each other and it's what brought out the best in him. In the picture, Shannon stood next to their daughter, Sal, who appeared to be a year or two younger than now. Sal wore one of Tage's button-up shirts and flexed her arms pretending to be her dad. They were both playfully posing in front of a glassy lake. Tage, as he continued to stare into the photo, taking in every minute detail, a divergence of peace and guilt battled within him. Everything suddenly fell silent as he slipped into their world.

~

Tai banged his fist against the outside door of the shack, the thunderous noise alone made adequate demand for the door to be opened quickly, but he shouted as well. Inside, Brandy relentlessly barked. Sal knocked rapidly, with as much force as she could muster; her small fragile hand barely registered sound against the solid wooden door. She cried out for her Uncle Hollie with a loud trembling voice, a seldom heard wail of terror that could stop the heart and drain the life from all who knew and loved her. She banged her palm harder on the door, turning and looking over her shoulder, her face tight with fear. Gina, wide eyed, looked out the tainted window. Hollie, with shotgun in hand and Brandy barking immediately

99

behind him, flung open the door, allowing Sal and Tai to rush inside to safety, to comfort.

Sal, who had been resisting the urge to cry, released all of the pent up emotions suppressed by her exodus of fear. She began to bawl almost inconsolably.

"Brandy," snapped Hollie.

As on cue, Brandy yelped into silence and moved to Gina's side.

"What happened, are you okay?" Hollie asked, terrified by the panic in Sal's voice.

Gina whisked Sal into her arms, trying to comfort her. She rolled her around in her arms scanning, checking, poking and prodding for any sign of injuries. She looked to Tai for answers.

"She's not hurt," he said.

Sal confirmed. "I'm okay, Auntie Gina."

"There's something going on in the clearing," Tai spit out, winded.

Hollie pressed for more detailed information, but there was nothing more to be rendered.

Every day, they lived in the fear of one day being found out, being hunted. They've experienced it before, and they knew it was only a matter of time before it happened again. Sal's breathing slowed enough for her to speak.

"There was something in the trees," she said.

Hollie kept his eyes riveted on her, while the others exchanged looks of concern, their unspoken words floated between them.

Hollie was less than satisfied with the extreme lack of detail. He often reminded them that what they all saw and heard in any given moment could be a matter of life and death. Nothing was to be disregarded or taken for granted.

"Erika went to check things out," said Tai.

Hollie paced the floor, his body tensed.

"You guys should have all come back here together, none of us are supposed to be in that area."

Hollie turned his attention to Gina and Audrey. "Make sure everyone is ready to move out if we have to... Gina, muzzle the dog."

Gina and Audrey ripped through the place, rehearsed, disciplined and militant.

"If you hear gunshots, head for the escape route and get to the cave."

"What about me, Uncle Hollie?" Sal inquired, wanting to be useful.

"You're in charge of Brandy, okay. If you have to leave, make sure he gets out of here. Okay, sweetheart?" Sal whimpers her okay.

"Tai, you're with me."

Hollie and Tai marched out the door. The fire pit, the one burning the animal carcasses was now on life support, struggling to stay alive. "Antonio needs to alert anyone camping within the perimeter about the possibility of cannibals, or God forbid... Hunters." Tai nodded his understanding.

"Position yourself in the middle of the camp. If you see anyone, I mean anyone suspicious coming at you before us, shoot first and screw the questions. You got it?"

Tai hesitated. "Yeah, uh... about that..."

Hollie shot him a look that demanded the immediate clarification of his last words.

"I don't have a gun."

"What do you mean you don't have a gun? You were on watch."

"Frank took it," Tai sheepishly replied. "Look, I was gonna beat

101

him down, but he started bustin' out with… This is my gun, there are many like it, but this one is mine." Tai's impersonation of Frank was impeccable.

"I was like, that's for a rifle, moron." Tai continued.

Hollie furled his brow as Tai continued. "And then he grabbed me, so I punched him. He must have started drinkin' early, 'cause it didn't even phase him… And I was like dang, boy, you strong. And he—"

"Okay, okay. Get Gina's gun and do what I told you. You think you can you do that?"

"Like Mountain Dew, baby."

Tai headed back towards the shack and Hollie lit up a path with the beam of his flashlight. He sprinted for the clearing, hoping for the best, but fully prepared for the worst.

~

A slew of officers surrounded the Nu-way Market and there was a city garbage truck parked halfway on the curb in front of the store. Glass lay on the sidewalk from the broken door. News reporters scurried about grabbing microphones, while their crews busied themselves with setting up equipment for a major broadcast. The reporters gathered appeared nothing like those of old, who were polished in their power suits and blazers, with styled hair, painted faces, million dollar smiles and body movements that were on par with runway models. No, those lining the sidewalks were found on a budget, and looked no more appealing than those who woke at 4am to deliver the morning paper door-to-door. Police tape sectioned off the area encircling the store, which served no purpose, due to the obvious absence of spectators, who were wisely locked in their dwelling places. After a distant flash of lightning crossed the ink black sky, a light rain, which was one of the few things that hadn't changed, began to fall.

Reporters rushed to grab their umbrellas. A spectrum of dull colored umbrellas soon appeared and congregated; one anxious reporter needing to outdo another for a story, that hadn't changed a bit either. Cords were strewn over the ground attached to microphones, cameras, and the heart of any mobile broadcast, the trucks, which looked more like vans kidnappers would use for their abductions. Satellite dishes stood at attention on top of the broadcast vans, which moonlighted as getaway cars, hungry for something tantalizing to transmit.

The camera lights shone brightly while reflecting on the wet streets. A clap of thunder and a downpour accompanied the arrival of a black sedan that was waved in and escorted through the police barricade. The vehicle pulled to a stop in front of the market. The driver, Rasul, a handsome olive-skinned man of Middle Eastern decent, quickly exited the car dressed in a black suit and wearing an ear piece. He rushed to the back of the vehicle with an umbrella in hand and after scanning the area, opened the rear door on the passenger side. He extended his hand inside the vehicle and retrieved a walking cane. He then patiently waited for the sole passenger to exit.

The walking stick was exquisite; the handle had a face on one side accentuated in gold, the top of which had been hand carved into the head of a serpent. The man exiting the vehicle was Goodwill Ambassador Kendall. He was a broad towering man with chiseled features and white hair neatly styled. He moved with power and grace in his tailor made European suit. His charm was as deceptive as a master illusionist; he was the epitome of Charisma.

Even though he walked with a noticeable limp, he carried himself perfectly.

Ambassador Kendall walked purposefully towards the door, shielded by the umbrella being held over his head by Rasul, who's every movement was methodical and sharp. Journalists pressed in like a pack of voracious wolves smelling the blood of a wounded bison, unleashing a flurry of questions they were dying to have answered.

"What did they want?"

"How many are dead?"

"What is the condition of the clerk they tried to kill?"

Reporters screamed with enthusiasm. Ambassador Kendall, fully aware of everything going on around him, remained focused and composed.

Sergeant Haims, the Sergeant in Charge, approached Kendall, who continued his brisk walk towards the front door.

"Is there something you can do about this, Sergeant?" Kendall, with a hypnotically soothing voice, inquired of the excitable Officer, who was relishing in the action.

"We're doing the best we can, Sir. It's been over a year since our last encounter with these people and—"

Kendall stopped and raised his thick eyebrows. He turned, beaming, and locked eyes with Sergeant Haims, who almost choked on the next words that were hanging on his lips waiting to be spoken. Blood drained from his mortified face.

Ambassador Kendall released him from his paralyzed state, "Please, mitigate this for me, sir." Haims was flooded by a short lived sense of relief. So much so, that his hands began to tingle. Falling over his words, he immediately barked out orders to any officers within earshot, and they subsequently converged on the news teams.

Kendall continued padding to the store's entrance. Sergeant Haims stopped for a moment only to think about the kindness of Ambassador Kendall. His countenance abruptly fell and he began to gnaw on the inside of his cheek, thinking it would have been better for him if the Ambassador lashed out in anger or threatened to have him executed. He was racked by the torturous thoughts of what could soon happen to him and what remains of his family.

A crime scene unit, spread throughout the inside of the store, gathered evidence. The items that were being purchased when Frank was killed had been set aside. Other items were already tagged and bagged, and Frank's body was being drained of what was left of his blood. The clerk, Robert Timothy, was being interviewed by a pair of officers.

While taking in his surroundings, Ambassador Kendall closed his eyes and inhaled deeply. He remained motionless, his breath held. He emptied his lungs and slowly filled them once again.

Kendall's breathing becomes more of a hiss as he audibly sniffed the air. His eyes rolled in his head and his lips began to babble incoherently as though he was chanting. A dark tangible presence filled the room, so thick, that not a step could be taken by anyone in the room without resistance. All inside the building except for Rasul nervously turned their attention to Kendall. Officers traded looks of curiosity and confusion, ultimately giving way to fear. Kendall's body moved with a slight twitch, and a painful look registered on his face as he peered around the room with only the whites of his eyes showing. His pupils had rolled into his head and he was using every sense, known and unknown, to absorb and ingest his surroundings. He drank in his setting like a demonic bloodhound preparing to stalk his prey. His hands begin to follow Tage and the others' path through the store, leading all the way up to the point where Tage whisked Walter out the front door.

The weighted presence lifted.

Kendall's breathing normalized and his eyes fell back in place as a look of gratification graced his face.

Everyone immediately returned to their respective duties, and no one dared consider inquiring about what had just taken place. The officers siphoning Frank's blood entertained themselves. They posed and took pictures of each other with Frank's lifeless body, as though he were a trophy or prize catch on a fishing expedition. This had become the norm when fugitives on the run were killed, those who had refused the implant. The more killed, the more they suffered, the greater the glory in the eyes of Demetri.

Robert stood behind the counter with several officers surrounding him. There was giddiness and excitement in his voice as he recounted the story of what transpired. The officers laughed as they hung on every word that escaped his drooling lips. He was especially excited about the forthcoming reward he would receive because of his actions. There was a time when every television and radio station, social media sites, internet chat room, and posters on every corner announced huge rewards for every capture, or information leading to the capture of anyone, dead or alive, refusing to take the mark and align with the one world society, with Demetri. With so much time having passed since the last capture or execution of this magnitude, Robert Timothy's reward would no doubt be substantial.

Those who called themselves Christians, and refused the mark on those grounds, held the highest monetary value because of their perceived messages of hate, division, and intolerance. It was amazing to think that the start and popularity of reality shows helped to condition and even usher in an era where Christians were hunted and killed for sport, all while being broadcast live around the world; without anyone batting an eye or thinking twice about the humiliation, suffering, and death those people experienced. It was entertainment at its best, with thirty second commercial spots easily going for upwards of four million dollars when the award-winning show, "Where's Your God?," aired. The program has since been canceled, due to a massive drop in ratings when the supply of worthy people to hunt had all but diminished. They tried using others but nothing could bring back the glory days of having a Christian cry out to their God, only to be answered by the report of gunfire riddling their body with bullets. Death was the only thing awaiting those who chose to go against the will of the government, and the slanted media crews outside would once again remind those in hiding that they too would end up like Frank.

Robert Timothy was a man of little self control, which people could tell simply by looking at him; overweight, slovenly and unkempt. He was the type that blew his nose into his hand, wiped it on his clothes, and then extended it fully expecting someone to shake hands with him. His parents raised him as best as they could, passing on their secret to rearing children; beat everything you don't like out of them. Robert Timothy was the model child for that school of thought and he swore by it, because he raised his kids the same way. You almost felt sorry for him as he told his story because the officers were laughing more at him than with him, but he was just too dumb to know it.

Ambassador Kendall strolled towards him, extending his hand. He spoke with a generous smile.

"Mr. Timothy?"

"Robert... You can call me Robert."

"Very well. How are you feeling, Mr. Timothy?" Kendall said.

"I, uh... fine. A little shaken up," muttered Robert.

"As you should be, under the circumstances." Kendall offered. "On behalf of the United Nations and Alexander Demetri, I would personally like to thank you for your service to your country and to the world."

Robert stood red-neck if-momma-could-see-me-now proud as he listened to Kendall's words. His huge smile showed his pearly brown and rotted teeth. Ambassador Kendall bid him farewell and headed for the door.

"Excuse me, your highness. I seem to recall something about a reward. Uh, what about that, bud?" Kendall stopped and turned, no longer smiling.

"Mr. Timothy, are you aware that possession of a firearm of any kind by any civilian citizen of the world is punishable by death?"

Robert responded only with a dumb stare.

Kendall glanced towards Frank's body.

"You did shoot that person, did you not?"

Fear prevented Robert from uttering a word.

"With a gun," continued Kendall.

"My Daddy gave me that gun a long time ago."

"Well, fortunately for you, your gun has been confiscated and will be destroyed according to the United World Peace Treaty." Robert moved only to wipe the sweat from his face. "The only reason you are not facing criminal prosecution and I am not carrying out your death sentence right now is because of your heroism. Shall I reconsider?"

Robert was a simpleton, but he knew that if he said the wrong thing, the next words that came out of his mouth would certainly be his last. "Well...uh...I guess that's enough reward for me," Robert stammered out.

Kendall smiled just as Rasul leaned in and whispered something into his ear. Kendall's face lit up.

"Alive?" Kendall exclaimed quietly.

"Yes, Sir."

They marched toward the door, leaving Robert behind with a vacant expression on his face.

Outside the market, lights flashed and camera's captured Frank's body being hoisted and tossed irreverently into the back of the garbage truck.

As Kendall rushed to his car, reporters scuttled towards him screaming out questions. "Ambassador! Ambassador! What can you tell us about the men that tried to rob the store?" As they advanced and officers attempted to maintain control, Rasul, at the Ambassador's side, searched the crowd and spotted, Haims. He casually drew his gun and put a bullet in his brain. The Sergeant never knew what hit him. It was simply lights out.

The crowd, stunned, looked on in horror and disbelief. Rasul then proceeded to shoot reporters and camera operators, starting with those closest to him. The crowd immediately took flight and dispersed; he even killed a nearby officer, who appeared to be doing his job, keeping people away from Kendall.

The crack of Rasul's gun rose above the high-pitched screams and gut wrenching yells, as people dropped dead one after another.

Rasul, poised, did not shoot wildly, but slow, steady, and certain. Every time he pulled the trigger, someone died. There was no opposition or resistance from the fleeing crowd because guns were taken; well, legislated away and freely given over to the government upon promises of keeping every citizen healthy and safe.

Once the crowd, running hysterically into the night, had cleared sufficiently, Rasul holstered his weapon and escorted the delighted Goodwill Ambassador to his car.

Kendall halted for a moment. "See that this place is burned to the ground," he said coldly. "And make sure that Mr. Timothy and his family are inside when it happens." Rasul acknowledged the order and then opened the car door to allow Kendall to slip inside. Rasul then jumped into the driver's seat and the vehicle sped away, leaving behind a number of dead bodies littering the street.

~

Tage was plagued by nightmares whenever he slept, another reason for the weary circles around his eyes, that and being severely malnourished. Somehow in the midst of all the waiting, the waiting for Walter to be killed, exhaustion had finally taken its toll and he was thrust into the realm of fitful sleep. He didn't know how long he'd been out, because time had become irrelevant to him. The ticking of each second that passed, pounded constantly in his head, like a leaky faucet with a drip that was boring a hole into his forehead.

Tage began to stir because of an unsettling silence. His mind was still in a haze and he groggily rolled his eyes as he woke, and he instantly felt trapped, failing to remember that he found shelter underneath a large air conditioning unit on the roof. The mental slip reminded him of times when he got off work in the middle of the night and he couldn't remember how he had gotten home. More times than he would care to admit, Shannon would have to wash all the bedding because he climbed into the bed and passed out fully dressed in his muddy clothes and boots. It was especially bad one day when he spent 36 hours straight in the middle of summer working on the septic lines at an old folk's home. And yes he did; as much as he planned and fought against it, he ended up in bed fully loaded. Shannon tossed ev-er-y-thing, and their room had never been the same from that day on.

Water from the passing rain had soaked through the bottom of his clothes and his body shivered uncontrollably. He felt the exterior of his pocket and found comfort in knowing that his watch was right where it should be. He listened for a moment, relieved not to be hearing Walter's screams. He was surprised that he was able to slide in under the air conditioner, because he knew full well that if he was his normal healthy size, he would certainly have been stuck out in the open. It was a tight fit for him and he was having difficulty breathing with his chest pressed firmly against the metal undercarriage. He was never one to speak of claustrophobia, but he felt as though walls were suddenly closing in on him; being forced in to crush and bury him in the open air tomb he found himself lying in. He quickly scurried out, lightheaded and faint. He sat up and took a few deep breaths and his mind began to clear. His inclination to rest was overridden by the sound of voices he heard down below. He crawled towards the edge of the roof and took a gander. His nervousness suddenly turned to alarm when he realized that it was not over yet. His eyes narrowed on an unforgettable face. He swallowed hard, with an audible gulp in his throat as a furnace of unresolved grief began to burn.

Ambassador Kendall stood casually in front of a battered and bloodied Walter, who was freezing more than ever from the effects of the rain storm that has passed. Soaked to the bone, he quivered as he knelt before the Ambassador, who lorded over him like a mythological god.

"Why are you making this so hard on yourself? You want to live don't you?" Kendall waited for an answer that never came. "All I want to know is where the others are hiding, and you have my word, I will let you live." Tage could barely make out the quiet voices, which added to his anxiety, but he heard enough to know that Kendall was asking about their home.

"I know you wouldn't last a day in the city without help, and only death awaits those outside the city limits, so I would really appreciate you telling me what I want to know," said Kendall. Aside from the sound of Walter's labored breathing and the chattering of what's left of his teeth, he remained silent.

Kendall calmly took one of Walter's arms and twisted it into an impossible angle. He continued to wrench the limb until something snapped. The pain was so intense, sound refused to exit Walter's wide open mouth.

"Where are the others, Walter?" Walter lay on the ground broken, his body contorted and misshapen.

"Kill me. Just... kill me, please." Walter begged.

"I don't want to kill you. I want to help you, Walter. Your life doesn't have to end like this." Walter managed to gurgle out a few inaudible words and scrambled to his knees. He lowered his head, not defeated, but ready.

"Very well, then," Kendall said, as he removed a sword from the inside of his cane and aligned the blade at the base of Walter's neck.

He slowly raised the blade, knowing that at any moment, he was going to be told whatever he wanted to hear.

Tage was saddened by the loss of his dear friend, but he was grateful, relieved that his suffering would finally come to an end. Tage turned to walk away, wondering how he was going to tell his wife that he failed to keep his promise. He only had time to take a single step forward before he heard Walter's bellowing voice.

"Wait. Please! Stop!"

Tage's blood iced over. In that moment Tage's heart felt as though it had been ripped violently from his chest. He rushed back over to the edge and saw Walter speaking to Ambassador Kendall.

Tage's eyes narrowed on Walter and Kendall. Everything else was a blur, and all he could hear was his heart thumping like a kick drum.

Every last bit of air in his lungs had been siphoned, eradicated, and he was afraid, deathly afraid. Through all that had happened since their deadly adventure began, for the first time, unmistakable terror had registered on his face and that dread was now squeezing the life out of him.

"What are you telling him, Walter?" He growled, seeing Kendall relay what was spoken to him to the surrounding officers, who then got on their radios, laughing.

Tage's existence was eroding, evaporating into thin air.

How could he stop the hemorrhaging?

He wanted so to scream. If only he could scream, "Stop! Don't do it, Walter!" But he'd be as dead as a stuffed animal with a hole in its head if he gave voice to his thoughts.

He had to survive, no matter what he promised himself that he would live. He promised Sal that he would be okay. Tage found it hard to concentrate, nearly impossible to focus, with the hammering inside of his brain.

"How could you make such a promise?" He asked himself, knowing he already failed with Walter. The exasperation of the moment was suffocating him.

Kendall stepped back, contemplating.

"Please, no," whispered Tage.

He wanted to shout, "Come back!" as he watched officers on their radios come and go. "Where are you going?" Tage cried out in his mind only to be answered, "To kill your family. To kill your daughter… we're going to kill, Sal."

Tage grabbed his head. He cursed the despicable voice that spoke those words. He hated himself for wishing that Walter had died sooner, but he did. Why couldn't the old man just die? Did he deserve what happened to him, no, but he had no sympathy for the wretched man now. "Oh God. They're going to kill my little girl. Why couldn't you just die Walter?"

Tage's mind spun out of control, then gridlocked. He was freezing, but his body was on fire. He wanted to sleep, but dared not shut his eyes. He wanted to fight, but was terrified. Every thought and emotion, the past and the present painfully collided, and all outcomes led to the brutal slaughter of everyone he loved and cared for. He had to get to his little girl. This was war. His war. The future was as distant and as untouchable as the past to him. There was only now. There is only now. There is.

Without waiting to see what happens to Walter, the Judas Iscariot who wouldn't just die, Tage frantically scrambles to the other side of the roof, and with each stride he takes, he curses Walter, spewing words of hate that cut bitterly into his soul. Tage quickly descends the building, and when he hits the ground, he takes off running for dear life; for his and for hers.

Chapter 6

Eʀɪᴋᴀ trudges through the thick brush and dense trees surrounding the clearing, her gun held steady, sweeping and leading the way. Her face is hot with expectancy. She steps crouched, treading softly, but each muffled crunch of dirt and rock under her tattered size seven shoe and every snap of twig announces her presence.

She hears a rustling in the trees up ahead and catches a glimpse of something in the branches above. She raises the muzzle of her gun and cautiously advances. No sooner than she identifies a possum hanging from a tree limb, it falls to the ground gasping for air, like a tortured fish deprived of water for someone's wicked amusement. The possum's body gradually seizes up and lies lifeless on the ground.

Erika moves on unfazed, the tortured and dying animals she lays eyes on are an all too common occurrence. What she is not use to seeing is, Sean Milhous, an 18-year-old curly brown-haired kid with freckles and glasses fogged from the clashing heat of his frail body and the cold dark air.

A stunning picture of innocence, lies on the packed dirt, partially inside a sleeping bag, convulsing.

The twitching of his body is almost rhythmic, even quiet, as he lies amid the fallen leaves, with his yellow-like complexion almost matching the foliage he may soon be buried in.

Erika slowly edges forward. Her eyes fix on him, just as his vacant eyes begin to dart back and forth. Erika comes within a few feet of Sean, with her gun still trained on him, when all of a sudden she hears the crackle of branches above her. She cranes up and spots a man flying down from the trees toward her. She has no time to raise her gun, but she manages to narrowly miss being struck by the crazed looking male. Erika gets a bead on him with her gun.

"Don't move!" She screams.

Brad is frail with deep-set eyes. His facial features are withdrawn from drug addiction. He is sweating and fidgety, a ticking time bomb ready to go off.

"That's my brother. We're just looking for help."

Erika scans the area as Brad begins to cough violently.

"Who's we?"

Erika shows no sign of sympathy or compassion.

"My brother, please help him," Brad pleads.

He's ready to come undone from the pressure.

Sean's body locks in a distorted fetal position as every muscle in his body contracts.

"Who's we? How many of you are out here?" Erika sternly repeats.

"I just want you to help my brother," Brad says, biting his filthy fingernails.

Before Erika can give any thought to her next course of action, Nevaeh Garret, a scraggly looking twenty four-year-old, wearing faded overalls, and a tie-dye shirt, breaks through the trees. Her matted hair makes her look much older than she really is. Catching sight of Erika, she partially raises her hands to show she is not a threat. Nevaeh, ghostly white, cold and trembling, is scared out of her mind, and Erika's gun pointing squarely in her face quite possibly has something to do with it.

Erika wheels around and positions herself where she can keep an eye on everyone. Her situation has gone from bad to worse. If things go sideways, without question she knows somebody is going to die, and her being on the fatal end of the equation is not an option. She has never killed anyone, none that she is aware of, but self preservation ranks very high on her priority list. There will be no hesitation in the pull of a trigger.

Sean struggles for each breath, wheezing loudly.

"How many more are with you?"

"Just us. There's nobody else. I promise," Nevaeh manages to squeak out. "My name is Nevaeh. That's Brad," she says motioning towards the bony volatile man staring at the sick boy on the ground. "And that's his brother, Sean. We don't mean any harm, please don't shoot."

Brad makes a sudden move towards his brother. "We don't have time for this, my brother is dying.

Erika yells. "Hold it!"

Brad stares her down, viciously. Erika doesn't budge, waiver, or show any signs of fear; her stony gaze locks eyes with Brad, who scoffs at her with a look of disgust on his face. He spits in Erika's direction and moves toward Sean, almost daring her to shoot him.

It's evident that he wants to be put out of his misery. Erika is forced to reposition herself. She makes Nevaeh stand alongside the others so she can easily keep them all in her sights. Brad kneels down beside his brother. He awkwardly begins to rub his head and sweeps the loose curls away from his sweaty face.

"I got you little brother. I'll look after you."

Hollie hauls through the woods with the beam of his light bobbing. Branches rake across his body and face as he runs, drawing blood, as his uncovered skin grinds against thorns and dry brush. He stops for a moment to get his bearing and to catch his breath. After checking his position, he takes off again at top speed, frantically trying to find Erika.

Sean begins to relax his tightened muscles at the sound of Brad's voice and his attempts to comfort him. Brad turns his attention to Erika.

"Do you have a medical kit?"

"Yes, but—"

"So why don't you do something?" Brad roars.

"I don't have one here."

Brad's agitation increases, seeing Sean writhe on the ground, tormented as though a highly corrosive acid is ingesting him from inside out. Sean's body suddenly jolts hard. He sharply inhales air with a gasp, as his body shrinks into a ball and his eyes lock onto Brad. Sean's eyes widen, his only means of crying for help. Death is prying him from Brad's trembling grip. Sean screamed in silence for his brother to not let him go. He did not want to be taken, but there was nothing for Brad or anyone else to hold on to. Sean's tightened form releases from its constricted position as he exhales his drawn breath. The air whistles from his mouth like the shrill of a boiling teapot. His yellow hued eyelids loaded with purple and blue spider veins lower like venetian blinds and close.

Brad shakes his brother, calling out, screaming out his name. He raises his hand and lightly slaps his face, lamenting. Groaning, he bellows for him to wake up.

"Sean. Sean! Come on, buddy. You gotta wake up."

Tears flow freely down Nevaeh's pastel face.

Erika's emotions stir, but she refuses to let her guard down. She notices the slight rise and fall of Sean's chest.

"It's okay, he's still breathing," Erika says.

Brad looks him over, assuming the worse. His dark skeletal eyes are puffy from fighting back tears. Brad leans over his brother to see if he's alive, too wired to see the slight movement of his upper body, but he can hear the faint wisp of breath in his ear, which he presses lightly against Sean's lips.

Sean ventures into another place, a place where any child who is afraid longs to be, in the presence of their mommy and daddy.

A four-year-old Sean creeps into a bedroom in the wee hours of the night, startling his dad, Mitch, who groggily tries to send him back to his room. But his mother, Corrine, will allow no such thing. She reaches out both arms and sweeps him up into the bed. She hugs him tightly and kisses him, placing him gently in between her and Mitch, who is no longer annoyed. Mitch places his own arms around his frightened child.

This is one of the few life scenarios where everybody wins; Corrine loves her husband more than ever, seeing Sean's hands on Mitch's smiling face, Mitch is stronger now than he's ever been, more powerful in this moment when he stands as protector and his fearful child feels safe and secure, and Sean who is peacefully soothed by the sound of his mother's heartbeat as she embraces him and the low rumble of his father's snoring. Sean rests in the belief that there is nothing that can reach him in this place.

Brad continues to try and wake Sean and fails to notice the fleeting smile that suddenly graces his face and then vanishes. Sean, unmoving, never wants to leave this moment. He can now let go and be free. He wishes that his heart would stop beating, that his body would no longer draw breath, forever finding solace, comfort and sanctuary in this eternal moment.

Sean finds himself pawing through years of memories that scamper through his mind. The now twelve-year-old boy, who actually really does know just about everything, like most adolescents mistakenly believe, jokes and laughs with fellow classmates and friends moments after his graduation ceremony. The school valedictorian has two leis around his neck, one made up of miniature candy bars and a second fashioned with paper money folded into the shape of diplomas and flowers. The grounds are packed with anxious children waiting in eager expectation for the official start of their summer.

Proud parents and relatives, with flowers and balloons in hand, impatiently wait for the future junior high school students to join them. Sean's father, who gained quite a bit more weight, and lost quite a bit more hair, holds a camcorder in his hand. Corrine, who hasn't seemed to age a single day, holds a certificate with Sean's name on it, the Presidential Award, an award for academic excellence signed by the current President of the United States or America, Barrack Obama. Corrine looks it over like a winning lotto ticket.

"Here he comes," Mitch announces.

Corrine's eyes eagerly search through the sea of people. "Where? I don't see him."

Mitch points for a split second before weaving excitedly through the crowd trying to reach Sean, who bids his friends farewell after being forced to pose for pictures by his nerdy friends' parents.

He then heads straight for his father and excitedly hands him his diploma. Mitch eagerly takes it and wraps him in a monstrous bear hug. Sean, red faced with embarrassment, tries to play it as cool as a freckle faced curly head geek with glasses could, because of all the people around, but it made no difference to his dad, he is proud of his boy, and wants everyone to know it.

"Way to go, buddy, you did it. The Presidential Award." Mitch shouts, beaming.

Corrine finally reaches them and pries them apart, only to take her turn in physically smothering him and lavishing him with praise. While still wrapped in his mother's arms, Sean scans the crowd.

"Where's Brad?"

"He'll be here, Sean," Corrine says tentatively, her words not ringing true in his ears. Sean slouches, bitterly disappointed. "He probably just lost track of time, that's all."

Mitch attempts to redirect his attention.

"Sean? Sean, come hold the camera. Get a shot of your mom and me."

"Really? Okay. Cool"

Sean jubilantly takes the camera from his father.

Mitch gives him a quick rundown on how it functions, and Sean humors him, knowing far more about anything electronic than anyone in his family.

"I got it, Dad."

Mitch and Corrine join together and unleash a barrage of loving humiliation upon Sean; talking, singing, dancing.

"Are you kidding me?" Sean thinks to himself, astonished by how much his parents didn't care about what others think about them; their antics being captured in front of the eye that never forgets.

"Mom? Dad? Really?"

He tried to get them to stop, by making idle threats about shutting off the camera, but he is secretly content with them being mom and dad.

Sean is wildly entertained, but wants more than anything, for his brother to be there, or to be where he is. Again, Brad somehow has found something else to do, somewhere else to be, or someone else to be with; this hurts Sean most of all.

"Westside Charter School, here we come," Corrine yells, giddy with excitement.

"The best is yet to come for you, Sean," Mitch shouts. "The best is yet to c—"

Mitch's words are suddenly cut off by the deafening sound of a blaring horn. It feels as though the scream of a jet's engine is firing in everyone ears causing every bone in their bodies to quake. The ground begins to shake like the plane of a still pond violently interrupted by a rock skipping across its surface. The earth rocks and twists as ripples of ground roll over the horizon. People look as though they are all standing on water-beds, swaying as though their equilibrium is off. Sean, deathly afraid, looks around while still holding the recording camera in place. Parents, teachers, and children, are all paralyzed with fear. Many cup their ears because of the piercing blast, but the shrill horn feels as though it is emanating from within each person.

Through the lens of the video camera, Mitch and Corrine can be seen holding each other tightly. They begin to move carefully towards Sean, whose finger is frozen on the slow zoom button of the camera that is still recording his parents. They call for him, but he does not hear them, his eyes swing about wildly taking in every moment of the surrounding terror and chaos. Sean looks towards the sky and sees the clouds pool together and recede like a scroll being rolled up, opening the heavens like the drawing of theater curtains.

His parents scream for him.

They reach for him.

They vanish.

The horn gradually silences, leaving only the sound of gut wrenching screams from adults cradling children's clothing and backpacks.

A handful of early teens, in a state of unfathomable disbelief wander about aimlessly, quietly crying out for their loved ones. Sean looks to his parents, but they are gone. Only their clothes, jewelry, the Presidential Award and his diploma remain as a silent witness. Sean, lost in this waking nightmare, steps toward his parents' belongings. He quietly calls for them. Horrified, he looks around unable to believe his eyes. There are cars and buses without drivers and car seats without children, only clothing still held firmly in place by seatbelts. Sean looks up to see a small private jet falling from the sky, spinning out of control. From someone who dreams of being an aeronautical engineer, he immediately identifies it as a Gulfstream G150. Moments later, he hears the massive explosion from it hitting the ground and sees the thick black smoke climb into the air.

He closes his eyes, believing this only to be one of the nightmares that leads him into his parents' bedroom.

Soon this will be over.

Soon he will find comfort and peace, when his parents assure him that everything is okay.

"Please tell me everything is okay," his mind pleads.

Sean opens his eyes and pays no attention to the people blowing by him in an effort to avoid an attack they suppose they narrowly missed. He knows what this is. Something bad didn't happen to his parents or those who vanished, something much worse is happening to those who remain. Sean drops to his knees, sobbing uncontrollably.

"Mommy?" Sean clings to his parents clothings. "Daddy?"

There is an icy chill in the air as the wind begins to pick up. Nevaeh wipes away the tears that continue to snake down her face.

Everyone looking upon Sean knows that his health is rapidly deteriorating. Erika, who remains tense and guarded, sadly contemplates how much longer he will be able to hold on.

Suddenly, Sean's eyes shoot open and he thrusts himself up, screaming.

"Mommy. I want my Mommy."

Brad is momentarily startled but then grabs hold of him and embraces him securely. Both are so distraught that tears even decline their appearance.

"I know Buddy, me too. I got you. Everything is going to be okay."

Nevaeh falls to her knees weeping and buries her face in her hands. Erika wrestles with her emotions, but she swallows hard and chokes back her feelings, fighting hard to maintain control.

Brad tries to quiet Sean. "Shhh," he whispers soothingly, gently lowering his brother back to the ground. Brad then springs to his feet and he begins to pace; eyes darting back and forth as if some maniacal plan is being devised. A plot to overthrow. Erika cautiously backs away from him with her gun lowered, but ready.

"Why won't anyone help us?" Brad yells out. He screams to himself for reason, for understanding, for cause, seeking rest for his afflicted mind but finding none.

"Everyone we've come across out here has turned us away."

He struggles to make sense of everything.

"They're afraid you're either going to infect them... or eat them," Erika says calmly.

They look at her as if the dumbest thing they have ever heard anyone say just came out of her mouth.

"I'm sorry about your brother, I really am. We have lived in these woods for a long time, and we've been where you are now—"

"Don't try to patronize me," Brad shouts, as he clutches his head feeling as though it's going to explode.

"Calm down, Brad," Nevaeh pleads.

Erika attempts to reassure him that she wants to help his brother, but insists that they wait for someone from her camp to show up. Brad's movements quicken as his mind and stability reel out of control, and he works himself into a frenzy.

Sean's eyes start to hover and lose focus.

Nevaeh quietly calls his name, "Sean, look at me. Look at me."

Erika glances over toward them and before she can swing her gaze back, Brad unexpectedly charges her. Erika doesn't hesitate, she aims to kill. She points her gun directly at Brad's heaving chest, but doesn't have time to squeeze the trigger before he tackles her with such force that the wind is immediately knocked out of her. She lifts off the ground and her body folds in half from the impact. She sails backwards anticipating, and so not looking forward to her forthcoming and inescapable collision with the ground. She slams against the unforgiving surface. The last pinch of air in her body

127

slips out, but she keeps a vice-grip like hold on the gun in her hand.

"Brad! Stop!" Nevaeh's cries are unheeded.

Hollie, dog-tired and running on fumes, hears Nevaeh's screams. He shuts off his flashlight and takes off running in the direction of the sound. He's tripping and falling on the uneven surface and the brush that catches and stalls his swiftly moving feet.

Brad climbs on top of Erika fighting to take control of her weapon. She struggles to take aim, but can't get a shot off, not directly at him anyway, so she tries for the next best thing, thinking that if she could just pull the trigger, the sound may startle him enough for her to do something, anything. She tries to squeeze off a round, but her crazed adversary prevents her. Brad, with great difficulty, manages to lift Erika's gun bearing hand into the air, and slams it against the packed dirt, causing Erika to growl in agony and anger as the gun topples out of her hand and out of reach.

Brad scurries like an animal and scoops up the gun.

"Brad, what are you doing?" Nevaeh yells.

"I'm doing what I have to, shut up."

Brad stands, winded and sucking air, and points the gun at Erika.

"Get up. On your feet!"

Erika slowly rights herself and stands.

Brad motions with the gun and directs Erika to move in Sean's direction. She reluctantly complies. Brad keeps the gun trained on her, and when she reaches Sean's side, he presses the gun firmly against the back of her head.

"Do something."

"I'm not sure, but we might have some of the antidote."

Nevaeh and Brad trade confused looks.

"Antidote? What do you mean?" Brad demands.

128

"Back at my campsite. For Sean... and for you two."

Brad continues to come unglued.

"What are you talking about? We're not sick. Only Sean is sick," Nevaeh says, as Brad looks tentatively into Nevaeh's eyes, the gun still held firmly against Erika's skull.

"She's just messin' with us," Brad snaps as he turns his attention back to Erika. "Not the smartest thing to do, lady, with a gun pointed at your dome."

"Listen to me," Erika says calmly. "All of you have been ingesting poison, probably from the moment you stepped out of the city. It may be too late for Sean, and I'm sorry. But I know there's still time for you two.

Brad fastens his eyes shut inwardly tormented, hoping to shake the words devouring what fragments remain of his guilt laden heart. The numbness that sweeps through his body is unsettling, even for him.

"No, not true. That's just a bunch of conspiracy theory crap that people talk about to keep us trapped in the cities and under control," Brad argues. "Like an electrical fence to keep sheep in the freakin' yard."

"I wish it was a lie," Erika says.

"If you don't help my brother, you're dead. Do you understand that?"

"I want to help you, but you don't have much time. I can tell by Sean's condition that you guys have been out here for about two weeks now, and the reason why you're not as sick as he is, is because of the drugs you've been taking."

The looks on their faces confirm her words.

"If you give me back my gun, I will get the antidote for you. I promise."

129

Brad deliberates, as he looks intently at his suffering brother.

"The antidote. You're going to take us to get it. Now!"

"Not with that gun in your hand, I'm not."

Brad thumps her in the head and takes a step back, ready to shoot.

He begins to weep shamelessly.

"God, please don't take my brother. It's all my fault."

Brad snivels, wounded from the conflict of extreme sorrow and furious anger.

"He looked up to me. I'm the reason he's here," he confesses to the wind. The emotional anguish and anxiety are crushing him. He must do as he must.

A decision has been made.

Brad instantly composes himself and he tightens his grip on the pistol.

"Step back, Nevaeh."

Nevaeh finds herself frozen in fear.

"Move!" Brad shouts.

Nevaeh jumps back away from him, terrified.

"I want to help you, Brad, I really do. I promise you that. But I can't risk the lives others for you."

"What about your life? Does that mean anything to you?"

Brad's eyes are bloodshot and twitching.

Strangely enough, Erika is somehow at peace, even knowing that in just a few moments, her life could be forfeit.

"Think about what you're doing, Brad. Just give her the gun!" Nevaeh begs.

"No," Brad snaps, with quiet rage. "But I'll give her what's in the clip... You have 'til the count of three."

"Don't do this, Brad," Nevaeh says, looking away and burying her face in her arm.

She wishes she could do something, but she's not a leader.

What value does her life hold?

What weight does she carry?

She has been a follower her entire life. No confidence. No self esteem. Just living in fear and going where others lead her because of it. Her only recourse is to do nothing but retreat further within herself.

Nevaeh is unable to hide her plagued expression as memories of abuse surface, forcing her in this solitary moment to relive the many years of mistreatment and cruelty she was subjected to in foster care. Both of her parents were killed in a horrific car accident when she was a child. As a result, she was moved from foster home to foster home until she became an adult; at least a legal adult. She has never been given the proper tools to mentally grow up, so in many ways, she is still a small child needing to be taught and cared for, and conflict, any conflict, she will avoid like the dad's in foster care who wanted to play house with her when their wives were not around.

It's easy for her to cower when feeling threatened or intimidated. In some odd way, she feels protected when she goes within herself, venturing into the shelter of her inner cave. It's a place of safety, where she becomes deadened to the world around her.

Standing there, all she can manage to do now is close her eyes and wait, and perhaps hope that Erika will not have to suffer.

She has nothing more than that to offer.

Sean stares up at his brother with his glossy eyes, pleading. He can't seem to formulate words to speak, but his expression is clearly and quietly begging his brother not to continue on this path.

Erika closes her eyes and softly says, "I'm yours God."

Brad begins to count, "One."

Crack!

A loud sound suddenly reverberates through the trees, and at the same time, Brad's body quickly rises. He is instantly unconscious as the stock of Hollie's shotgun hits full force on Brad's head.

Hollie, completing a monstrous follow-through swing, wields his shotgun like a baseball bat.

Erika's eyes flutter open. She remains still. Unsure.

Hollie calls to her. "Erika?"

She slowly turns toward the sound of his familiar voice and she locks eyes with him.

"Are you okay?"

She struggles to find her voice.

"I'm okay," she says. "I think… yeah."

She then begins to tremble uncontrollably, everything flooding back to her mind in an instant. Hollie places his hand on her shoulder and squeezes as he looks her in the eyes.

"Thanks," she says softly. A grateful smile graces his face and she manages a tired grin in return.

Erika breaks away and picks up her gun, the gun that almost ended her life. Hollie checks on Brad and searches for a pulse. After finding one, he rolls him onto his stomach. He then pulls some nylon fishing line out of one of his coat pockets and ties Brad's hands securely behind his back.

"What's going on here, Erika?"

Erika explains only what she must, knowing that they needed to get Sean back to the shack.

Erika kneels down by Sean. "Hang on, Sean. We're going to try to get you some help." She speaks softly and with compassion, and the faintest light of hopes twinkles in his eyes.

Hollie throws Brad's limp body over his shoulders into a fireman's carry, and Erika and Nevaeh drag Sean back towards the campsite.

Chapter 7

Tᴀɢᴇ tears through the streets as if nothing else around him existed. Panting and out of breath, he continues to sprint for as long as he can. He stops for a moment and doubles over, spitting the excess moisture from his mouth. He quickly scans the streets and spots the vivid glow of red and blue flashing lights several blocks away. He considers his options and chooses the road less traveled. He psyches himself out and makes a run for it, bolting in the direction of the lights, all the while thinking to himself that he's lost his mind.

Wheezing heavily, with a torrential downpour of sweat gliding down his discolored face, he stops just around the corner from a police cruiser. The officer on watch, standing outside his car, is built like an Abrams tank. He realizes that his chances of overpowering the beefy officer is right up there with him winning a Miss America pageant, but desperate times call for desperate measures.

He looks around for anything he can use as an instrument of combat; something that can inflict great bodily harm upon those on the wrong end of it. He scours the area and sees only a pile of small rocks used for road repair. He picks up the first one. No weight. No substance. What he needs is a boulder the size of a fist, so he could knock him senseless, not pebbles, but apparently advantages are for the weak, because he wasn't finding any.

He stops for a moment and allows his mind to race, but no plan he concocts grants him a favorable outcome. Tage sits down, keeping a watchful eye on the officer a short distance away. His pant legs rise, showing of his formally white mismatched tube socks. "These things have seen better days," he thinks to himself. His mental wheels begin to grind out and he quickly sheds one of his gnarled shoes. The smell of his moist sock hit him like a whiff of smelling salt. He loads up his sock with the small rocks and ties it off at about three quarter capacity. He then holds the makeshift weapon of mass destruction in his hand with pride. He removes both of his shoes and socks; his concern is that his shoes against the concrete may draw attention to himself before he is within striking distance. He considers double nunchuckin' him like Bruce Lee in Enter the Dragon, but his other sock is riddled with holes.

Officer Nash, a corn-fed southern boy, six foot one, neck thick as a tree branch, looks as though he is excellent at what he does, punching sides of beef and wrestling alligators. He stands adjacent to his patrol car drooling over a Guns and Ammo magazine.

Tage slowly inches forward, walking as soft and silently as he can on the wet, grimy surface. He has no idea of what he's stepping in, but that is the least of his concerns. He slips and slides on the slimy street surface like a clumsy first time ice skater; looking as ridiculous as a mugger on a budget with his body flailing, carrying a rock filled sock.

He tiptoes forward like a frightened animal and comes to within a few feet of the massive officer. His heart is clacking like a Wheel of Fortune game wheel. Each step forward becomes more and more difficult. He secures his sock firmly in his right hand and prepares for the swing. Just as he slips to within arm's length of Nash, the officer spots him in the reflection of his patrol car and wheels around.

Heat drains from Tage's face.

He takes a winding swing, but Nash blocks it with his wrist that is as thick as a bowling pin.

Pebbles inside the sock shoot out onto the asphalt and skip along the concrete. In any other situation, this would be funny, hysterical even, but not now.

Tage brandishes his padded sock, to Nash's amusement, and he attacks again, missing so embarrassingly bad he is ashamed of himself. Rocks continue to spill out of his sock through the growing holes.

Nash launches his beefy fist and lands a crushing blow to Tage's kidney, forcing a squeal out of him he's never heard before. The pain is almost debilitating. He considers making a run for it, believing that someone Nash's size couldn't possibly catch him, but he didn't think he could outrun a bullet twice in one day. He knows sooner or later he will have to turn and fight and now is as good a time as any. Tage grits through the pain and prepares to bring the thunder. He swings madly with his sock over and over, some missing, others landing, but the impact is not even enough to warrant being taken seriously. Nash seems to be enjoying himself, smiling and laughing, toying with Tage, which causes Tage's blood to boil.

Nash pulls out his baton and a knife and throws a quick glance at Tage's limp sock; giving him the professional courtesy of letting him know that he is empty, no more rocks in the sock. Tage drops the sock just as Nash charges him with his baton in one hand and the knife in the other. Tage is frozen by the sight of death quickly approaching; the confusion of not knowing what he should fear more, the knife or the baton, causes him to do nothing but stare with a stupid, I'm-a-freshman look on his face.

The sound of Nash's monstrous footsteps approaching, pounding hard against the pavement breaks Tage out of his daze. He miraculously avoids Nash's initial attack and then responds by rushing him, screaming like a possessed banshee. Tage catches him off guard, takes him down hard, and proceeds to rain down blows like a freak of nature. Tage is riding an adrenaline dump like a bull. Nash smashes Tage in the head with the back of his hand, which stuns him, and follows the blow with a thrust of his blade. Tage angles his body and the knife lodges deep into his coat just above his shoulder. A split second later and it would have been buried in his neck. The close call triggers insanity. Tage freaks and he goes ballistic; his wild and unpredictable, yet effective strikes, connect hard with Nash's basketball sized head.

Nash throws him off, but Tage swoops back on him like a duck hawk and pummels the giant with hands so fast they are almost a blur. Nash can barely get his bearing and a gash above his brow streaks blood down his face and nearly blinds his left eye. His right eye is nearly swollen shut, making it almost impossible for him to see anything. Nash tries to curl his large frame into a fetal position to weather the beating. Modern breaking news would say that David is miraculously beating the tar out of Goliath.

Barely conscious, Nash summons his remaining energy and

draws his gun. With every ounce of strength Tage could muster, he tries to force Nash's rising hand back down, but the gun slowly but surely rises and turns toward him. Nash pulls the trigger and a bullet rips into Tage's side, launching him backwards. Tage's mouth opens wide, and he howls in pain. He rocks back and forth with his hand on his side like a six year old that gets hurt and can't remember how to breathe.

Nash's body slinks to one side. The broken and bloodied officer tries to fire off another round, which infuriates Tage, who then scrambles to get up, disregarding the fissure in his side and the agony. Nash steadies his gun and prepares to pull the trigger and with an animalistic yell, Tage rushes towards Nash and delivers a vicious soccer kick to his head that has him seeing stars just before going black.

Tage grips his side as blood oozes through his fingers. He hunches over, his body feeling as though hot coals are torching his insides, and his head is ringing at such a high pitch frequency his head feels like it's going to shatter like glass. He staggers forward and grabs Nash's gun and his keys. All he can think about is getting home.

Home...

He is going home... and in style.

He tries all the keys in the key hole; one fits seamlessly in the door and looks as though it's moving the locking mechanism, but does nothing more than that. Tage resorts to using the bone shattering baton to try and smash the window, but it barely scratches the surface of the glass. He then points the firearm squarely at the glass, attempts to squeeze the trigger, but it doesn't budge. He checks to see if a safety might be engaged, but there is no such feature on the gun. He aims it at the window again and squeezes against the trigger with all his might. Nothing; not even the slightest of movements. He even tries putting both fingers on the trigger. He squeezes, applying pressure, grunting and growling like the matting call of a Wookie, but no go. Angry, frustrated, and bleeding, he chucks the weapon as far as he can possibly throw. He weakly retrieves his shoes and staggers back down the alley, having no clue as to how to get home, but knowing that he must. The old man that just wouldn't die, told them how to find his daughter.

To be back at square one was disastrous enough, but now he was not even on the stinkin' map.

The longer he went, the more his legs wobble. Traversing through a back alley, only minutes after having been shot, the fatigue, pain, and blood loss catches up with him and his body begins to shut down. The head splitting ring in skull continues to grow louder and his motors skills are failing. His face painfully grimaces before he collapses to the ground, struggling to breathe.

"Get up. Get up, Tage," he tells himself, but his body refuses to obey his command.

He stares upward as his world spins out of control. His face tightens as he squints, trying to block the incessant and maddening tone which grew louder as his world suddenly goes dark.

~

Gina and Audrey anxiously await Hollie and the others' return. Gina stares out the window holding an ax in her hand. Nervously she runs her fingers through her hair. She would normally bite her nails, which is always her first instinct when she worries, but because there is so much to worry about all the time, she never has any nails to gnaw on when she needs them.

Sal has fallen asleep with Brandy on a sleeping bag in the front

140

room. Audrey sits at the table thinking about Walter and the others. She tries to pray and desperately wants to trust. "Why have they been gone so long?" She ponders. Antonio peers intently out into the darkness with his gun ready. All of them are fighting the same battle, the fear of the unknown. "God, please take care of them." Gina quietly prays.

Suddenly, Brandy starts spinning donuts in the middle of the floor.

Antonio blurts out, "I see them. Here they come."

Gina is flooded with a sense of relief when she sees the smile on Antonio's face. All the activity causes Sal to wake from her restless sleep. Antonio takes another look out the window, noticing that there are other people with them. The mild change in his expression is read clearly by Gina, so she rushes to fling open the door.

Everyone converges on the entrance.

Hollie, deflated, enters with Brad across his shoulders, still bound and unconscious. Nevaeh timidly files in afterward, nervously taking in her surroundings. Hollie props Brad up against one of the walls. Brandy busies himself snooping around Hollie, and at the same time, trying to sniff out the newcomers.

"Sal, take the dog and get him out of the way," Hollie says flatly.

"Yes, Uncle Hollie."

Erika and Tai carry Sean inside and they drag his wilted body into one of the makeshift rooms and lays him on one of the beds.

Erika searches frantically for the medical kit, while Tai covers Sean with a blanket. Nevaeh leans into the far corner of the room. She slides down to the floor, and sits, trying to warm herself by tucking her hands in between her knees. She watches and waits as Sean is being tended to. She looks around the room, and sees the

141

walls are covered with colorful pictures; posters of angels, and a variety of butterflies from all around the world. There is a Goliath Birdwing Butterfly from the tropical forests in Indonesia, the Tiger Swallowtail, found throughout the USA and Canada, a Ulysses, a blue butterfly from Australia, and the Monarch, found all over the world. Butterflies and more butterflies. She is blown away by the colors, the vibrancy, and the life she sees within the pictures.

Nevaeh turns her head to another wall, only to be staring straight into the eyes of a warring angel with his foot on the neck of a defeated spiritual being. The picture is so lifelike she is startled. She takes a few deep breaths to allow her heart to fall back into rhythm.

Awestruck, her eyes scan the posters on the wall now covered with angels. Next to that poster is another one of two Cherubs sitting with each other on a white, rod iron bench. Each one holds a single flower in its hand. She pries her eyes away from the pictures and turns her attention to Tai, who is wiping Sean's forehead with a washcloth.

Then as if in a most welcome daze, she swings her eyes back to the artwork. Glancing upward, she sees colorful drawings methodically stapled and taped on the ceiling. There are angels flying; one carrying a closed scroll, another with an open one, and yet another with a silver and white gift box in its hands. There are two more blowing horns placed in the center of the ceiling, and all around them, more butterflies. She can't take her eyes off the drawings, nor does she want to. She ponders where they came from and what they mean. They make her feel as if she is escaping from reality for a moment. However fleeting, she wants to fly with them, to turn from the ugliness in the real world and find refuge in theirs; a world filled with beauty, color and safety.

Gina presses Hollie for answers. He tries to distance himself and stares blindly at nothing in particular.

"What happened, Hollie?"

"Nothing. It's fine," he says absently

He sighs and rubs his eyes.

"What do you mean, fine? Who are these people? Are you okay?"

Hollie gives in to the battering of emotions that seizes him. "No, Gina. You know what? I'm pretty stinkin' far from okay."

Gina reaches for him. She desperately wants to hold him, but Hollie, unsure of himself, keeps her at bay.

"I watched this addict almost kill Erika. She almost died because I couldn't take that boys life. I sat there in the shadows with my gun on him, ready to shoot, and ready to end that boy's life, but I couldn't pull the trigger. I couldn't. I tried, mom, even knowing that Erika, who's like my little sister, was going to die if I didn't do something."

Gina tries to cut in, but she knows that he has to release whatever is boiling on the inside of him, the gut wrenching emotion causing his hands to tremble and his heart to quake.

"When I looked at him, I saw my kids… I was paralyzed. Frozen. When I heard him speak, all I could hear was the voice of my sons… They're just kids, Gina, like Matthew, Mason, and Raven." Hollie groans, his aching body, almost doubling over. His eyes swimming in tears.

"Honey, don't do this to yourself."

"It's been almost seven years, and I can't stop thinking about our little ones. I can't take this anymore," Hollie confesses.

Gina stares compassionately into his eyes and places her hands on his face.

"Do you think about Seth?"

"Every day," he lovingly whispers back.

"Well, I'm sure he's thinking about you right now. He might even be watching you and feeling the same love in his heart for you as you feel for him."

"What about Matthias and Jeremiah?"

"Not one moment passes that I don't think about my kids." His voice cuts in and out as he speaks.

"Dad, they are all thinking about you right now. They love you. They believe in you. I believe in you."

Hollie weeps.

"And you know what honey?" Gina looks straight into his eyes. "You know what I think?"

Hollie stares, his eyes red and stinging from tears.

"I think we had a lot of kids, dude."

Hollie can't help but to respond with laughter. "We sure did, didn't we?" Hollie chuckles.

"They are all in heaven waiting for us. Safe. Our babies are safe." Hollie looks away, the pain too great. "And until the day comes when we are with them again," Gina says softly, lifting his face and staring deeply into his eyes. "You keep being the man you were created to be, the man of my dreams."

Hollie holds tightly to his wife and weeps unashamedly. Hollie tries to speak, he wants to, but words held no value in this moment.

Erika continues to rip the place apart looking for the antidote.

Sal sits on Audrey's lap, and listens intently as she tells her story. Sal's radiant smile lights up the room. She is a gift. A treasure. She is their treasure.

The cold is numbing, and its nip penetrates the cracks and crevices of the decaying shack. Antonio gathers some wood for the fire that has been stacked on the front porch. He carries it inside and places some by the wood stove as Gina stokes the fire. The warmth in the shack is needed now more than ever. If Sean is to get better he needs warmth, that and of course the antidote that Erika is tearing the place apart looking for.

The smell of the burning fire brings a small measure of comfort to everyone inside. In these days, you learn to cherish even the smallest of things.

Audrey continues to sit with Sal, who especially loves hearing about the ocean and the sea life that used to be abundant. She can hardly believe that a third of all living things in the ocean and seas died almost overnight... and she still weeps over the loss of life.

As Erika searches through box after box, bag after bag, she stops to listen to the radio that quietly plays nearby. After a few moments, she wishes that she hadn't. Her head drops, overtaken with sorrow.

She slowly approaches Hollie and Gina, her shoulders hunch and her head hangs low. They both look at her and immediately know that something is terribly wrong. She lingers in their presence for a moment, reluctant to speak.

"You guys need to listen to this," she says somberly.

Hollie and Gina follow Erika into the kitchen area where the emergency radio is located. An emergency broadcast is interrupting every station. Audrey and Tai follow and Sal edges in, stepping carefully over Brad's leg, unaware that he is beginning to stir.

Audrey covers her mouth with her hands, trembling as she listens to the reporter's message.

"Preliminary reports indicate that there were three suspects involved in this attack, none of which survived."

"What about the victim?" The Anchorman asks.

"The victim was forty three year old Robert Timothy, a clerk at Nu-way Market. He sustained moderate injuries fending off the initial terrorist attack, and was later killed along with his family when they were locked inside the market, which the terrorist then set on fire."

Sal looks around at the stunned faces, trying to make sense out of the setting. As brilliant and gifted as she is, her mind refuses to process what she is hearing. No one utters a word as they continue to focus on the broadcast.

"What we know at this point is that the suspects reportedly entered the premises by disabling an outdated referencing system. They began to ransack and plunder the store, shouting religious expletives, and eventually Mr. Timothy was forced to defend himself."

"What a tragic loss of life for Mr. Timothy and his family. He was a true hero," the Anchorman says.

Hollie flips off the radio as it begins to repeat the breaking news. Gina held Audrey in her arms and she weeps bitterly.

"My Walter is dead," she says repeatedly.

Everyone is devastated by the broadcast.

Hollie looks at Sal, who begins to cry only because Audrey is crying. She does not yet understand that her daddy will not be coming home... Ever.

Gina holds Audrey and reaches out her hand to Sal.

"Come here, sweetheart." Sal moves in close and they hold one another.

~

Streaks of light penetrate the darkened litter-strewn alley as Tage slowly begins to regain consciousness. He clinches his eyes and shakes his head to clear his mind, still hoping to somehow escape this nightmare. The sound of a scuffle around him interrupts his thoughts. It suddenly registers that a fight, an all out brawl, is taking place practically on top of him. He tries to rise, forcing himself to stand, but he swiftly collapses back down to the ground. He tries to scoot out of harm's way, but every reach, every stride and every movement made all the nerve-endings in his body scream.

Tage's eyes narrow and focus on a mysterious man, Jacob Hollis, who looks to be several years younger than him. Jacob is waging a ferocious and bloody battle with Officers Mitchell and Stevens.

Jacob is significantly smaller than his opponents, has dark slicked back hair, an athletic build, and looks to be more like a lover than a fighter. It is clearly a fight to the death, but the two brutal officers are no match for Jacob who moves with almost inhuman quickness and precision. Stevens draws his gun, but just as quickly as he flaunts the weapon, it's taken away from him faster. Mitchell attacks Jacob from behind with his baton, but his night stick is stripped from his hand and used against both of them. Mitchell wisely pulls his gun, but the man in black immediately hones in, and with a few choice movements, sends the weapon flying.

The right side of Tage's body feels like he is getting a deep tissue massage from Edward Scissorhands, a reminder of the bullet still lodged in his flesh. He lifts his blood stained shirt to survey the damage and sees that a dressing has been placed on his wound. He wonders how it got there, but his thoughts are interrupted by the thunderous bang of Stevens being flipped up and against a trash bin in the alley. Tage forces his body to crawl after Stevens' gun. He reaches the weapon and points it at Mitchell. When he thinks he has a clear shot, half excited about payback, he attempts to pull the trigger.

Nothing happens.

Tage lays on the ground, once again in unwanted territory. Helpless.

Sirens whoop in the distance, closing fast. Mitchell and Stevens are now reeling on the ground in agony.

"You're a dead, man." Mitchell shouts to Jacob, while spitting up a stream of frothy blood on the ground.

Jacob walks purposefully over to Tage.

"Excuse me," he says, as he removes the gun from Tag's grasp.

He coolly points to Mitchell and fires two rounds into his chest. In like fashion, he then turns the gun on Stevens who throws up his hands in surrender.

"No. Wait."

Without so much as a thought, Jacob pops three rounds into him, center mass.

Tage is in no condition to celebrate, but there is a sense of relief in knowing that two of the men who killed Walter, the old man that just wouldn't die. He knows as sure as death and taxes that the two officers who are now dead, would have been heading to his home.

Tage hears the screech of tires drawing closer and the wail of sirens growing louder by the moment.

Jacob approaches Tage and helps him to his feet. He is anxious to get him walking and away from the area that will be swarming with cops in no time flat. Tage quickly pats his clothing and discovers that his watch is missing.

"Wait," Tage insists.

"Unless you know something I don't, we need to get out of here."

Tage breaks away and scours the area with only one thing on his mind. "My watch," he says, as he stumbles over to the place where he woke. His watch is nowhere to be found.

Distressed, he throws himself to the ground, looking anywhere and everywhere, but he sees nothing. As he lays prostrate on the ground, searching for his most prized possession, a stubby boyish looking rookie with an oversized uniform rounds the corner, out of breath and his gun drawn.

"Freeze. Don't move," he screams, with a noticeable measure of fear in his voice.

From his position, he can't see Tage on the ground amid the debris around him. The flashlight in his hand is focused straight ahead.

"Put your hands in the air. Now!"

Jacob has his back facing the officer.

While lying on the ground, Tage sees his watch next to one of the officer's batons.

The rookie slowly advances forward, nearly stepping on Tage. All he has to do is look down.

Tage holds his breath. He almost convinces himself to whisper a word of prayer, but that wasn't for him. Not anymore. All he can do is hope he's lucky enough that the rookie treading only inches from him would not look down.

"Turn around!" The rookie demands, but Jacob does not comply.

The rookie spots the two officers on the ground and immediately realizes he's way out of his league. He hears a faint moan from Stevens.

Tage slowly, ever so carefully takes hold of the baton lying next to his watch. He then quietly grabs his watch and slips it into his pocket.

Out of the corner of his eyes, Tage sees the unsteady and shaking arms of the rookie.

"Turn around! Last chance," he barks.

Click! He pulls back the hammer of his gun.

Jacob slowly, reluctantly turns around, shaking his head.

The rookie stares at him, looking intently into his face with utter disbelief. Contempt.

Tage picks up on the sense of familiarity. There is an unmistakable expression of recognition on the young officer's face. Tage lifts himself quietly to his knees just as the rookie passes beside him.

"You? How could you?"

"It's not what it looks like, okay. I can explain," says Jacob.

The confusion on the rookie's face tells Tage, it's now or never.

Tage rises like the dead, wielding the officer's club.

"You're a traitor," shouts the rookie.

With that, Tage lunges for the young officer. He swings the baton and smashes the stick against the rookie's wrist. The sudden snap of his bone accompanies a speedy drop of his gun.

Tage immediately follows up with a strike to his neck and the rookie buckles to the ground clutching his throat. Tage tries not to look at the damage he's done, but can hear the strangled gasps for air. Jacob kneels down by the rookie's side, but the fallen rookie turns away from him, gurgling, barely able to get air through his crushed windpipe.

"Don't touch me", the rookie groans out almost inaudibly.

Patrol cars screech to a halt in the area.

"We have to move," Jacob commands, as he drags Tage's weakened body out of the alley. "You should not have done that," Jacob scolds.

"I had no choice. I can't let them take me. My family is in danger."

"You're in no condition to help anyone right now. We need to get you fixed up."

As the two head out of the alley, Jacob takes a final look back at the rookie who lay motionless on the ground.

~

A spirit of heaviness fills the shack. The words spoken on the radio celebrating the death of their loved ones, linger in the air like puddles of reeking perfume sprayed liberally by those with a diminished sense of smell. Gina consoles Sal as she sits on her lap crying.

"Why did he go, Auntie Gina? I told him not to go. His angel wasn't finished yet. I didn't finish painting his angel. It's all my fault."

"No, sweetheart, don't say that. It's not your fault."

"But I didn't finish him. His guardian..." she interrupts, pointing her shaking finger to a picture on the floor of an angel hurling towards the earth with a single wing; his right arm extended as though he is leading with a sword not yet painted by the artist.

Gina is undone by the thought of this little one feeling responsible for the death of her father.

"Your dad, my friend, went into the city because he loves us. There is nothing on earth that could stop him from trying to provide for you, because he loves you more than life itself."

"Now I have nobody," Sal says with a broken voice.

"Sal, you will always have people in your life that love and care about you. Always. I promise you that. We love you, honey, and people that love each other, take care of one another."

Sal buries her face into Gina's chest and Gina wraps her arms around her.

151

"It'll be okay honey. We will get through this together."

After a few moments, Sal wiggles free from Gina's grasp and she stands to her feet. She steps to her painting and hovers over it, staring. Her tears fall from her face and drop onto the picture of the unfinished angel. Sal lowers herself to her knees, reaches for her art supplies and begins to work on the picture.

Nevaeh remains by Sean's side. She makes sure he's comfortable and tries to help him sip some water. His eyes are barely open, but he is able to respond with a whispered, "Thank you." Erika enters with a vial in her hand and calls for Nevaeh, who quietly leaves the room with her. No one in the shack is aware that Brad has regained consciousness. He slips a razor blade from his back pocket and begins cutting at the line binding his hands. He sees Erika and Nevaeh approaching and closes his eyes. Brad holds still in his slouched position, but continues to work on the restraints around his hands.

Erika and Nevaeh sit within earshot of Brad.

"Here take this," Erika says, as she places the tiny bottle in her hand labeled Nathancleovoxalyne.

"What is it?"

"It's the antidote to counteract the poison that's in your system," Erika says.

Nevaeh looks at her confused.

"What about Sean? He's the one who is sick. I feel fine."

Brad, still pretending to be unconscious, listens attentively as he continues to awkwardly slice away.

"We only have enough for two of you, maybe. Sean is… We don't think he's going to make it, he's too far gone."

Brad can't believe what he's hearing. He tries to swallow, but the dryness in his mouth seizes his throat, like a fool trying to swallow a spoon full of cinnamon on a dare. He wants to scream, he wants to cry, but he remains still. He tightly fastens his eyes, hoping that the nightmare will be over once his eyes reopen.

"At this point, all we can do is to make sure he's comfortable." Nevaeh shakes her head in disbelief. "If we give Sean this antidote, more than likely he will die anyway. You and Brad will die right behind him if you don't take it."

The line Brad chips away at can easily be broken now, but he does not move. He sits in quiet and tormenting anguish. He understands that Sean having the antidote does not mean he will survive, but not having it came with the certainty of death.

"Nevaeh, listen to me. You have to make a decision. Brad will have to make the same decision when he wakes. If you don't take this, you will die." Nevaeh struggles to wrap her mind around the situation.

"Why is this happening? I don't understand why someone would poison us."

"This is not just about you. Anyone this world government can't control, they kill. The President of the United Nations brought world peace at the expense of all our lives, our blood; those who want to live free. Alexander Demetri is the god of this world, and he will kill anyone who gets in the way of his plans and purpose and refuses to receive him as Christ."

"No, that can't be true," Nevaeh reasons.

"He said it himself, Nevaeh. I shouldn't have to argue that point."

"If there really is a God, He wouldn't let this happen. I don't believe it."

"Not believing something doesn't make it untrue, Nevaeh. I didn't believe in God six years ago, but that didn't stop Him from

153

taking hundreds of millions of people off this planet, like He said He was going to do. It was right there in black and white, until Demetri had all the Bible's burned."

"Do you really think that was God?" Nevaeh questions

"I wouldn't be here right now if I didn't; every child in the world, every baby..." Erika hesitates. "Including the little one inside me, vanished without a trace..."

"But that's not what Demetri said."

"It really doesn't matter what anyone else says, but I will tell you what settled it for me. I had a few close friends before the vanishings... and afterward, they..."

"They were all gone?" Nevaeh interrupts.

"Oh, God no. Not one of them was gone."

They both laugh quietly.

"I realized that it didn't matter what others labeled you, or what you ran around calling yourself. It didn't even matter what you claimed to believe; Baptist, Catholic, Muslim, Buddhist, Christian..."

Nevaeh plays with her matted hair.

"Aside from the children... the babies, only those that had one thing in common, a real, genuine relationship with Jesus Christ, went with them."

Nevaeh's eyes search Erika's.

"The Bible said it was going to happen and it did. That's all I needed to know. " Grief and regret pours over Erika as she thinks about her family, her friends... her baby. "Better late than never I suppose." She says with a forced smile.

Nevaeh tries to smile, but can't. The information has her hippy like circuits fried.

Erika then rises to her feet. "Let me know what you decide, okay.

But please don't take to long." She then grabs the vial, but Nevaeh's fingers won't let it go.

"I don't know what to do. Please tell me what to do."

"This is something you're going to have to decide for yourself."

Nevaeh releases the bottle, and Erika leaves her to grapple with the life and death decision she is forced to make.

Chapter 8

THE mysterious cop killer in black, Jacob, continues to drag Tage through the streets of the city. Tage's leg stalls as he hobbles along, and Jacob's firm grip around him is the only thing that keeps him from plummeting to the ground. The cold air in this part of the city miserably failed to dampen the hovering sticky odor of feces and urine. There are open fires in garbage cans that the street dwellers use to keep warm, and the shadows of those cast on the nearby walls appear to take on a life of their own, somehow separating from their hosts. The shadows seem as though they are calling to one another, their eerie presence following, whispering. Tage isn't sure if his mind is playing tricks on him, but he desperately wants to believe that the razor sharp teeth and the claws that look like Ginsu knives are only his overactive imagination.

It is startling for Tage to see such a large number of lost and broken people gathering hopelessly around trash barrels. They are wraiths, the living dead, those who blend into the shadows. Their skin is splotchy and peeled back, revealing flesh that looks like raw hamburger meat, perpetual reminders of a mysterious incurable tissue eating bacteria that invades their hosts and excretes a brownish curdled fluid from the resulting open sores.

Scientists, chemists, and doctors, some of the greatest minds in the world are baffled, to say the least, and are also heavily affected by the disease; some likely standing around these same containers. The cellular composition of what's known as, Rev-192 is unlike anything else. Many believe its origin is extraterrestrial because nothing in its chemical makeup appears on the periodic table. It spreads like an unseen fungus whose spores feed off everything the world has become, and to this day there is no vaccine or cure.

The government went to great lengths to cover up the fact that only those with the mark are susceptible or affected by the plague, but an overly ambitious journalist covering another piece on health and human services caught wind of the tempting tidbit of information and let the story fly; reporting that the contagion is somehow connected to the implanting procedure, and instead of the coveted anchor spot for the piece as promised by her network, everyone, right down to the receptionist and mail clerk, are publicly executed on live television over the course of three days and nights.

The street dwellers who stand around the burning trash containers wear filthy garments that are shredded and ragged. Tage's clothes are in similar condition, but he at least makes a conscious effort to maintain some sense of hygiene and cleanliness. Refuse lays all over the yards and sidewalks, and steam rose from the dumpsters along with a foul, putrid smell that cannot be mistaken for anything else except heavy amounts of human waste. Community cleanup efforts are nonexistent where they travel. It is a forgotten wasteland where survival is all that matters.

Trust did not come easy in that world, for anyone. Because anyone with nothing will sooner or later turn someone in for something. Especially when starvation is one of the leading causes of death after a severe famine fell upon the face of the earth and wages are barely enough to provide for a single individual, let alone an entire family.

The seasons of the world have shifted. Earthquakes, tornadoes and other natural disasters regularly occur where they have never been before, and the weather is not only unpredictable, but goes from one deadly extreme to the other; either hot enough outside to cook your insides, where it wouldn't surprise anyone to see the devil himself at Ace Hardware buying an air conditioning unit, or cold enough to where cops no longer yell "Freeze," they shout, "Go outside!"

If you are not properly prepared to brave the elements, you die, period, and that is considered mild northern California weather, so one could easily imagine the weather in other parts of the world.

In the beginning, soon after the vanishings, Demetri signs a seven year peace treaty with Israel, and in signing this covenant, he brings peace and prosperity to the entire world. During the first 3.5 years everything is seemingly perfect; there is no unemployment or welfare, not a person on the planet is without insurance, medical or dental benefits. Everyone submitting to Demetri's lordship is free to do as they pleased, with acceptance and tolerance removing any and all lines of right and wrong. Crime is virtually nonexistent because no one has need of anything and people all over the world are truly their brothers' keeper.

After 3.5 years of a virtual Utopian society, Alexander Demetri breaks the peace treaty that united humanity, establishes himself in

Jerusalem to be worshiped, and the world changes almost instantly into what it is today. Peace is ripped out of the hands of civilization and nearly 1.2 billion people kill each other, die of starvation and disease, or are torn to pieces by wild animals in a few short months; a fourth of the world's population, dead. Matthew the Apostle writes about this time saying, "There will be great distress, unequaled from the beginning of the world until now—and never to be equaled again."

During this time, many seek to end their own lives; they cry out for an end to the suffering and for some unexplainable reason, none, not one single solitary person is able to take their own life, to commit suicide. Some attempt to overdose, blow their heads off, slit their wrists, or throw themselves off cliffs or into oncoming traffic, no matter what heinous plan one can devise, when the dust settles they continue to breathe; their bodies, their spirits refuse to die. It's as if something supernatural is preventing anyone from killing themselves. Because of the severe shortage of food many resort to eating their own children in order to survive; it becomes common place to overhear one neighbor say to another, "Today we will boil my son, and tomorrow let's bake your daughter."

The Bible warns of this hell on earth, and provides a way of escape; those who vanished are the ones who found it, or better yet, found Him. John the Apostle prophesies that a time will come, which he calls, "The Great Tribulation," but Tage can testify that there is nothing great about it. He thinks the name, the Great Tribulation, is more akin to a card trick by a magician in Vegas or the sixty dollar grand finale firework you buy at a Phantom Fireworks booth to wrap up your 4th of July block party. Even so, in the midst of living out what's left of their lives in a world that is no longer going to hell in a hand basket, but is pulling up to the gate, people curse God and run from Him, just as Tage continues to do.

Fires ravage the land and one third of all the trees and all the green grass in the world are consumed. A third of the rivers and bodies of water become blood and every living thing in them die, and one third of all ships in the world are destroyed.

Again, war breaks out all over the world, and soon, another billion and a half people die; a third of the human population, dead. Missiles fired to initiate or respond to attack fall like stars from the heavens and a third of all bodies of water become bitter; all who drink from the contaminated waters, die. No country or nation is in a position to do anything about the breaking of the peace treaty because Alexander Demetri himself has become the only world superpower. He has become god, and none dare to openly oppose him. His power lies in a lie and the Truth is the only thing, the only One, he will ever fear.

The world government under Demetri's orders raid houses and dwellings in search of Bibles, and other religious material. If something turns up, anyone found within are taken into custody for propagating hate crimes against humanity. During transport, the prisoners will be driven down a seemingly endless stretch of road, a road that Demetri named La Via Dolorosa, which means the Way of Suffering. Driving slowly down this path, prisoners will see truckloads of bodies in various stages of decomposition stacked high and wide, all of which are missing their heads. The seats and floorboards of the transport vehicle are covered in plastic because it was unlikely that with the sight, smell, and the terror of what is to come for those inside, that anyone can make it through the Way without violently throwing up.

161

Officers will often place bets as to how many times an individual will puke, what color it might be, and would even go so far as to try and guess ahead of time what the person may have eaten last. Just when the prisoners begin to wonder where the heads are, they would see them; hills made with only the heads of those who refused to conform, who refused to be implanted. The heads and faces, contorted and twisted, with mutilated mouths and eyes or only sockets staring at those who will soon be staring at those who will come after. Either that would be their end, or they will walk away as marked members of society, but with the sentence of eternal judgment upon them according to the Unbelievers.

By the time the mounds of heads are seen, many already decide that they will renounce their God and worship Alexander Demetri. Statistically, for every one body seen along the Way, a hundred choose to conform. When they enter the prison, rows of proud guillotines present themselves as the welcoming committee, and the masses seeing them are usually fully convinced that they will stand by their decision and surrender whatever belief system they held.

Bibles are gathered together for burning in the city's bonfire celebrations. The festivities last for days; depending on the amount of what they call religious propaganda is collected. It is mandatory that citizens attend, but to force anyone is unnecessary. There is no other place anyone would rather be; food and drink, music and dancing, drugs, free flowing alcohol, which is scarce, is made available to all. The debauchery detailed in Sodom and Gomorrah pales in comparison to the shindig sponsored by Alexander Demetri; men laid with men, women with women, humans with animals, whether living or dead, nothing is frowned upon or off limits, if it feels good, indulge, with or without anyone else's consent.

To accommodate everyone, bonfires are set up throughout the city, so everyone can participate in the Bible burnings. Anything religious is burned, but the Holy Bible is prized above all. In the beginning there was an abundance of books, but now, to find a whole book from the Bible or even multiple pages stuck together and used in an underground church or held by someone in hiding is a rarity. Rewards are still promised for Bibles and for turning in those living outside of society, but more often than not, the only reward for services rendered is to share the same fate as Mr. Robert Timothy.

Jacob drags Tage through what he explains is a rough part of the city; as if there is only one area of the city to be avoided. The neighborhood is known as Del Paso Heights. Tage's body is becoming unresponsive and he desperately needs to rest, but it becomes evident by the look on Jacob's concerned face and the feverish pace he keeps, that they are now running from something. Someone or something out there even has Jacob spooked.

Tage's body suddenly goes limp, but Jacob has no trouble managing his dead weight, slowing is apparently not an option. Jacob eyes swivel cautiously; eyeing shadows, listening to sounds, feeling the air. Tage's body is hot with fever so he dismisses the returning hallucinations that catch his eyes as he scans.

"We have to pick up the pace." Jacob speaks with an air of grimness that causes the hairs on Tage's neck to stand upright.

Tage jerks his head back and looks over his shoulder when he hears a cryptic voice, neither male nor female, the sound of many voices speaking as one, whisper, "Stayyyyyy," into his ear as if someone is walking directly behind him. Tage buttons his eyes and tightens his face, attempting to shake the perceived nonsense from his thoughts and regain himself. His legs stretch further apart as his stride widens to keep up with Jacob's hurried tempo. Thick clouds of frost bellowed from their lips as the temperature suddenly plunges another fifteen degrees in a matter of seconds.

"Where are we going?" Tage whispers, feeling so disoriented he is unsure of who he is actually talking to.

"Away from here. Keep moving."

Tage begins to resist the forward motion, pulling against Jacob as he continues venturing forward. With each step, Tage's foot plants and slams against the unforgiving concrete in an effort to back pedal. With each thump of his shoe, a shockwave of anticipated and excruciating pain shoots from the bottom of his heel to his hair follicles which feel like pins and his head is the pincushion.

Tage is intimately acquainted with the darkness of this world, but he knows this is somehow different.

"I don't want to go," Tage utters, quietly at first, then again in spastic protest. "I don't want to go. I don't want to go. I don't go. Don't go. Don't go."

Every cell in his body is being pulled in the opposite direction; he feels as though his flesh is beginning to tear, like one being drawn and quartered.

"No. Not now," Jacob screams into the cold darkness.

Lights flicker and street lamps explode, torturous shrieks coming from nowhere, but feel as though they're everywhere, pierce their ears. Tage is being swallowed by the darkness.

Jacob jabs his fist into Tage's wounded side, forcing a harsh guttural growl to expel from his tightened lips.

"Keep moving. Keep moving—faster," Jacob shouts, trying to force Tage's protesting body and dragging legs to advance.

"I don't want to go. I want to—"

"Stayyyyyyyyyyyy," a deep breathy voice that both Tage and Jacob could hear, eerily finishes Tage's request.

"You got a light, junior?" The voice belted again in a tone chillingly similar to Frank's voice.

"Oh crap," Jacob snaps, just as an unseen force blows through and splits them like an ax splintering wood.

Jacob is knocked into the street; a graceful shoulder roll prevents him from taking a vicious spill. Tage slams against a wooden fence surrounding a boarded up and condemned preschool building. His right hand steadies himself against the fence, and his left hand reaches for his neck. Tage gasps for air as something tightens around his throat, squeezing, crushing his windpipe. Tage thrashes his body, drawing only short staccato like breaths; his hands pull downward by his throat as though he is struggling to pry unseen hands coiled around his neck.

Tage drops to his knees, oxygen depleting. Jacob rushes to him, stopping only for a moment to determine what, or if anything could be done. He glances at the fence where Tage had steadied himself, and notices Tage's smeared blood was disappearing and the wood was chipping as if it is being gnawed on.

Jacob quickly moves in, cuts off a blood soaked strip of Tage's clothing and wipes it along the fence. Teeth marks begin to surface on the wooden boards. Jacob grabs both of Tage's arms, pulling. Tage shakes his head, indicating the obvious, that he can't breathe.

"I know. Trust me. Run. Come on!"

Tage, with Jacob's help, gets his wobbly legs underneath himself, and follows Jacob's lead. He bolts.

They both run for all they're worth.

The farther they get from the area, the easier it is for Tage to take in air. Jacob cranes his neck to take a quick look back and sees Tage's bloody hand print being licked up by whatever entity that had attacked them. The piece of Tage's shirt is being tossed about as if it's being fought over.

Tage plods along as though he has been walking aimlessly for days in a dry and barren wasteland. The outside temperature has returned to normal, but the cold does little for his blistering fever. His body aches as though he has been beaten with a bat to the sound of kids screaming, Piñata.

Jacob shuffles Tage up the walkway of a decrepit one story, three bedroom house, with steel bars on the windows. A three feet tall chain-link fence surrounds the house, and a red mailbox with no name inside the corroded name plate holder stands next to where the missing entry gate should be. The concrete pathway is uneven, cracked and broken by tree roots and grass growing underneath and jutting up to see for itself what the world has become. The house is Jacob's own private fortress in the middle of a physical and spiritual war zone. The paint used to be white, but is now brown, peeling and damaged from years of neglect.

Sorrow washes over Tage like a black tidal wave when he thinks about the home he was forced to leave behind; a home that could very well be standing, but one that will never be what it was again. Not what it was for him and his wife. Tage looks over the landscaping of the house; overgrown and unkempt bushes, low hanging trees, and thick waist high weeds choking the life out of any grass that might even think of making an appearance.

Jacob helps Tage up the creaking steps and leans him against the railing. The dark and dingy porch has spider webs hanging everywhere, and the eight-legged masterful creators suspended in the center of each one makes his stomach queasy.

In one blink of an eye, the spiders as if on cue, rain down on him, hundreds of them, crawling all over his body like bees covering a honeycomb, hissing, biting, stinging. Tage flails his arms, frantically jerking, beating his body.

Smack. Smack.

Out of breath and wide eyed, Tage suddenly focuses on Jacob standing before him with his hand raised, ready to slap him again to loose him from his distorted sensory experience brought on by his elevated temperature.

"Sorry," Tage says, tensed and embarrassed.

Tage is apprehensive to say the least, being taken to an unfamiliar place, by an unfamiliar man, that he is forced to trust; it isn't like he can just part company and skip merrily along on his own. It's a miracle, a term he uses rather loosely, that he has made it as far as he has with the bullet still lodged in his gut. He imagines the damage that is being done internally, with every step, twist, and turn. He tries to shake the uneasy feeling of where he is by telling himself he's with a cop killer. As far as he is concerned, Jacob is one of the good guys. He hopes.

Tage watches closely as Jacob swipes his wrist in front of a panel next to the main door of the house to gain entrance.

"Nice. A high tech ghetto," Tage says, wanting to laugh, but too busted up to enjoy the snide remark.

"I'm glad you still have a sense of humor. You're going to need it," Jacob responds.

He twists the door knob and throws open the door.

It's pretty remarkable really. You can't even open up a simple door these days without an implant."

Tage turns back and scans the area outside. He locks eyes with a pipe smoking elderly man living across the street. The old man eyes them suspiciously from a curtain drawn window. The elderly man then lifts his right hand and makes the shape of a gun with his fingers. Tage squints to get a better look at the man who then aims his finger at him and pulls the trigger. He follows the shot with a blow of his finger. The gust of his breath blows away the imaginary smoke from the barrel of his gun. He then steps back and allows the curtain to fall back in place. Tage has no idea what that is all about and wonders what he is getting himself into.

"Come on, let's get inside," Jacob says.

He does a quick check of the street and helps Tage inside.

They retreat behind closed doors. Tage immediately hears the clanging of pots and pans.

The house is sparsely decorated with Goodwill's finest. Tage faintly makes out where the couch is in the darkened room. He staggers over to it and collapses.

"Honey?" A woman's voice calls out from the kitchen.

"I'm here, love," Jacob replies. "Grab me a blanket. Hurry." He says with urgency in his voice.

A scented candle burns on an upside down wine barrel being used as a coffee table. Tage hasn't smelled anything like it in a long time. It almost made him smile. How incredible is it that something as simple as a smell can take someone back in time, wielding the power to unlock memories.

In his mind, he can see Shannon sitting by the fireplace on a cold winter's night and remembers how beautiful she looks bathed in the glow of candlelight. He is instantly jolted back into reality from the searing pain shooting through his body brought on by Jacob ripping off his coat to get a better look at his wound.

Amanda, Jacob's wife, is a svelte, fair skinned brunette in her late twenties with mysterious gray eyes. She strolls down at a snail's pace, carrying a blanket in one hand and a seven-month-old baby boy in the other. Her bright floral formfitting and laundered dress is as out of place as a box of Twinkies at a fat camp. Her hair is cut short and neat, fingernails painted, and she's wearing shoes suited for a night on the town. The theme song to Three's Company plays in his head, seeing the spitting image of Janet now standing before him. Tage's guess is that she was either born or married into money and she is used to getting what she wants. He can tell by looking at her, she would never miss a day of Zumba and that taking care of herself is of utmost importance.

"Thank god you're back, I was so worried," says Amanda.

The first thought that comes to Tage's mind upon hearing her voice is, spoiled. Jacob takes the blanket from her hand.

"I'm fine, babe. Bring me the first aid kit." He tosses the peach colored thermal blanket over the couch and helps Tage to remove his blood soaked shirt.

"Where have you been? Mother has been expecting us for three days now, and my father has been scouring the streets looking for you," she heatedly says, as Jacob contemplates how to treat Tage's wound. "You could have called, you know. Father's been checking the hospitals, the morgues—"

"Amanda! I need that first aid kit," he demands.

Amanda, embittered, reluctantly turns and slowly walks off. Jacob presses his hand on Tage's wound, who gasps for air. Tage fights to catch his breath, and before he could lean forward to see what Jacob is doing, Jacob rips off the two strips of blue tape that hold the compress in place. Tage bellows out in agony.

Amanda struts defiantly back with the medical kit.

"Amanda, I'm working here, okay. I need you on the same page with me, do you understand?"

"Fine," she replies. "But why did you bring him here? Do you know what they will do to us if we're caught?"

"We can have that discussion later. Give me the kit." Amanda stares at Tage with disgust.

"Amanda!" She breaks out of her trance and practically throws the supplies at Jacob.

"Next time call," she says, storming out of the room.

Jacob is oddly amused by the outburst. He's half tempted to go after her but knows he must remain focused. He quickly opens the case and the supplies are abundant. He has everything he needs for practically any given situation, just short of open heart surgery. Not only are the medical supplies ample, the couple has stored up enough food and water for their family for months, their walls lined with boxes of food, water, and supplies. Tage is curious as to why their excess has not been seized by the government, every citizen is given only a small amount of rations to live off of. Too late to complain now. The "people" voted for this; to have the government provide for and run all aspects of their lives. Tage then recalls how he met the mystery man and figures that being a cop killer apparently comes with benefits.

Jacob tries to peel the compress away from Tage's open wound, but dried blood and skin surrounding the cut has adhered to the old dressing. He reaches for a pair of scissors then slowly lifts the gauze until it gets to the point where his skin begins to rise as he pulls. Tage's fist clench tightly as Jacob reaches in and begins to cut away at the flesh that is sticking to the fabric.

"I apologize for the rush job I did on this field dressing," he says, as he continues to snip. "I was listening to the police scanner and I heard about your 'terrorist' activity." He snickers. "I'm grateful that I found you before they did."

"Yeah, you and me both," Tage says through gritted teeth.

Jacob instructs Tage to prepare himself.

The slug has to be taken out of his side, and he is concerned about the possibility of infection. Tage steals a glance at the cloth removed from his side. Seeing the crusted blood and fragments of skins that refused to part, he knows he is in for the ride of his life. He nearly loses consciousness when he sees Jacob thread the needle that he intends on using to sew up his gaping wound.

"You're not afraid of needles are you," he jests.

Jacob slips away for a moment and quickly returns with a bottle of whiskey and two shot glasses. He fills both vessels and offers one to Tage first. He takes notice of his hesitation.

"What? Drinking against your religion?"

Jacob tosses back both shots and pours himself a third.

Tage begins to get lightheaded.

"Suit yourself," says Jacob.

"Just get this over with, okay. Please. I have to get home to my family."

Jacob chokes down a third and pours himself another. Tage is now starting to worry just as much about Jacob's liquor intake as he is about the bullet inside him.

Tage's temperature climbs, sweat pools on his flush face. "How many of these things have you done?" Tage nervously questions, trying to lay claim to some measure of reassurance.

"One, including this one. That's the reason for the booze."

Jacob throws Tage a mischievous grin as he retrieves a pair of clear latex gloves from his medical stash. He forces his bruised hands inside and snaps them around his wrists.

Tage lays his head back on the couch and closes his eyes. If he is going to find a happy place, he needs to start looking now. Jacob retrieves a bag that contains a syringe packaged inside and he tears it open with his mouth. Amanda comes back into the living room after putting the baby down.

"Perfect, grab that flash light and shine it right here." Jacob directs Amanda's attention to the hole in Tage's side, which dribbles blood.

Jacob loads the syringe with the clear contents of a vial and angles himself to inject the liquid directly into Tage's wound.

Out of the corner of his eye, Tage catches sight of the needle nearing the crevice in his side and he flips out. Pain or no pain, he shoots up and smacks the needle out of his hand, sending it flying across the room.

"Are you crazy?" Jacob shouts.

"What is that? What are you trying to do to me?"

His racing heart fills the reservoir in his side with red.

"I'm not trying to take out a splinter, my friend. You do understand that, right? I need to put you under." Tage locks eyes with Jacob.

"No needles." Tage groggily says.

"It was just a local anesthetic."

"If you want to help me, just get me out of here," Tage groans. "No needles. No drugs." He is not in a position to be making demands, but he feels he needs to clarify his unwavering objective.

Jacob is surprisingly with all that. Because... at this point Tage

172

has lost count of how many shots of alcohol he's downed, but half the bottle being gone seems to be a reasonable indicator of how much is now in his field doctor's system.

Tage quickly snatches the glass Jacob is filling and he tosses it back. The whiskey is so dry it practically evaporates in his mouth, but he can feel the smoldering liquid travel down his throat and into his body, leaving a burning wake along its path of travel.

Tage isn't much of a drinker, but he figures the more he can consume of the disorienting drug, the less will be available for the one who will soon be sticking sharp pointy objects into his body.

Jacob is already beginning to appear overly relaxed, and Tage nervously questions whether it's a good thing or not. Amanda rolls up a towel and tosses it at Tage.

"Try not to let the whole neighborhood know you're here," she chides.

Just then, the baby begins wailing in the bedroom. "There's more at stake here than just you," Amanda points out, as she lays the flash light on the wine barrel, still pointing at his side, and rushes out the room.

"You ready?"

Tage hesitates then manages a nod, granting him permission to commence. He fights to slow his erratic breathing. No sooner than he places the towel between his teeth and bites down, he feels the coldness of the needle nose pliers in Jacob's hand against his flesh.

Jacob digs into the cavernous hole in his side. He tries hard to quickly sop up the blood that continues to fill the yawning wound, so he can better see what he is doing. Tage writhes in mind splitting pain.

"Be still. You have to stay still. I don't want to push the bullet further inside."

Jacob continues to probe as Tage tries to lie motionless; not an easy task when seemingly every muscle in his body violently contracts at will.

He tightly fastens his eyes. Panic grips Tage as his heart pounds out of rhythm and the left side of his body suddenly goes limp. He just knows he's going to die. His head screams over and over, "Cardiac arrest." The right side of his body loses feeling and his eyes spring open. He is unable to move and all sound ceases. His body becomes so relaxed that the towel he is chewing on releases from his jaws. He feels as though he is being overcome with the sensation of a dream world, but all he can see is darkness. His thoughts begin to escape and a barrage of sounds fill his ailing head; the sound of car horns and heavy street traffic, voices and laughter. Music, oh the sweet sound of Johnny Cash crooning the Ring of Fire... It would not have been his first choice, considering all he's been through, but the song is still legendary.

Tage is overcome with the sounds of life.

Life how he remembers it.

His vision soon returns, but Jacob and the gloomy room is now nowhere to be seen. Not even a distant memory.

He escapes.

His mind slides back and he remembers days gone by. Every sense in his body is filled with the hustle and bustle of everyday life in a city looking so strong and beautiful that day, with such magnificence, that even the buildings stand clean and proud. The city is full of energy as people flood the streets, busy about their daily activities. Different smells fill the air as the vendors sell a variety of fresh cooked foods that represent countries from around the world.

A cornucopia of cultures floods the streets.

The weather is beyond perfect; a soft breeze blows, and the warmth of the sun kisses his skin. The few clouds above only serve to enhance the brilliance of a sky saturated in blue.

Then everything suddenly changes.

The sky becomes dark, as if a net of evil is cast upon the city.

The clouds begin to roll, unsure of which direction to flee. All of a sudden people begin screaming and pushing one another for no apparent reason. Car horns blare and vehicles veer out of control, viciously and purposely running over people; men, women, and children, without so much as a brake light shining in their wake to indicate even a fleeting thought about stopping. Car doors are opening while still in motion and people are literally being thrown out of speeding vehicles.

Terrified citizens charge into buildings to escape the hysteria, hoping for safety and refuge, and others drag people out of buildings only to beat them openly in the streets. A city bus jumps the curb and careens into a bench at a bus stop, crushing and instantly killing an old light-skinned black man who fails to get out of the way in time. The bus barrels down the sidewalk, mowing down people, running over bikes, magazine and advertising racks, newspaper bins, tables and chairs outside coffee shops and bistros, destroying laptops, iPods and cell phones, anything left by frightened patrons who dart out of the way. The driver loses control of the bus and plows into a tree. The driver of the bus, a forty something year old light-skinned heavy-set black male with chicken pox scars and a birth mark on his left arm, stumbles out of the bus dazed from the impact. His Regional Transit uniform is soaked in blood from the gash in his head and deep cuts in his shoulders and leg. He slowly rights his bent glasses that rest crooked on his face, the left lens, which had been super glued in place, barely hangs on.

When the driver comes to his senses, he limps toward the back of the bus and forcefully grabs the lone passenger, who bears an uncanny resemblance to himself.

"Hey! What are you doing? Don't you recognize me." The passenger shouts, as the bus driver muscles him to the door.

"Leave me alone. I don't want to go," screams the passenger. "It's me. It's me..."

The bus driver throws him out the door and the passenger lands hard on the ground.

"Please stop. It's me... I'm you--"

The driver clutches him by the throat, cutting him off. He then slams the pleading passenger against the heavily damaged bus, and chokes the life out of him with his bare hands.

The bus driver, chest heaving, looks over the dead man on the ground thinking about what he has just done. A smile that could light up a room traipses across his face, and he hobbles away relieved, repeatedly chanting, "The old man... The old man... The old man is never so dead that he can't be resurrected at a moment's notice." He gives little thought to the chaos ensuing around him.

Jacob continues to fish for the bullet; poking, prodding and twisting, wading through the crater filled with Tage's blood.

Tage's face contorts, not from the anguish of the procedure, but from the events unfolding in his mind. He doesn't want to remember, but unfortunately for him, he can never forget the events over three years ago that forever continues to alter his existence. So extraordinarily vivid are the details of yesterday.

Tage slips back in his mind to the time when he and Shannon are driving through the city streets in their car, hastily stuffed with bedding, clothes, camping gear, canned food and water; everything they could get their hands on in a hurry. Sadly, they stripped their home of pictures, heirlooms, trinkets and memories, knowing full well they are never coming back. They walk away from the house they have shared as husband and wife for twelve years, leaving the front door wide open.

Tage is not one of those kids who grew up in front of a television, but he's seen his share of emergency broadcast center tests; the ones encouraging people to store up extra food and water, clothing, medical supplies and various survival goods in case of earthquakes, floods, hurricanes, tsunamis, or anything else of that nature. But for this, there is no such thing as preparation.

He remembers every word of the news broadcast that seemingly set everything in motion. He and Shannon decide to leave everything they own, everything they love and worked so hard for, and to purposely lose themselves. They are going to vanish from society; Tage, Shannon, and his parents who are going to rendezvous with them at the place where his dad used to take him fishing in Tage's younger years.

Tage and Shannon try to calm their minds by listening to oldies, a time when music was music. A couple of songs into their exodus a high pitched tone belts from the speakers. The voice of a news reporter breaks through. Tage smiles wryly to his wife who nervously turns and met his eyes.

"In just a few moments, the U.N. spokesperson will be taking questions regarding the new law that has now gone into effect... for those of you who are just tuning in with us, in an unprecedented move to protect world peace, head of the United Nations, Alexander Demetri, has just signed a bill officially sanctioning the capture, and execution of anyone who refuses to embrace our new way of life. Anyone not submitting, any unbeliever refusing to be governed by Demetri or confess him as Lord, is now wanted dead or alive."

Shannon dips her head in utter disbelief.

In silence, Tage calmly drives the vehicle laden with their belongings. He is careful not to draw any undo attention to themselves.

Car horns begin sounding off, one after another, glass and windows shatter, and voices rise into a chorus of howls and screams. Tires screech. All around them are the unmistakable sounds of wreckage; metal against metal, twisting and grinding. Bone shattering explosions can be heard all around, and dark plumes of smoke rise one after another. The car fills with the smell of smoke. Tage's heart races and he accelerates. He tries hard to look calm, all the while his mouth rapidly fills with salty saliva. The acidic bile stings the back of his throat.

Horrified, they witness a shop owner being dragged out of his store, begging and pleading for his life. A mob of angry businessmen force him to the ground and beat him mercilessly.

Glass begins to rain down from the heavens, lightly sprinkling and dancing upon their car, then shards of glass pour like spring showers, followed by a hail of bodies falling to the ground with such force that it feels like the impact is rattling the car; the "Thunk" of the flattened, nay, exploding bodies reverberate on contact, immediately accompanied by pools of blood. "Oh my gosh," Shannon says with a hollow tone as her eyes float up and she sees people smashing through high-rise windows screaming and flailing as they plummet to the ground. Tage's mouth hangs open as he glances up and sees people throw, nay, launch, others out of the towering buildings. He argues with himself that they have to be jumping, they must be; there is no other explanation. What kind of people would throw someone out of high-rise windows?

Some of those falling from the smaller buildings, those who did not die when they collide with the street, lay disfigured with their head's cracked open and broken bones protruding. They cry out for help, but are only cursed and yelled at from those standing in the open windows above, those who hurled them out, wanting, longing to see them dead; angry that the broken bodies on the ground are still clinging to life.

All around them, people are screaming, fighting, slashing, and stabbing at one another as if in a single moment no one knows anything but hate. The shocked silence in the car is broken when the broadcast concludes with, "All we can say here at the United News Network is… it's about time. One World. One Religion. One Lord, Alexander Demetri."

Tage is thrust back into the reality of torturous pain. Jacob opens his grip, which widens the mouth of the pliers piercing the hollow near Tage's stomach. He clamps down on a .45 caliber round which he extracts with sense of satisfaction. He slaps a compress over the rising reservoir of blood and takes a moment to admire the bullet against the beam of light from the flashlight. He drops the bloody bullet into a silver dish that is shaped like a miniature bed pan. Sweating profusely, Tage's eyes begin to focus and his breathing slows. Jacob then leans over him smiling, "You still with me," he says rhetorically. Jacob then picks up the needle and thread he had previously prepared.

"Halfway there," he says blissfully as he forces more whiskey down Tage's throat, most of which is spit up. Jacob sterilizes the massive needle by running it back and forth through the flame of the candle. Jacob pinches the folds of Tage's skin together, which sends his pain meter off the charts.

Tage slips away once again. He sees himself barreling through a side street in the city. Shannon holds on for dear life, as they swerve to avoid people, cars, and objects that seemingly appear out from nowhere.

His grip is tight on the wheel and his gaze fixed ahead, unsure as to what awaits them around every corner or turn. With a quick turn of her head, Shannon spots a black woman wearing an overcoat being pummeled in an alley by three white construction workers wearing old worn and dirty blue jeans, brown boots, and bright orange colored t-shirts.

Shannon screams, "Stop the car!"

It takes him a moment to register and respond. "What? I'm not stopping this car."

"Now!"

Tage recognizes the looks, Shannon is going to jump out whether the car is moving or not.

He slams on the brakes, mind racing. "What's happening? What did I miss?" He thinks to himself.

Before the car comes to a halt, Shannon's seatbelt is already undone.

"What are you doing?"

"There's a woman that needs help." She flings open her door.

"It's too dangerous. I'll go."

Shannon is already out and tearing down the street on foot, a straight look of crazed fury in her eyes.

"Shannon!"

All she can hear is the sound of her own will. Her face is flushed red from the heat and anger rising within her. Tage reaches over, frantic, and pulls the door closed that she left open. He slaps the car in reverse and hit the gas. Shannon rounds the corner and disappears from view.

Shannon yells like a spider monkey as she advances on the workers who are beating the helpless woman with tools from their utility belts. The woman fights with every ounce of her being, backed up against a storage shed that she refuses to move away from. The men repeatedly knock her aside and she quickly returns to fight them in front of the maintenance door.

Shannon picks up a bottle lying on the ground as she charges forward, and smashes it into the head of the worker nearest her, the one with no business wearing a pony tail. She then begins to wail on him.

Tage overshot the alley and sees his wife sitting on a man's chest, pounding her fist on the guy who lays motionless on the asphalt. Tage floors the gas pedal and peels out towards them.

He honks his horn, yelling like a crazed groupie, desperately trying to get her attention, hoping to distract the man with a yellow hard hat, heading straight for his wife.

As Shannon rises, she barely has time to lift her hands to defend herself when she is struck in the side of head with a wrench. A cut instantly opens at the point of impact and wet warm blood trails through her hair and down her face. Instead of withdrawing or cowering, Shannon advances on the man, clawing, swinging, and trying to gouge out his eyes. The man strikes her repeatedly and bashes her again in the head with his improvised weapon. Shannon staggers back. She looks around, faint, everything she sees has a ghostly echo, disorienting her. Her attacker simply watches with a crooked grin on his face. With her arms outstretched, she stumbles over to the woman being beaten on the ground, whispering her plea for the man to cease his vicious attack. Shannon collapses on top of the battered and bloodied woman, and begins to bear the brunt of the man's attacks.

The man who struck Shannon marches in to finish what he started, but suddenly goes airborne, catapulting into the air from the impact of Tage's car against his now broken body. The man smashes up against the windshield and sails wildly over the top of his speeding car. Tage stops the car and jumps out. He grabs the only worker who remains standing, the one beating on his half-conscious wife, who is still trying to protect the woman beneath her. The man seems almost possessed; his eyes are vacant and lifeless and register only a blank stare that sees through whatever he fixes his eyes on, unaware of anything else around him except for his insatiable desire to inflict great bodily harm or death upon this woman, and now his wife. Tage unleashes a fury of blows on this man that he never knew he could summon. He then smashes the man's face against a concrete wall and did it again for good measure. The man begins to lose consciousness, but Tage didn't stop, he couldn't stop. He straightens him up and he jabs his fist repeatedly into his face. The man's body drops to the pavement like a stone. Tage quickly spins around, breathing heavy, anxious to take on the next one, but there is no one left.

Tage rushes to Shannon's side. "Please be okay," he whispers as he throws himself to the ground and carefully rolls her over, instantly relieved to see her force a smile.

Tage checks the pulse of the black woman beneath her but is unable to find any signs of life.

Shannon speaks faintly. "Her mother. She calls her, Sal."

He shakes his head, confused, not able to process what she is attempting to communicate.

182

"She said it's short for Psalm. What a pretty name."

Her words slur and he struggles to make sense of what she is saying. Shannon slowly, painfully reaches up and points towards the door of the storage room. She lowers her hands and her eyes fall.

Tage is reluctant to leave her side, but Shannon's grin and the slight nod of her head tells him that he needs to. He rises and steps towards the door. Cautiously he opens it and sunlight floods the darkened room. He peers inside and his eyes widen as he takes a sharp unexpected breath, which makes his heart skip. Inside the dirty maintenance room, hidden in the shadows, he sees a little black girl, she can't be more than four years old, wearing Dora the Explorer pajamas, sitting with her knees tight to her chest in a ball. She is rocking back and forth in the corner, crying hysterically. She has two braids in her hair, both tied together with colored yarn.

Tage speaks with a soft, quiet voice. "Hi Sal. My name is Tage."

Sal tries to stop crying; she whimpers between each breath.

"Sal, your mother asked me to come get you. She wanted my wife and me to take care of you. Would you like to come out from here?" Sal nods her head, still wiping away her tears.

"I think Psalm is a beautiful name."

Sal tries to smile.

"I've never heard that before." Tage continues.

"It's from the Bible," she says.

"That's right. It's from the Bible."

"Do you know what it means?" She says, shyly.

"What? The Bible?"

"No, my name. Psalm?"

Tage thinks for a moment and then glances back to check on Shannon and his surroundings. He knows they are not safe, but understands that this moment must not be rushed.

183

"No, sweetie. I don't"

"It means poems. Poems to be sung with music."

Tage immediately realizes there is something special about this child. "That's wonderful, sweetheart. Come on let's get you out of here, okay?" Sal nods her head, but doesn't move. For a moment she simply stares straight into his bright blue eyes. Tage feels like everything about him is being revealed to this child and his discomfort is noticeable by his expression.

He did not know how to respond to being forced into a position of transparency.

Tage imagines what it's like to be on a witness stand being cross examined by a shrewd attorney who knows how to get information that someone is not wanting to share. After what feels like a lifetime of having the sum total of his existence picked apart and scrutinized, Sal, as if on cue, as if she hears the call of an expected and familiar voice, rises to her feet and wipes the remaining tears from her eyes.

A tight lipped smile graces her face and Tage responds with a smile of his own.

She then takes off running towards him with her arms open wide, and new tears... tears of joy flood her eyes. Tage's heart flutters as he lifts her into his arms. He is surprised by the smothering hug she gives him as he cradles her. The moment she places her head on his shoulder, her eyes peacefully close.

For Tage, it is love at first sight.

Jacob stares at Tage, passed out on the couch. The look of tranquility on his face puzzles him. Even with the needle and thread zipping in and out of his skin and being yanked forcefully to close up the wound, he still manages to muster a wide and peaceful smile.

Jacob thinks the whiskey may have something to do with Tage's unusual sense of tranquility, but as he takes another drink from the bottle, he realizes how little Tage has consumed, especially in comparison to himself. The smile is a mystery to him.

Tage lies on the couch, physically there, but his mind so far removed from the agony of being sewn up like a torn garment. He remembers sitting parked on the side of a deserted two-lane highway, trying to catch his breath, trying to stop shaking, trying to digest everything that has and will now happen as a result of the new laws that now govern the world. Little did Tage know, that on this particular day, he was going to become intimately acquainted with both death and life. Shannon sleeps in the front seat holding Sal, who is awake and staring wide eyed at Tage. She waves at him with her tiny hands and Tage waves back at her, grinning ear-to-ear, his heart soaring.

She looks as though she is mimicking his every move.

The only thing that is able to pull her attention off of him is when a butterfly flies in and out of the window. She follows it with her eyes for as long as she can.

Sal raises her hand up, with her palm facing Tage. He looks at her curiously.

"Now you do it," Sal says to him in a chastising tone. As far as she is concerned, he should have already known what he is to do.

Tage raises his hand. Sal, still being held firmly by Shannon, reaches as far as she can towards him with her hand, but it is still not enough to bridge the gap of empty space.

She motions with her eyes and facial expression and the slight tilt of her head, that she wants their hands to meet.

Tage eventually catches on and presses his hand to hers. Her entire hand barely covers the corner of his palm. Sal giggles at the sight of seeing his hand engulf hers. She then makes a sweeping arc motion with their hands together and melodically says, "I love you with my whole heart." Tage's heart melts, especially after she scolds him for not saying anything. Tage quickly apologizes and initiates the motion, realizing that she has drawn the shape of a heart in the air with their hands. He repeats, "I love you with my whole heart," with the same melody, but slightly off key. Tage blushes at the words as they draw their hearts.

"That means forever and ever", Sal says in a whisper, not wanting to wake Shannon. "Even if we have nothing, we have all that we need, as long as we're together."

Tage is clearly out of his element but loves every moment of this new experience; this extraordinary view of life through her eyes. He does not question what is being unlocked within him, he simply embraces it, and all he can do is smile.

"Do you get it?"

"Yeah, sweetie, I think so." Tage speaks softly, utterly amazed by everything about Sal; the little green-eyed girl that he already loves with his whole heart.

"Good," Sal excitedly says.

Her frightened gaze immediately turns to a speeding jeep that passes closely by them, shaking the car; a reminder that they need to keep moving. Aside from his parents, everyone is a threat and no one is to be trusted. It is a mistake to be stopped anywhere for too long, but he would happily live or die for this mistake.

This moment he would not trade for anything.

Tage jumps out of the car and gently pries Sal from Shannon's arms. He kisses Sal's forehead and places her in the seat behind

Shannon, into a car seat he snatched from an abandoned wrecked car he spotted on his way out of the city.

"Rule number one… Seatbelts." He straps her in with a click. "So we can be safe."

He closes the door and his countenance immediately falls as he looks back towards the city. He wishes they could have saved Sal's mother, or at the very least did something more than just cover her body. Now all that he can hope for is that Sal's mother will be honored by the way they raise her little girl.

His thoughts return to the moment and he shuffles back to the driver's side door and hops in the car. He closes the door and secures his seatbelt. Shannon's hand moves on top of his. He lightly massages her hand with his fingers and his eyes swing up to meet Shannon's as she mouths the words, "I love you." Tage quietly responds, "I love you with my whole heart." Out of the corner of his eye he sees Sal give him a thumb up. He starts the car, shifts it into gear and takes off down the road with his family.

Chapter 9

EXHAUSTION takes its toll on Hollie and Gina; more mental than anything else. Both are sluggish, running only on fumes. They move slowly as they approach Brad, who still appears to be unconscious. Hollie is holding a familiar vial in his hand. He takes one look at Brad's ghostly white sallow complexion and immediately knows that something is wrong. Brad doesn't appear to be breathing and his lips have a bluish tint. Hollie quickly lowers himself and checks Brad's neck for a pulse. He looks up at Gina and slowly shakes his head.

"I don't understand. He was fine when I brought him in here."

"Move, Hollie," Gina barks, pushing him out of the way.

She kneels down to get a closer look at Brad and his body slinks to the side. She reaches behind him and quickly withdraws her fingers, which are now covered in blood. Seeing the blood streak down her hand, Hollie panics and reaches for her.

"Honey, relax. It's not mine," she confesses, disgusted and fearful of the potentially drug tainted blood on her skin. She jumps to her feet and rushes to the kitchen area to clean herself.

Hollie reaches behind Brad's body and pulls on one of his arms, which easily comes free. He takes a look at his arm and cringes. He rolls the empty, shell of a body over and sees that both of his arms have been cut to shreds; the flesh on both forearms look like chunks of diced ham.

Hollie, overcome by guilt, slumps back against the wall, wrestling with what he could have done differently, perplexed as to why a man would take his own life, leaving his little brother to face his fate alone. He thinks of how precious life is and thoughts of his own children came rushing into his mind. Gina returns and covers Brad's body with a sheet. She sits down beside Hollie, saddened, and they cling to one another.

Nevaeh sits alone on the porch steps outside of the shack, bundled in a blanket, but still shivering from the cold. Her eyes, filled with sorrow, reflect a life of rejection and regret. The blanket slips from her shoulder and as she tries to throw it back over her neck, the sleeve of her shirt briefly rises. She stares at her arm, solemn. She lifts up her right sleeve and slowly traces her fingers over the many scars running up and down her arm, scars resulting from self prescribed therapy, which involves the cutting of her own skin. Like so many who yield themselves to this form of self mutilation, she feels that if she is going to suffer, if it's inevitable, than she is going to suffer under her own terms, at her own hands. Erika exits the shack and Nevaeh quickly lowers her sleeve, but she fails to hide anything that Erika has not already taken notice of.

Erika approaches her and sits down beside her. Only the sound of silence is shared between the two as they look out into the darkness and gaze upon the haunting stillness of the blackest of skies and a pale cherry colored moon.

Nevaeh breaks the quiet. "I've decided not to take the antidote. I want you to give it to Sean. He's a good kid. He deserves a second chance." Her voice is strained, broken.

She knows what her decision means. She wasn't ready to die, but she didn't know how to live either.

Erika considers her words. "And so do you, Nevaeh. You deserve a second chance."

Unbelieving, tears instantly begin to stream down Nevaeh's face.

"You know nothing about me," Nevaeh says defensively.

"That's true, but I'm hoping that will change. I'd like to get to know you."

Nevaeh turns away.

"The only people that take the time to get to know me are people that want to use me. That's what kind of person I am," She says. "It's the only purpose that I serve."

"I want to know you because you are a person worth getting to know," Erika says with sincerity in her voice.

Nevaeh struggles to believe her words; they are foreign to her, never spoken to her without an ulterior motive.

"And what makes you think that?"

Erika thinks for a moment. "Because I believe that God created us and made each and every one of us special. We all have purpose and significance, even when the life we've lived so far tells us otherwise."

Nevaeh scoffs.

"And we are all worth saving. You, Nevaeh, are worth saving," Erika says as she hands her the antidote.

Nevaeh looks away. "I've made my decision, Erika. Give it to Sean."

"We already gave Sean his dosage."

Nevaeh looks at her, surprised.

"Brad?"

"He made his choice," Erika responds. "For himself… and for his brother."

Erika gently takes Nevaeh's hand and gives her the vial. Nevaeh simply stares at the bottle inside her open palm.

"Giving Sean any more of that is not going to help him. His life is in God's hands now."

Nevaeh ponders for a moment, and the closest thing she can muster to a smile graces her face.

"That doesn't sound so bad, y'know." Nevaeh says, staring at the vial in her hand.

Erika reaches for Nevaeh's palm and folds her fingers around the vial. Erika then puts her arm around her and just holds her.

Nevaeh stares at her clinched fist and begins to perceive something in herself she has never allowed herself to see… value.

~

Jacob stands inside of a partially open bedroom door, having a quiet but heated conversation with his wife, Amanda. Tage, body glistening from sweat, forces his weak and depleted body to swing his legs off the couch and sit up. He immediately feels the blood sloshing through his limbs like a half filled water bottle being tilted back and forth. The crimson liquid of life courses through his starving vein, which selfishly engorge themselves. An irritating tickle races through his arms, which he scratches feverishly. He then counts to three in his head and lunges forward, clumsily trying to stand.

Jacob, hearing him growl, rushes over. "Hey. Easy. You're not out of the woods yet. You've lost a lot of blood".

Tage slouches and peers around the room, feeling nauseous, everything spins sickly before his eyes. He reaches for the arm of the sofa to stabilize himself, then falls back onto the couch. Looking down, he buries his face in his hands, hoping that the world will soon slow, and better yet, stop moving altogether. Amanda has something cooking on the stove in the kitchen and the aroma flooding the house serves only to add to his queasiness.

"I guess now would be as good a time as any to formally introduce myself. My name is Jacob." He speaks in a tone which is low and nonthreatening. "My wife, Amanda, and our son, Cameron, are in the other room. You saw them earlier?" Tage searches the fragments of his blurred memory.

"Yeah, that's right. I vaguely remember something like that. I'm Tage... Tage Craddock." Tage extends his rickety hand towards Jacob, but suddenly begins to dry heave. He withdraws his hand and Jacob takes a cautious step back, thinking Tage just might manage to get something to come up. Jacob has no intention of wearing the contents of Tage's insides. Tage's spasms subside and he wipes the spittle from the corner of his mouth.

"So what's your story? You some kind of Good Samaritan?" Tage says with his eyes barely open.

"No, not exactly, I don't believe like you do." Jacob responds.

His statement gives Tage pause, but he chooses not to take offense; being that he unquestionably has saved his life on more than one occasion.

"And what exactly is it that I believe, Jacob?"

"You are a Christian, are you not?" Jacob probes with confidence.

Tage is unsure about going down this road with Jacob; an avenue which requires him to grapple with his own personal thoughts and beliefs regarding religion and faith. So he makes his long story short, "No, I'm not a Christian," Tage says coldly, trying to mask the conflicting feelings of rage and regret. "I thought I was at one point, but it never... I never..." He stares at the floor as if he can look to it for understanding. He searches for words that easily evade him. "I had all I needed in life, and God, religion... Jesus, was for those who couldn't make life work on their own. If that makes any sense."

Jacob nods his understanding as Tage continues.

"I was raised in Church. I figured that would count for something."

Sorrow begins to consume and suffocate him as his thoughts suddenly become clear.

"God was just someone I bumped into every now and again... and it wasn't enough."

Jacob takes another long drink of whiskey straight from the bottle. "My apologies for the confusion, it just seemed evident that you were not a member of our society," Jacob says directly.

"Last I remember it looked like society was tryin' to kill you too." Tage quips. He nearly breaks out into laughter but his body rejects the outburst, offering only a snicker instead. A smile flashes across Jacob's face, finding humor in his truthful statement.

"What we've done to you people..." Jacob starts.

Tage gives him a look that causes him to be more selective about his choice of words.

"I'm simply referring to those who do not embrace our way of life. I've had a chance to reevaluate some things. We've made our decision and I am at peace with that. We were all implanted. I didn't know that things were going to end up like this but, we couldn't buy, couldn't sell, we didn't have a place to live... I couldn't work or provide for my family, so what choice did I have?"

"There's always a choice," Tage interjects.

"Well, we're living with that choice now, but rather than withdraw ourselves completely, we've chosen to help people like you from within the system."

Amanda marches in and tosses a clean button-up shirt on the arm of the sofa, and without so much as a pause, she heads straight for the kitchen. As she walks away Tage thanks her, and she responds with a gruff "You're welcome." She then disappears through the old western style swinging doors leading into the kitchen.

"You think you can keep something down?" Jacob asks. "You look like you could use something to eat."

Tage takes a moment to listen to his aching body, and before he can formulate a response, Jacob tosses a can of mixed fruit on the couch next to him. Tage's stomach is upset, but he knows he is in dire need of nourishment. He uses his right hand to crack open the lid on the can, but a surge of pain seizes his right arm. He switches to his left and completes the task, then precedes to greedily devour the contents. It takes him longer than usual to eat because he has to repeatedly swallow the same bite several times, determined not to allow it to come back up. He is blown away by the sweetness of the syrup and the luscious clumps of fruit that has every taste bud in his mouth screaming. He wishes that Sal could be with him right now, to share something like this with her would be a dream come true. His parents always stressed the importance of the simple things in life, and the power they possess to change perspective, but never would he have imagined something like this. In a way he feels selfish, scooping the remainder of the can into his mouth using his finger.

"Thank you," he says, still savoring the lingering taste of the fruit cup.

"No, thank you," Jacob responds, which causes Tage to return a puzzled look.

"Thank you for not dying on my couch."

Tage leans forward, grunting, and checks out the bullet Jacob retrieved.

"Can I ask you something?" Jacob says with a serious look on his face. Without saying a word, Tage fixes his eyes on him, anxiously awaiting the words that are forthcoming.

"I honestly can't believe that you went through that procedure the way you did. In all reality, I'm surprised you even made it here alive."

"So what's your question?"

"I don't know if you are aware of this or not, but you were actually smiling most of the time. Grinning ear-to-ear most of the time, even when I was really digging in to you. What were you thinking about?"

Tage releases the breath he's been holding and slowly reaches for the shirt left for him by Amanda.

"I was thinking about my wife… and my daughter."

He carefully puts one arm in and then the other, not wanting to engage in something so personal with someone he knows little about.

"Where are they now?"

"They're waiting for me."

He muscles his way off the couch and his hands fumble through the process of buttoning the baggy shirt now covering his body.

Tage can only imagine how much time has passed since the old man who wouldn't just die, sang like a choir boy, probably telling Kendall everything he wanted to know. He is anxious to get moving.

"You need to rest," Jacob declares.

"I need to leave," he quickly responds, as he hastily grabs the rest of his clothing. "I need to get home. How far are we from the police impound yard along the river?"

"A couple of hours on foot, but in your condition, there's no chance you can make it there," Jacob says emphatically.

Tage lifts his eyes, his hands still clumsily working on the shirt buttons. "There's no question about me making it, not when it comes to my daughter." Inwardly he struggles with the fearful reality that his motor skills and body are not up to par.

He shakes the vile images of him dying in the street from his mind, though the odds are, that's exactly what will happen to him. Nevertheless, nothing will keep him from making a go of it. "Thanks again, for everything," he says, finally able to extend his tingling right arm to shake hands with Jacob.

Driven by sheer will and determination to get home to his child, he turns and charges for the door. He knows how much she needs him, but the truth is he needs her so much more than she needs him. She is everything that is good in him.

Tage takes heavy, dread filled steps towards the door; each stride carries heartbreak within it and he feels as though a lifetime is passing. Not his, but his daughter's. He unexpectedly discontinues his advance and slowly begins to turn, unsure, uncertain as to whether what he just heard was real or a figment of his hopeful imagination.

"What?"

"Let me help you," Jacob repeats. "I want to help you. I'll take you to the station."

Tage reasons in his mind that it is most likely just the booze talking, but before he can at least enjoy a fleeting moment of elation, or begin to explore the possibility, the feeling is immediately drowned out by Amanda marching towards him, holding their crying son.

"Honey, no," she snaps. "You're not going with him. You don't owe him anything. It's too dangerous and you have already done more than you should."

"She's right," Tage admits, repulsed by the words he knows he rightfully should speak, though everything within him unanimously shouts, yes. "I can't let you risk your life, or your family."

Jacob tries to calm his wife. He wipes away the tears that glide down her face, carving a line in her thick makeup.

"Honey, look at me." Jacob tries to redirect her stabbing gaze away from Tage.

Amanda's contempt for Tage is obvious and deserving as far as she is concerned. How can someone like Tage possibly understand or relate to what she is feeling right now in this moment.

She despises him.

She detested him from the moment he entered.

Tage didn't know why.

He didn't ask to be brought into their home.

The only thing that makes any sense to him is that Amanda's bitterness is attributed to the feeling of vulnerability. To the dismay of those around him, Jacob probably picks up people, like those who pick up stray animals. It's a calling he lives out apart from Amanda.

Tage wants to explain to her that he is not looking for a hand-

198

out, he wishes he had the time to tell her about his losses, about his suffering; how he would give anything to erase the memories that drown him every day, how daily his mind will chase him into a dark sadness that would route his pathetic attempts to recapture his life, by mocking him with the screams of those he loves and those he's lost.

"We've been doing this for a long time, right?"

Amanda grudgingly nods to Jacob. "I just need to get him to the police station, that's all. After that, I'll put in for some time off. How about that?" Amanda's face lights us.

Jacob, taking it a step further, says, "we can even spend some quality time with your family." Amanda's broken grin turns into a smile. "Really? Oh, honey. I really do miss my father."

Jacob drops his head down with mixed emotions, and raises it with a forced smile. "Okay, let's talk about it when we get back home. I have to do this. I don't want my son growing up in a world like this. I have a chance to make a difference. I'm doing this for you, honey, and for our family."

Amanda, fighting to control her sobs, responds with an, "Okay."

Jacob whispers, "I love you," to his wife and he kisses his son.

"You sure about this?" Tage asks, fairly certain that he would not risk his life, or the lives of his wife and daughter for someone he doesn't know.

Jacob turns to him with determination in his eyes. "Let's go get your family."

His confidence and resolve brought strength to Tage's weakened body.

"Okay," says Tage, with an indebted smile.

He turns and reaches for the door but Jacob stops him.

"Remember?" He points to his wrist.

Tage steps back, shaking his head, realizing once again that without the implant you don't exist in this society. Amanda can hold her peace no longer. "Jacob, please don't do this," she pleads again. "It's okay, love. I know what I'm doing." Even with Jacob running interference, Tage still cannot be shielded or avoid the burning hatred contained within Amanda's frigid stare as they left. Tage glances back before the door closes and Amanda snarls at him before withdrawing into the darkened room.

A harsh wind blows outside as Jacob and Tage make their way a few blocks down the street to retrieve his car from a locked garage. The broken windows in the vacant buildings rattle from the impact. Debris flies through the air. People are scarce; some huddle together in the entryways of buildings, feeling a false sense of safety when staying together in groups, others hide until the darkness passes, fearing the worst. Broken down and stripped cars line some of the streets. Only the bravest of rodents forage in the open, because most are eaten raw and alive when captured by the demonized masses that don't know any better; and as far as far as pets are concerned, they don't exist. Man's best friend is now man's main dish.

The atmosphere is filled with sadness and despair and with each passing moment, the once thriving city looks more and more like a graveyard, a war torn city from an old eighties apocalyptic movie.

Jacob and Tage drive cautiously through the underbelly of the city, taking side streets, back roads, and altering course anytime a set of headlights approach, in an effort to avoid crossing paths with the police. Tage looks intently out the passenger window, staring out into nothing, caught up in thoughts of getting back to Sal. Ja-

200

cob observes him carefully and then reluctantly decides to break Tage's concentration with a question.

"Are you sure about this?" Tage does not turn nor flinch, his settled determination unwilling to entertain doubt.

"That's something you need to ask yourself, Jacob," who swings his attention back to the road. "If you're not sure, this is where we need to part company." Tage slides his eyes towards Jacob. "I can't afford for you not to be sure. There's too much at stake."

"I'm sure. I'm just wondering if you're ready for this." Jacob says extremely relaxed and at ease.

"Well, that's not what you asked." Tage says sharply. "If you can just get me to the yard, I can get a car and make it home."

"I'll get you to where you need to go," says Jacob.

As they continue on, Tage reflects on what's taken place over the last ten hours.

"There's something I've been meaning to ask you," Tage says, ignoring the pain in his side, but getting annoyed with the intermittent twitch in his arm. Jacob senses the seriousness in his voice and gives him as much attention as he can manage while still keeping a watchful eye on the road.

"That officer back in the alley, why did he call you a traitor?"

Jacob hesitates as he weighs the question. "Because of exactly what I'm doing right now. As you've heard me say earlier to my wife, I've been doing this a long time. They know my name. They know my face. My wife and I, we never stay in one place too long."

Tage's eyes drift to Jacob's hands on the steering wheel.

"What about that thing in your wrist? Surely it must be used for tracking people. Doesn't that give you away?"

"There are ways to block the transmission. As a matter of fact, with the right person and a laptop computer, the signals can be altered. I can essentially become whoever I want to be," he says with a sinister smile.

"Must be nice," Tage says, trying to digest everything he just heard.

He desperately wants to believe there are still good people in this world, but that comes at a price. The hesitations and questions that fire away in his mind can't take away from the fact that this man is a life saver; a savior of sorts.

"So, tell me about your family." Jacob says.

Tage's heart begins to speed up. He pauses, unable to speak freely and unsure of exactly what to say.

Tage is still not fully convinced that he should say anything.

He looks at Jacob for any sign of assurance, something that communicates to him that he's okay, or something to the contrary that tells him that he is not to be trusted. But all he can see is a man selflessly risking his life and his own family for him.

"I'd like to help you, but you're going to have to let me," Jacob says as Tage wages his inner battle.

Tage exhales a deep breath and slowly removes his watch from his pocket. He fixes his eyes intently on his wife and child. "My wife, Shannon, is already gone, and I don't want to put my little girl in danger, let alone, the rest of the people out there in the woods." He says quietly, even regretfully.

Jacob explains to Tage that the neighborhood they are in has other people just like he and his wife, and like those in Tage's position. He tells Tage they can provide him and his entire family with food, water and shelter, and can also offer them protection. Tage relishes in the thought of starting a new life, to bring some sense of normalcy to his daughter's existence.

"We've been on the move for years," Tage says, his words flowing easier from his lips. "We were fortunate enough to stumble upon an old ranger's shack. Been there for close to two years now, but we've been together as a group since the beginning of the end, when peace... when peace was taken from the world."

"When Demetri broke the peace agreement," Jacob mutters with a quiet rage. "Nearly three and a half years of hell on earth, some say."

Tage grumbles through his clenched jaws. "Every moment of that time, we've been surrounded by death... So you can see why I'm so cautious about..."

"I understand," Jacob assures him. "You don't have to say any more."

Tage takes a moment to reflect, and turns toward Jacob with a grin on his face.

"The people I live with, one guy in particular, his name is Hollie, they are a lot like you," Tage says, finding it strange that he is now wanting to talk. "We've helped a lot of people who are on the move and want to escape the oppression of the government."

"You don't see too much of that these days," Jacob adds.

"Maybe that's why you found me. It looks like things just might be looking up for me," Tage says as he ponders the hollowness of his spoken words; speaking as though there is a silver lining, while staring at the contrasting devastation and decay of the city and existence. "What comes around goes around. I firmly believe that," Jacob says as he takes a long look in his rear view mirror.

"Luck, karma, fate, you reap what you sow; call it what you want, I'm just happy to be going home. I don't give a rip how it happens, as long as I get there."

Tage uses the inside of his arm to wipe the sweat off of his face. He is feverish and his breathing is labored.

Jacob reaches back into the backseat, and the car veers to the left, riding the bumpy divider lines until he corrects course. He retrieves an unopened bottle of spring water and hands it to Tage, who looks at it in disbelief.

"Are you sure?"

"It's all yours," Jacob says.

Tage slowly reaches for the clear bottle and takes it in his hand; the weight of the 16 ounce bottle rest firmly in his palm, and that alone brings a smile to his face. He turns the bottle over and examines the label.

"You need a hand with that?"

"No. No, I'm just. It's been a long time. That's all."

Tage holds the bottle firmly in his left hand and with his right hand grips the white cap. His muscles tense as he twists the top; the crack of the tiny plastic tabs securing the cap being broken, sound off like beautiful music to his ears. He savors the sound of the twisting of the cap as it winds its way off the bottle. He raises the bottle and rests the tip of the bottle on his cracked bottom lip. Tilting the bottle and leaning his head back, the cool refreshing liquid flows into his mouth and he closes his eyes as the water pours down his throat and revitalizes his body. Tage continues to drink, nearly half the bottle is gone in an instant.

"Easy. You don't want to hurt yourself," Jacob warns.

Tage heeds his words and reluctantly stops drinking. He sits in silence for a moment, wanting to enjoy the feel of the water in his body. He puts the cap back on and fastens it tightly, not wanting to risk losing a single drop.

"I had forgotten what it's like to drink pure, untreated and natural God given water." Tage wipes a drop of water that hangs from his lip.

"Would you risk arrest and execution to have that?" Jacob asks.

"You know what? I think I would."

Jacob laughs.

"The closest thing we can get to safe drinking water is in the neighborhood of a tan, off white colored water from a muddy spring."

"How many of you are there?"

"There used to be nearly twenty of us who lived together, and dozens more all around us living out in the open. We do what we can as people come and go, but..." His words and his thoughts begin to drift.

Jacob is impressed with their resourcefulness.

"What can we do for you? How do you eat? How do you survive like that?" Tage cringes at the thought of what he is about to say, about what their lives have become. "We can't," he says with a wavering voice, his sorrowful eyes fixed on the top of the water bottle. "At least not anymore... Our numbers are getting smaller and the needs are becoming greater. Food, water, medical supplies are harder, nearly impossible to come by." The grief gradually passes when he begins to thinks about the alternative. "But there are no regrets. Not about how we live. We don't get caught up in what's going on in the world. All I care about is my little world. People have made their choice and so have we... My daughter, if something happens to her, there's nothing for me to live for."

Tage slinks back into his seat, thinking about Sal, who he imagines is sitting at the kitchen table right now painting; her smiling face, her trusting eyes, her innocent expression. His eyes begin to get misty, but he knows this is neither the time nor place for tears. He needs to stay strong and not allow his emotions to interfere. "Tears will not fall, because I will not fall," he repeats in his head.

"Do you guys have any weapons?" Jacob inquires.

"Yeah, a few. But it's not our thing," Tage says in a disinterested tone. "Now, if you want to know about sewers, water lines, ditches, stuff like that, I got you covered," he says lightheartedly. "We can take care of ourselves if we have to, but if people are out where we are, it's because it's their choice. They want to be there. They're not really threats to us."

Jacob listens attentively. "The impound yard has guns, old guns that you can use without needing an implant." Tage turns to Jacob straight-faced and direct. "I just need a car. If they want to come after us... let them come."

They drive along the dark river and the air around them carries a stench of decay. Tage is surprised to see the trees and plant life flourishing in the area; a stark contrast from the woods that struggle to survive where he lives. A grayish hue covers the sky. The lights from the impound facility can be seen a short distance away. The yard, located to the east of the police station, is teeming with old cars of every make and model, tightly packed together on the grounds.

They pass by the unmanned entrance to the impound yard. Tage looks curiously towards Jacob and then back towards the entrance. They cruise by the twelve-story police building and continue west toward an adjacent parking garage.

Jacob pulls inside the parking area.

"Why don't we go straight to the impound yard?" Tage questions. "There was nobody there."

Jacob continues driving to the second level.

As they rise, so does Tage's heart rate. His senses are on high alert.

"Don't worry. I've got a plan," Jacob tells him.

"What do you mean? What plan?"

"Remember when I told you I could become anyone I wanted to be?" Tage looks at him suspiciously. "Listen, all I want is a car. I'm not trying to wage some stinkin' war or make a statement."

"Trust me," replies Jacob with an arrogant smile, as he pulls the car into a parking space near the stairwell and elevator entrances on the third floor. Tage nervously surveys the area, grateful not to see anything unusual, but knowing somehow that everything is wrong.

"Now this is where things get interesting, Mr. Craddock."

"Just take me back to the impound yard," Tage demands.

"I can't do that. Do you have any idea of what's waiting for you out there?"

"I don't care!" Tage yells. "So, you're trying to protect me? Is that what this is about? You know what's best for me?"

"Something like that, yes," Jacob boasts.

"Get me out of this garage, Jacob!"

"Like I told you before, you can't make it. Do you know what's going to happen to you—"

"They'll have to catch me first," Tage barks out.

"But that's exactly what you don't understand... You have been caught."

Tage's mind feebly tries to process Jacob's last statement. He stares at him with a blank expression on his face.

"What? What did you say?" Tage stammers, as a crushing reality sets in.

"I said..." Jacob starts, and then finishes his response by brutally smashing his fist into Tage's jaw.

The violent and unexpected jolt of his head renders Tage unconscious and he slumps forward, still held securely in place by his seatbelt. Jacob studies him with disdain.

"Where's your sense of humor now?"

Jacob checks himself out in the mirror, runs his fingers through his hair, and then calmly exits the vehicle, slamming the door behind him.

He strolls casually to the stairwell, playing with his keys and whistling Ring of Fire by Johnny Cash. He opens the large metal door with the red number three painted on it and descends the stairs. The door squeals as it slowly closes, and the thump of Jacob's boots against the metal stairs fade away into silence.

Chapter 10

A sharp "Ding" sounds off in Tage's ears, and a green circle illuminates above the elevator door behind him. His eyes refuse to open, and all he can hear now is the sound of his own breathing. He groans, unsure of his whereabouts, but immediately he feels the pain in his jaw, which looks and feels crooked. A cloud of darkness and despair takes up residence within him. He briefly considers crying out to God, but wonders where He's been through all of this; the words will not form in his mouth even if he wants them to.

The elevator doors slide open and a slew of officers exit and step lively toward Jacob's car with weapons at the ready. The lead officer opens the door with one hand, and with the other, trains his service automatic on Tage, whose glossy eyes remain unfocused. He orders Tage not to move a muscle, threatening to blow his head off. Tage, who resigns himself to defeat, nods sheepishly, his body limp and deflated. The officer reaches inside the car to undo Tage's seatbelt. Just as soon as Tage hears the click of the belt's release,

Tage throws a barrage of punches in rapid succession on the unsuspecting officer, giving no thought or consideration to his weapon or any of the other guns leveled on him. If he is going to die, he is at least going to have a say in how it happens, and being tortured, dismembered, or decapitated doesn't rank high on his list; maybe somewhere in the area of being eaten by a shark.

The surrounding officers simply watch, entertained, as the lead officer violently pistol whips Tage, who is still crammed in the passenger seat of the car. Tage is bashed repeatedly in the head and beaten into a daze, allowing the officer to easily yank him out of the car and onto the ground. The ambushed officer wipes the blood rafting from his nose. Awkwardly Tage stands. He hunches over with his hands on his knees, confused, not knowing whether to hold his bust-a-cap side, his pistol whipped head, or sucker punched crooked jaw.

Tage's cloudy gaze catches the parting of the officers and his sight clears to catch a glimpse of Jacob...

In a police uniform...

Jacob in a police uniform with lieutenant bars...

And he is coming up fast, looking pissed.

"No freakin' way," Tage spits out, literally.

First he saw him as a friend. Wrong.

Then he pegs him as a man who lives the high life by turning in Unbelievers, which would explain the spoiled trophy wife. But he's wrong again.

Tage, judging from the look on Jacob's face, deduces that he is about to go airborne, and before he takes off, he thinks to himself, "Man, this is really going to hurt."

Jacob lands such a vicious blow to his face, he knocks Tage out of one of his shoes. This time he was right. Every wisp of air vacates his lungs when he pounds against the pavement. Trying to catch his breath is a losing battle, but he gasps for every ounce willing to enter.

Jacob kneels down. Tage stares wide eyed at him in a state of shock. He then turns away from Jacob, wheezing, and Officer Stevens, one of the "dead" guys in the alley, bends over him and pushes a long gooey glob of spit through his lips. Tage, sucking air, manages to throw his body to one side and turn his head just before the discharge fell into his open mouth.

"You miss me, sweetheart?" Stevens jokes.

Tage questions his reality. Nothing is making any sense to him, but he can't shake the nagging voice inside his head telling him, "I told you so." Maybe he is still lying on Jacob's couch being tended to and this is all just a dark fragmented shock induced nightmare; an enormously painful one. Tage rolls his eyes and wheels his body around, only to see Officers Bell and Mitchell, laughing.

"The officers you thought I killed are all part of my team," Jacob says, before violently grabbing Tage's face, and forcing him to look straight into his cold dark eyes, his face so close, that his hot breath stings Tage's eyes. "That young officer that you attacked in that alley, died en route to the hospital. He was my nephew."

Jacob strikes Tage again and the force makes him slam the back of his head against the concrete.

"Enough with the hitting already," Tage can't help but to say out loud.

"You haven't even began to pay for what you did; for who you are." Jacob warns, wanting Tage's mind to begin conjuring his darkest fears. "Up until now this was just another day at the office and you were just another misguided nobody whose file came across my desk. Now, it's personal. Your family and your friends are going to die and your daughter will suffer unimaginable pain at my hands."

Tage grits his teeth in anger. "If you go anywhere near my daughter, your nephew will be the first of many to die. Hell's waiting for you, Jacob, and I'm gonna see you off."

Jacob smirks with skepticism as he motions towards Stevens, who forces a brown bag over his head, plunging Tage into a world of darkness.

The burlap bag is musty and rank; a combination of sweat, snot, blood and tears, no doubt. The rope inside the bag tightens around Tage's neck, severely reducing his already limited air supply. He begins to think about Walter, the old man that just wouldn't die. He doesn't want to, it infuriates him, but he knows firsthand what follows after you get a bag like this shoved over your head. His chest gets hot as he fumes on the inside; a furious anger boiling into a rage.

"You better kill me while you can. 'Cause if you don't, I'm coming after you." Jacob draws his arm back to hit him, but playfully pats his face instead. Tage responds with a split second head butt he launches towards Jacob's face. Jacob turns, showing off his incredibly fast reflexes once again, and the blow catches him on the side of his face; not a breaking of his nose like one would hope, but Tage still feels pretty good. "I'll see you soon, Jacob," he says with conviction.

"Maybe in the afterlife, Mr. Craddock, but I wouldn't count on it."

Jacob motions for Tage to be taken away.

The heat generated from his heavy breathing inside the bag

makes him lightheaded. Stevens and Mitchell enjoy the task of strapping Tage to an old wooden chair. He takes several blows to the face and gut before he is left alone in a dark dungeon-like supply room.

Splintered wood from the worn arms of the chair dig into his sweaty arms. His circulation is being cut off by the rope cinched tightly across his bare chest. The bindings on his wrists are so tight all he can feel of his hands is the stinging throbs of his pulsating fingertips. He strains, pointlessly, to pull free from his restraints and his squirming rips at his stitches drawing forth blood.

An overwhelming sense of defeat serves notice to every last shred of hope to vacate. His battle seems futile, inane, but hope refuses to dislodge from his thoughts, though he sees no way of escape. No way humanly possible for him to get home.

The menacing darkness swallows him, and the gloom of despair that spreads throughout his body like a cancer is crippling. His thoughts then turn to his daughter, Sal, his light in the darkness. His mind has become his enemy, it challenges even his will to survive. He grunts, trying to force the low breathy voice inside his head repeating, "She's going to die. Die. Die," like a broken record. "You will never see her again. She's going to die just like your wife." The voice says with convincing believability. Tage rocks in his chair. A darkness that is as black as oil envelopes him.

"Come on! Keep it together, Tage." He growls out loud. "There must be a way," he reasons with himself. Violently he shakes his head, forcing his runaway mind to submit to his will. He arrests the criminal thoughts that try to sentence his daughter to death, and issues orders of his own. He demands that he find a way, nay, that he make a way to get home to Sal.

The battle inside his mind tosses him like a paddle boat lost in an ocean storm as the interrogation of his limits presents its opening arguments.

"What are you prepared to do?" He asks himself as his head dips and he slowly throws it back.

He lets out an audible wail as he ponders the question spoken and answered in his mind.

"Anything—I'll do anything," he responds with barely a whisper trickling from his lips.

"Not good enough! What are you prepared to do?" His mind quickly shot back, causing his fist to tighten and his entire body to tense as he screams out. "Anything! Anything!"

Sobs break through as he pants like a thirsty dog. "I'll do anything."

He mutters in a way that sounds more like a mingling of laughter and crying. His body sways as if he is in a drug induced stupor.

"I'll kill them," he spews resolutely. "If they go anywhere near my daughter, I'm going to kill them." He barks out sternly as if someone is in the vacant room with him. "I'm going to kill you! Do you hear me?" He yells into the air at nobody. At everybody.

"I can't hear you! LOUDER!" His mind commands like a master drill sergeant.

"I'm going to kill you! All of you!" Tage screeches, his body constricts, veins thick on his neck and spit hanging off of his lips. For a few moments, only the sound of his heavy breathing can be heard. His mind pierces the silence and serenely says, "So be it." Upon hearing those words in his head, Tage gradually begins to relax and his mind becomes still, calm, his ally once again.

The hallway outside of the darkened room where Tage is located resonates with the clacking of footsteps against the cold gray concrete floor. The crack of the lock is like the starting gun for the seasoned runner, it is his signal, the moment he is waiting for. It is his time to run.

When the door creaks open, as far as he can tell, a handful of people file in. His ears tune in to the flick of a light switch and the blackness seen through the bag covering his face lightens to a haze of charcoal, which allows him to make out only shapes directly in front of him. The large metal door slams shut and locks. His eyes squint, trying to make out something, anything, but the solitary swinging light above his head and the bag that is nearly suffocating him, doesn't help.

He knows someone is watching, and the thought of being on display sickens him, but not as much as the two voices he can hear quietly talking about him. The exchange of dialogue ceases and shadowy figures approaches him. He can sense and barely make out that someone is reaching for him. He pulls his head back, trying to resist being touched. Rasul unties the rope securing the bag and rips it off of Tage's head. The salty sweat raining down his wet and battered face stings as they trail across every cut and washes over the rope burn around his reddened and raw neck. Forgetting for a moment where he is, he closes his eyes and savors the freshness of the unobstructed air, allowing himself a couple of deep breaths before letting his eyes peel open. Greeting him, is the condescending smile of Goodwill Ambassador Kendall.

Seeing the sight of pure evil before him, up close and personal, almost takes his breath away. Buried memories too painful to access are forced into his mind and every fear he's ever known suddenly juts to the surface at the mere sight of this man. Things long forgotten, childhood terrors he'd outgrown and stored in the shadowy recesses of his mind, he now relives in the presence of this man; but in spite of everything that would cause him to cower, hatred, retribution and revenge rose above all. He wishes for Kendall to draw even closer, so that he could somehow lay hold of him.

"Mr. Craddock, I am Goodwill Ambassador Kendall."

"How can you even say that with a straight face?"

"Are you prepared to be cleansed?"

"Is that what you call murder these days?"

"Sir, I make no apologies to you for devoutly following the word of my god. We must purge the evil from our society if we intend to reach our full potential as a people." Tage feels as though Kendall's words alone possess the ability to choke the life out of a man.

Kendall continues. "When we as a people have one mind, one purpose, one voice, then nothing shall be impossible unto us. We ourselves shall become gods.

"Are you serious?" Tage stares in disbelief. "You want to be a god? And as flippin' stupid as that sounds, you go about it by slaughtering innocent men, women, and children."

Kendall calmly continues, unfazed by Tage's outburst. "This is our time, Mr. Craddock, when all of creation is put under our feet. Where we can now be glorified and become the exalted ones; Greater than even the God of the heavens. We shall reign and rule with our god, Alexander Demetri."

"Well, I don't believe any of that crap." Tage belts, "but when I get out of here, I'm going to arrange a meeting between you and the only God there is, then we will see how things work out for you."

"I'm here to present you with an option. A choice," Says Kendall.

"Don't bother," Tage snaps.

Kendall slowly circles Tage, rather enjoying the moment and relishing in his position. "Because we serve a great and merciful god, I have been placed in a unique position, one that would extend to you forgiveness. One that would pardon you—"

"No! The answer is no."

"Sir, I haven't even asked you any questions."

Kendall doesn't skip a beat, but continues on, smug and arrogant, strutting around with nauseating pride. "...One that will pardon you for your transgressions against our messiah, the only man in the history of the world to have ever brought peace."

Tage fights against his bonds, enraged.

"Peace? Under your orders my wife and parents were murdered. What kind of peace is that? You tortured an old man to get what you wanted, and thousands upon thousands before him. Is that an act of peace? You are nothing but the devil's puppet!"

"Mr. Craddock, I am trying to be a reasonable man. By extending mercy—"

"Why? Why did you kill them?" Tage waits for an answer that never comes. "You killed them because they had a different belief, a different faith than yours?"

"I am a patient man, but I will no longer tolerate your interruptions. I am trying to offer you a new beginning; food, shelter, clothing, insertion back into our society... I'm trying to offer you life, Mr. Craddock."

"No," Tage quietly responds, his mind in a tailspin. "No. No." His head shakes, eyes burning and unblinking. He's heard the Truth, knew the Truth... He's rejected the Truth. "No. No." He screams. "There is only one God. One! Not you. Not Demetri. One God.

Kendall's eyes narrow. "You don't have life to give, you miserable piece of-" In a fit of sudden and blinding rage, Kendall thrusts the end of his cane deeply into Tage's side, ripping through the stitches that hold his flesh together. Tage squeals, his teeth clamp and grind so hard they feel as though they are going to break.

Kendall flicks open Tage's treasured pocket watch, the only tangible reminder, other than his daughter, of a world that is beautiful. Upon seeing this, Tage yells and grunts, rocking the wooden chair to get loose and screaming from the cane still piercing his side. Kendall speaks directly and quietly into Tage's tortured face. "I recognize her. Your wife, Shannon, right? So pretty. They both are; at least she was." Tage is seething. The pain from his wound is now a distant memory. "You know, there aren't too many females around these days. Your daughter will be very well taken care of. You have my word." Tage furiously thrashes about, straining to reach for Kendall with his hands that refuse to move. His mind explodes with thoughts and memories, plans that he has made with his wife in days gone by. Plans centered on their collective future. Plans interrupted, butchered, plans that will never be.

"Someone must pay," he tells himself. "Kendall will pay," his mind screams.

Love and revenge are powerful motivators and Tage is determined to exact vengeance on those responsible for the senseless murder of his wife and parents. Love will be the driving force to get him home to his daughter and retribution will take care of the rest.

Kendall removes the cane from the deep crevice in Tage's side and he hands it to Rasul who wipes the blood from its tip. Kendall muses over Tage with pompous satisfaction, standing tall and superior.

"And I suppose I should thank you for telling us how to find your daughter and the rest of your group. We've been looking for you for quite some time." Kendall says quietly, anxiously awaiting his response.

Tage is blindsided by his words; leveled by the 300-mile-an-hour bullet train that shatters every bone in his body. Tage knows what he heard, and what it would mean, and because Kendall has just rendered him speechless, he hocks an angry loogie and discharges it into his face. Kendall, who is not surprised, poetically smiles and wipes the spewed slime with his fingers and sucks it like he is tasting homemade frosting.

"And who shall I Kill first, huh? Hollie and Gina? Erika perhaps?"

"What is this? What are you talking about? You knew."

Kendall turns to walk away.

"You already knew where to find us."

Kendall and Rasul exchange looks. Rasul smiles as he continues to clean Kendall's walking stick and Kendall wipes the remaining spit from his face with a handkerchief.

"We knew nothing until you told Jacob everything we needed to know."

Tage stares at him speechless. His denial momentarily hangs in his windpipe. "No, you're lying. I was there. It was Walter. He told you."

"You sure you want to try to blame this on the old man? There was a strength and conviction in him that I admired. He was not weak and easily manipulated like you."

Tage's body begins to shake. He is scalded by Kendall's words; and to think that he had considered and even cursed Walter for such a betrayal is devastating.

"Your Walter spouted off a few tired scriptures, and even told me before I severed his neck from his shoulders that he forgives me." Tage wishes he could plug his ears and block the razor sharp words that are cutting him to shreds.

"Out of respect for him, I gave ear to his words. He didn't beg for his life as I thought... He begged for his friend's life... Yours."

Tage's mind unravels and his heart thumps like sneakers in a dryer. Ever muscle in his body is tense, and veins protrude out of his neck as he thrashes in the chair. His eyes flutter and he calms only to watch the room spin out of control before passing out.

Kendall turns his attention to Rasul, who hands him his cane.

"Get him to the medical room and see that he gets proper care," Kendall instructs. "If he dies. You die."

With the flick of Kendall's wrist, the guards stationed at the door cut Tage's restraints. They lift his still body up between them, and drag him out of the room to the click clack of their steel toe boots against the ground.

Jacob stands in front of an open locker in the police armory, checking the growing bruise on his face in a mirror. Mitchell, Stevens and Bell are close by. They sift through an impressive array of weaponry and arm themselves with their weapons of choice. An additional four officers, dressed head-to-toe in black special forces gear, enter the room. Their goggles rest on their helmets, leaving only their eyes uncovered and visible. They methodically file in and march straight for Jacob. Bravo Leader, the tallest of the crew, snaps to attention.

"Bravo team, reporting for duty, Sir."

"Your reputation precedes you, Sergeant," Jacob responds as he looks over the group. "We are going to take care of this nest once and for all. The sooner we get rid of this filth, the better."

He releases Bravo Team, instructing them to ready themselves.

Bravo Leader then directs his crew, Davidson, Gomez, and Boyer, to secure weapons.

Jacob's adrenaline flows as he anticipates the thrill of the hunt. A new sense of strength and power flows through his icy veins. His cell phone rings, but he continues to order his officers around as it does. He checks the screen on his phone, which registers a private number. "Lieutenant Hollis," he says sharply into the phone. The voice responding back is his wife, Amanda.

"It's me… Hi, honey. How are you? Are you okay?"

Jacob moves away from listening ears .

"I'm fine, just busy... Who's phone are you calling from."

"Mine," Amanda quickly replies. "I just blocked the number because I know you wouldn't answer if you knew it was me."

"Don't be ridiculous, of course I would answer," he says trying to sound believable.

"Well, when are you coming home?"

"Soon, honey, but I have to go, I can't talk right now. I'll call you later. We've got to wrap this thing up," Jacob says, frustrated.

"Cameron said his first word. I'm almost positive he said, 'Daddy'. Isn't that wonderful?"

"That's great, honey. Give him a kiss for me, okay," he says with an annoying snap.

Kendall enters the room while Jacob is talking. "Great," Jacob says quietly, in response to seeing him. He then turns his back to Kendall.

"What? Are you talking to me?"

"No. No, I really have—"

"Did you get the note that I left for you?" Amanda says with excitement.

"Yes, thank you. I have to go." He rolls his eyes.

Kendall makes his rounds, shaking hands and talking with officers in the room.

Jacob awkwardly gathers his equipment, trying to be discreet about being on the phone.

"Okay, but remember what you promised me, okay. We're going to spend some time with my parents, and you are going to try to get along better with my father."

"Yes. Yes. I have to—"

"How did I do? I've been working on my tears."

"You did great, honey, we got him, but you've got to stay focused."

"What?" Amanda begins to pout. "Baby, I really missed you."

"Your attention was more on me than on what you were supposed to be saying." Jacob says, irked. "I know, baby. I'm sorry, okay. It's just that I get worried when you don't come home like you should. And I just want to get out of this filthy, whatever this is we had to stay in... How do people even live like this? This place is disgusting and I can't wait to sleep in my own bed, and... I can't believe I let you talk me into bringing our son—"

"You know what? That's a great idea. Why don't you just grab the baby, head back to our place, and get yourself cleaned up. I'm going to finish up here so I can come home."

"Hold on, Cameron wants to say hi."

"Honey. Honey. Honey, I really have to go. I'm working," he says as he thumps his head against a wall and leaves it there.

"Fine!" Amanda belts out with hurt feelings. "I won't call you anymore."

Jacob fights to maintain his composure. An involuntary growl of frustration escapes his lips. He turns and leans his body against the wall as his eyes scan the room.

"I'm not saying that you can't call me." Jacob makes eye contact with Kendall. "Amanda, I have go. Love you, bye."

Jacob abruptly ends the call and shoves the phone in his pocket.

Kendall peers around the room. He swells with pride as he gazes upon his elite instruments of death. He loves death almost as much as he loves himself. He saunters over to Jacob, fiddling with Tage's pocket watch in his hand.

"Lieutenant. May I have a word, please?"

The slip away from the surrounding officers.

"Do you think it would be prudent to take more officers?"

"All things considered, we have more than enough officers, Sir. My guys works very hard. They deserve to have a little fun every now and again and blow off some steam."

"I'm terribly sorry to hear about your nephew; only three weeks out of the academy, what a tragedy."

Jacob clinches his jaw at the thought of revenge. "And from what I understand, he had no idea of what you do within our organization."

"Not many people do, Sir. He thought I was a traitor."

The word traitor, and the thought of being one, stabs Jacob's heart.

"That boy had a bright future ahead of him, and he died at the hands of a Christian. How does that make you feel?" Jacob is amazed at how Kendall always seems to get a sick satisfaction from hearing about someone else's pain.

Jacob is infuriated by the question.

"He wasn't a Christian," Jacob says respectfully but direct.

Kendall calmly looks at Jacob, "Whoever is not with us is against us. There is no middle ground. Remember that. You're either one or the other."

"Yes, Sir," is all that Jacob can muster.

"Now, I'm sure you understand that we cannot afford any missed opportunities."

"Of course, Sir."

"I want you to bring that man's daughter back here, unharmed. Do I make myself clear?"

"What? What do you mean? What about my nephew?"

Kendall's eyes narrow. "Vengeance does not belong to you, Lt. Hollis. It belongs to god."

"But..." starts Jacob.

"You have your orders, Lieutenant. Is there anything else that you wish to say?"

There is so much he wants to say, needs to say; so much that he intended on doing, but he wisely shakes his head.

"Now, get it done, Lieutenant!"

"As you wish, Sir."

Jacob mutters as he walks away, disheartened.

The only thing helping him to keep himself together with the loss of his nephew is the thought of making Tage's daughter suffer. He had no intention of simply snapping her neck or putting a bullet in her head. He wants her to experience the pain of death before it comes calling, he wants to break her; slow, methodical, detailed. He wants to appreciate every cut, every tear, and every scream, but there is no going against the Ambassador.

Kendall moves to the center of the armory, and he calls for the officers to gather 'round. Jacob, still seething, is slow to fall in.

"Gentlemen, you are fighting for our freedom and our liberties against terrorism of the worst kind. Many of you, including myself, have been where those people are now, following God, preaching the 'good news,' only to learn through Alexander Demetri, that all along, we were spreading a message of exclusion, division, intolerance and hate."

Kendall walks toward Mitchell and points his finger at him saying, "Your mother and father died believing that you, their son, hated them because that Book told you that you had to." Approaching Bell he continues, "You walked away from your family and your friends, because that Book, their 'God', told you to have nothing to do with them. 'Luke 14:26, if anyone comes to Me, and does not hate his own father and mother and wife and children and brothers and sisters, yes, and even his own life, he cannot be My disciple.' Tell me, where is the love in that?" A demon spirit sweeps into the room and ushers in an unholy exchange. Good becomes evil and evil becomes good. All become one in agreement with Kendall as he continues to misinterpret and use Scripture out of context to those who once called themselves Christians, but having no idea of what it is to be one. Every spin, slant, every lie and misquote are absolute and indisputable truths to those in the room under the influence of the demonic anointing operating through the Ambassador.

The officers sway with eager anticipation.

"These Unbelievers, know nothing of love, acceptance, or forgiveness and it is all they ever talk about. The very thing they preach against and say amen to in their churches, are the very things they run out to do the moment their service is over. We have been used and we have been betrayed by what we all once stood for, and the payment for that is blood, and their blood shall be on their own hands. They are the only things standing between us and once again having world peace. So you find them, and you kill them, knowing you are doing your service to god, our god, Lord Alexander Demetri. The officers charge out of the room thirsting for blood.

Jacob watches their enthusiasm, feeling embittered and torn. He too is influenced by Kendall's words, but he secretly loathes the Ambassador.

Jacob plods to the door but Kendall swiftly intercepts him.

"Oh, and one last thing, Son, I received your request for time off and it's been approved."

Jacob shakes his head, confused. "But, I didn't put in for time off, Sir."

"My daughter called me before you got here, so I've already taken care of everything. We're planning a little family getaway. What do you think?"

"That's fantastic... Uh, well... thank you."

"It will give us more time to spend together, and I sure do miss my Grandson. Cameron is getting so big and... Well, enough of that, we'll talk more about it when you get back."

"Looking forward to it, Sir."

Jacob has gotten so comfortable with lying over the years, he almost believes everything that comes out of his mouth; and truth be told, lying comes easier to him than telling the truth.

"Happy hunting," Kendall says, proudly.

Jacob nods and exits the room thinking he just might kill Tage's daughter anyway; an eye for an eye, a tooth for a tooth, her life in exchange for his nephew's. Just the thought of it brightens his day. A smile traipses across his face as he rounds the corner.

Chapter 11

Rᴀsᴜʟ pushes Tage in wheelchair down a long stretch of hallway. The environment is cold and sterile, and as lifeless as Tage's body appears to be. His hands are bound together and resting in his lap. The only sound that can be heard is the clap of Rasul's shoes on the checkered tile and the rhythmic squeal of one of the wheels of the wheelchair.

Tage's body begins to twitch as he is being pushed along, and then suddenly he begins to shake violently. His body convulses, every muscle within him contracting to the point of snapping. He jerks about so wildly that he throws himself out of the rickety chair. Rasul grabs his cell phone and quickly dials for medical assistance.

"I need a medic on the second floor, main corridor, now!"

Panic grips him as he recalls Kendall's words.

The guards have been relieved of duty, not needed for such an easy assignment; escorting a wounded prisoner to the infirmary. With a keen understanding of who Kendall is and what he is capable of, if anything happens to Tage, Rasul knows he will suffer a slow painful death, along with anyone or anything he's ever loved.

Facing Kendall's wrath is not something to be wished on anyone, so there is only one thing on his mind, keeping Tage alive.

Working with Ambassador Kendall has its obvious advantages, but comes at a hefty price. The greater your position, the greater you suffer at his hands if you fail him. He is second only to the most powerful man in the world, Alexander Demetri himself. Rasul is bred from good genes, his father is a Professor at Harvard, and his mother has her Doctoral degree in Psychology. Even so, extreme intelligence is not needed to understand that Rasul's world is quickly starting to implode. Kendall will turn on anyone in an instant. He has witnessed Kendall's anger forged on many occasions with other employees, and he himself is routinely called on to bury all sense of decency and boundaries, to erase all lines of humanity and do the unthinkable without question or hesitation.

Tage's body ceases to twitch and he lays motionless on the ground. Wondering, praying to his god, that Tage still lives, Rasul draws his sidearm and lowers himself to the ground to check his pulse. As he reaches out, in a flash, Tage shoots his tied hands up and over Rasul's head and pulls him in to a ferocious head butt, smashing his head directly into his face. Rasul's nose breaks with a crunch, but he is still composed enough to point his gun into Tage's side.

"If I die, you die. Remember?"

It suddenly dons on him that Tage feigned his epileptic episode, and the briefest of hesitations gives him his window of opportunity. Tage repeatedly plows his head and knees into Rasul. Swinging his hands like a mallet with the strength of a wild ox, he quickly renders his escort unconscious.

Tage grabs Rasul's gun, even though he knows it's only for looks. He scrambles toward the door heading west. Just as he nears the door, a doctor comes through the door at the east entryway with a medical bag in hand. Tage hits the brakes, skidding to a stop, and quickly reverses course. The doctor spots Rasul lying on the floor unmoving and sees Tage running full speed towards him. He wisely retreats, heading as fast as he can for the door.

"Stop! Stop right there, Doc," Tage shouts.

The doctor reaches for the door. "Hey! Do it and you're dead."

The terrified doctor halts, allowing Tage to close the distance.

"Please, don't hurt me," the cowering doctor begs.

Tage presses the gun into the small of the doctor's back. "I don't want to shoot, but I will. I will, uh…shoot you, Okay?" Tage flinches at how stupid he sounds trying to sound threatening. A look of bewilderment registers on the doctor's face.

"Open the bag," Tage demands.

The doctor complies, fearing for his life.

"Cut these things off of me."

The doctor quickly grabs scissors from his bag and cuts the bindings off Tage's hands.

"How long will it take for you to clean up this wound and patch me up?"

The doctor removes the bloody gauze from his wound and examines the hole and the stitches. The doctor's face scrunches.

"Who did this to you?" The doctor looks angry. "A first year medical student could have done a better—"

"How long?"

"Um…about eight, maybe ten minutes."

"Okay…well you've got three. A second after that, I will karate chop you in the throat, and… and I will bust a cap for you, at you, in you… Understand?" The doctor nods his understanding.

Tage quickly concludes that trying to sound gangster didn't work for him. He was overcompensating in his theatrics because he knew the gun wouldn't work, but after hearing himself he figures it will be best for everyone if he just keeps his mouth shut.

Tage scans the halls and points to a closed door along the corridor.

"What's in that room?"

"On this floor, I think it might be an interrogation room."

Tage forces the doctor to assist him in getting Rasul into the wheelchair. The doctor opens the door and they wheel Rasul into the interrogation room.

From the moment Tage sets foot into the tiny gray room, he experiences the psychological effects of the area designed to manipulate him. The dreary walls with no patterns or pictures on them, and the two-tone gray carpet that has to be a throwback from the 70's makes him feel trapped, isolated and exposed. In the center of the drab room is a large metal table, two cushy brown chairs without armrests, one positioned directly across from a gray metal folding chair with no padding; the hot seat. An oversized observation mirror, the crown jewel of any worthwhile interrogation room, is mounted along the longest wall in the room, and four closed circuit TV cameras with lights flashing red are affixed to each corner of the room, which increases Tage's heart rate and his anxiety. Tage's eyes swing to a round charcoal colored clock hanging above the entrance door and his heart sinks when he sees that it is nearly 12am. Tage could only hope, or dare he say, pray, that Jacob and his men are not able to find his home. Tage cannot shake the feeling that he is being watched. At any moment, he believes that a team of murderous cops itching for payback are going to burst through the door, guns blazing.

"Get up on the table," orders the doctor, which lifts him out of his stifling cloud of thought.

They push the chairs out of the way, and Tage climbs up on the wobbly table. One of the table legs is shorter than the others so even the slightest of movements causes the table to constantly knock against the hard floor.

"Don't try anything, Doc. I'd hate to have to shoot you in your spleen."

"I'm just going to patch you up," the fearful man responds. "I just want to get you out of here. That's all."

Tage confides. "I didn't do anything wrong, I'm just trying to get home to my family." Tage lays down, drained and weak. "I just want to go home. I just want to go home," Tage quietly mutters as his mind drifts. The doctor quickly goes to work patching up his side. At this point, both Tage and the doctor know that he can easily be overtaken in his condition. The doctor can do anything to him, and Tage honestly wouldn't know any better. But for some unexplainable reason, the doctor is doing exactly what he has agreed to do. Tage shakes himself out of his fog, knowing that he cannot allow himself to lose focus.

"This will only be temporary. It needs to be stitched again."

"Ten seconds, Doc." Tage barks, with surprising conviction in his voice. The doctor, taken back, works feverishly. "Three. Two. One." The doctor is nearly finished.

"Good bye, Doctor."

The doctor cringes with a squeal.

"I'm just messin' with you, Doc. Hurry up, okay."

The doctor applies one more bandage and then signals that he's done. Tage throws his legs off the table, relieves the doctor of his jacket, and sets it aside. He looks around the room searching for something useful for restraining, but sees nothing. He checks the doctor's bag, but the meager amount of tape inside would not serve its purpose. Tage makes his way over to Rasul, who is still unconscious. He holds the gun firmly in his hand and takes a couple of practice swings at Rasul's head.

"Where is the best place to hit this guy to knock him unconscious, to where there's no permanent damage?"

The doctor looks strangely at Tage. "He's already unconscious," he stammers out.

"I know, but I don't have anything to tie him up with, and I can't take the chance on him waking up. So I need to hit him again... So where should I hit him... again?"

The doctor looks at him and Rasul, confused and hesitant to say anything.

"Come on, Doc. I'm running out of time," he snaps.

The doctor points to the back of his head. "Um... Most likely here."

"You sure?" Tage quickly responds.

The doctor nods, with a measure of uncertainly.

Tage draws a deep breath. "How hard?"

The doctor racks his brain, trying to think.

"Come on, Doc," he says impatiently.

"I don't know. I've never knocked someone out by hitting them in the head. Gimme a break."

"All right, calm down."

Tage takes a huge swing at the back of Rasul's head with the butt of his gun. He sends enough force through him that raises him up out the wheelchair and sends him sailing hard to the floor. Both Tage and the doctor cringe. "That might have been a little too hard," the doctor says.

"Yeah... Wow. Never mind that now. Sit down," Tage says as he motions to the wheelchair.

The doctor reluctantly sits.

"You like rides, Doc?"

He thinks for a moment, puzzled by the question. "uh… Yes, I guess so."

"Good," Tage responds, suddenly taking a somewhat smaller swing at the back of the doctor's head.

"Ow! That hurt," The doctor cries out, holding his head.

Tage rolls his eyes then follows immediately with a heavy strike to the other side of the doctor's head and he goes out like a light. This time, at least Tage's victim remained in the wheelchair.

Tage grabs the doctor's stethoscope and hangs it over his neck. He quickly puts on the doctor's jacket and he wraps the doctor's entire head as best as he can with gauze, to give an appearance of a head injury. Tage stops for a brief moment and snaps his fingers, thinking to himself that he could have tied Rasul up with gauze. Oh well, he made a mental note, then proceeds to roll the doctor out of the room, leaving Rasul behind sprawled out on the floor.

Making his way down the hall on the first floor, where the main entrance is located in the police station, Tage spots the night watchman out of the corner of his eye. He keeps his eyes focused on the exit and continues moving ahead, calmly. The night watchman watches him with extreme curiosity.

"Can I help you with something, Doctor?"

"What? Me? No. I'm just… my patient just needs some fresh air, that's all."

"Looks like he needs a lot more than that."

The men chuckle at the not so funny attempt at a joke, as Tage continues to push the wheelchair through the main entrance, and exits the building.

Rasul moans as he stirs. Slowly, he sits up. He pulls open his jacket and sighs deeply, seeing the empty gun holster. Putting his hand to his throbbing head, he stands. He stumbles to the door, dizzy and feeling faint. He contemplates going after the wounded fugitive that he has allowed to slip through his fingers and escape, but even if he is successfully recaptured, Rasul knows that he has already shown his unforgivable incompetence. Rasul makes his way out the door and down the hall. A battle of fear continues in his head, thinking about Kendall's wrath. In a muddled stupor, he continues down the hall and he stops at a water fountain. He brushes his hair back and takes a long drink, enjoying the cool water as it makes its way down his throat.

He casually strides to a stairwell and climbs the stairs to the roof. He throws open the door and takes a step out into the dark winds of night.

As he walks towards the roof's edge, he stops to light a cigarette. He takes a deep drag and lets out a puff with a look of utter satisfaction. He continues to walk, smoking as much of the cigarette as he can before reaching the ledge. Once he reaches the ledge, he takes a final toke, allowing the wind to gracefully play against his body. Rasul, without expression, then leaps from the roof of the building. His body falls with poise and grace towards the ground, and just as his crushed body caves in a parked car, a skeletal cloud of smoke escapes his parted lips.

~

A trio of black SUVs slices through the darkness, weaving their way along the river road a few miles from the police station. Stevens pilots the lead vehicle with Jacob riding shotgun. Jacob's phone rings. So caught up in the moment, so focused on his mission, he fails to hear the My Little Buttercup ring tone from the Three Amigos movie. Steven's finally speaks up, laughing.

"You gonna get that?"

Jacob shakes free of his mental zone and grabs his phone.

"My wife did that. I don't know how to change it," Jacob says to Stevens, who continues to laugh.

Jacob, enraged, glances at the caller ID that reads, "Amanda". He presses the power button on his phone and shuts it off, having no desire whatsoever to talk to her or anyone else for that matter. He picks up the handset for the radio mounted in the car. "Adam four to all units. Adam four to all units. Switch to tactical channel David two seven, now. I repeat, all units, switch to frequency David two seven." "Bravo team, copy. Switching to David two seven," Bravo Leader responds. Jacob slams down the receiver and turns to Stevens. "All work and no play, makes Jacob a dull boy." Jacob says with a crooked grin. "No more interruptions… from anybody. This is our time."

"Copy that, Sir," Stevens says, eagerly.

~

Tage walks steadily towards the wrecking yard when an alarm suddenly begins to blare. The whole compound lights up. He looks around, scurrying faster as he pushes the knocked out doctor in the wheelchair. He nearly loses the doctor and Rasul's gun when he zips around the corner of a building. He quickly bolts around another corner and comes face to face with a posted guard who is startled by his sudden appearance.

Knowing that his gun is only for looks, Tage chucks it at the head of the officer, who ducks and avoids it easily. The gun goes sailing by the untouched officer. The officer tries to take aim, but Tage hunches his body behind the wheel chair, trying not to give him a clear shot as he continues to barrel forward. Tage, running as hard and fast as he can, rams the chair and the good doctor into the officer. While the doctor and the chair are piled on top of the officer, Tage snatches the officer's baton and cracks him over the head. Tage then takes off running, leaving the two unconscious men behind.

There are office buildings and warehouses stretched down the river port. Forklifts, pallets of goods, and barrels are scattered throughout the area. The air is damp and chilling to the bone. Dark clouds hover in the blackened sky ready to bring forth rain. There's a short pier and a boating dock stretched to the south above the dark murky waters. Officers converge on Tage's position from all angles. As he rockets towards the water, officers open fire, stopping only to position themselves for a clearer shot. Tage races along the dock. Wood splinters all around him from the bullets narrowly missing him. Tage launches himself off the pier as bullets whiz by, following him on his speedy descent towards the dark choppy waters.

He tries to draw a long purposeful breath before he hits the surface of the deep, but his nose and lungs are assaulted by the putrid stench of the waters below. He smacks hard against the surface of the murky waters. The air his body tried to reject, the air that makes his lungs declare mutiny and seize, is forced out of his body on impact. His body spins underneath the water as he sinks.

He struggles to fight his way back to the surface so he can breathe, but all sense of direction is lost. He opens his eyes for a brief moment hoping that somehow he could catch a glimpse of bubbles rising to the surface, but he slams them shut when the pain of pins and needles stab into them. His hands instinctively press hard against his eyes as he tries to block whatever he is swimming in from seeping in again. He keeps telling himself to be still. He scolds himself for panicking, which he knows will do him no good. He allows his body to relax, fighting the desperation to swim in any direction, knowing that not even a single morsel of air is still inside his lungs for him to breath. He unbuttons the jacket he is wearing and strips it from his body. He relaxes, taking the time to remain still. The jacket slowly begins to rise. Once he detects the subtle tug of the surface upon the jacket, his arms and legs flail wildly to get topside. He knows he is suffocating, and not knowing how close or how far he is from the surface, is breaking him. As he continues to claw his way up, his eyes peel and the foul liquid once again creeps into and sears his eyes.

Tage's inability to see suddenly throws his mind back in time, back into the blinding rain of the darkest hour of his life. He remembers how the wind and rain battered the frayed tents of his campground. Tage and Sal playfully cover their eyes because of the heavy downpour. They can barely see inches in front of their face, but they sing and dance. Sal is dressed in her dad's button-up shirt, the one she is wearing in the picture found inside his watch. They walk along a muddy trail that leads back to their camp. They are

237

oblivious to anyone and anything, until the flashing of red and blue lights arrest Tage's attention.

Panic immediately begins to set in as his breathing quickens. His legs turns to rubber and wobble as he hurries Sal towards the commotion occurring a short distance away.

"What's that, Dad?" Sal asks tentatively.

Unable to speak, his pace steadily begins to hasten. A look of hopeful and wishful curiosity becomes fear as he sees a black government vehicle, patrol cars, and a garbage truck positioned along the water's edge.

Colored lights flash and reflect against the lake and puddles of water on the ground. Hollie, Gina and Walter come out of nowhere and stop him. Tage looks around. "Where's my wife? My mom and dad?" Hollie stands in his way, his hands up. He gently pushes against Tage's chest.

"It's too late, they're gone. I'm so sorry," Hollie says, as Tage edges himself forward.

Gina takes Sal into her arms. She shields her from seeing her Grandparents' bodies being hoisted into the garbage truck. Tai and Antonio came out of the bushes and join Hollie.

Rasul stands in the rain holding an umbrella over Kendall, who is being interviewed by the press. A female reporter holds a microphone in front of his face and a fellow media jockey positions a large black umbrella over her head. "Just how many Unbelievers were found hiding here within this camp?" The reporter asks.

Tage tries to break away, he has to see her, to see them, but the men prevent him.

Tage yells, "Where's Shannon?" He cries out in desperation to anyone willing to answer him. "Where's my wife?"

238

"She's gone, Tage," Hollie repeats. "They're all gone. They're dead."

Tage, like a bull seeing red, charges forward. He drags the men who are fighting to contain him. He collapses on the slick muddy ground and the men pile on top of him. Tage claws at the ground, inching towards Kendall, and screaming for Shannon until his vocal chords are shredded. He lifts his head and his eyes narrow on his beloved wife; his best friend and soul mate. The love of his life, Shannon. Officers lift her into the air and ruthlessly throw her into the garbage truck, an image forever etched and seared into his brain. "Shannon!" Hollie is forced to cover his mouth. Tage wails loudly through Hollie's fingers, eyes red with tears, body heaving from agonizing sobs.

"Quiet. Come on, Tage. They are going to find all of us."

Tage's piercing cries become deep groans as Hollie's words miraculously sink in.

"I'm so sorry, man," laments Hollie. Tage lies face down in the mud, broken.

The relentless canopy of rain beats against their drenched, mud covered body. Kendall turns and stares in the direction of the group, but the weather and terrain obstruct his view. He senses their presence. He can feel their sorrow; and the anguish to him, is like an illicit drug. He smiles towards Tage who stares back with vengeful and hatred filled eyes. Kendall then turns his attention back to his interview.

Tage surfaces from the dark waters thirsty for air. He rubs his burning eyes and allows them to open, only to see that his whole body is a deep red and covered in what looks to be blood. He is surrounded by all manner of dead sea life, floating upon the river's surface. His stomach instantly becomes nauseous and he violently gags as he wades in the warm crimson pool surrounding him.

Spotlights mounted to the pier suddenly shine on him and he sees that the entire river, as far as his eyes can see, is blood; an ocean of thick oily blood. Shots ring out and he plunges himself under the surface of the red currents. Bullets streak by his submerging body. He swims tirelessly beneath the surface, completely unaware of his heading. He comes up for a breath of air and his mouth fills with the ruby fluid; knowing that he has to immediately dive again to avoid the gunfire, he is forced to swallow the repulsive liquid. He pushes himself through the river of blood and swims in the direction of the wrecking yard.

Swimming mostly underwater, he manages to swim to one of the docks with the crackle of gunfire behind him as officers shoot blindly, unaware of his position. He lays hold of one of the wooden crossbeams and climbs up to an unmanned pier near the impound yard, feeling like an egg coated in red dye for Easter; only this is not a holiday and it is rich, vibrant, blood that clings to his body. He scales the beams to the surface and drops to his hands and knees, coughing and vomiting up milky ruby colored mouthwash.

He stands up, unsteady, and beats his hands against his body trying to remove whatever blood he can, as he takes in his surroundings. Officers still scan the waters below, unaware that he has surfaced.

Peering around the corner of the yard, Tage spots two officers conducting a routine foot patrol. He quickly pulls his head back out of sight waiting for an opportune moment to do something, anything. As soon as they begin heading away from him, he breaks from his cover and sneaks up behind them, leaving a trail of fading red footprints in his wake. Tage goes primal on the surprised officers, mercilessly beating them into a heap.

Tage drags the smaller of the two officers to the back door of the wrecking yard. He is spotted in route and all units advance. He lifts the officer's hand to the scanning device on the door, and with the sound of a click, he is able to pull open the heavy metal door. He drops the officer, scurries into the yard, and the door slams shut behind him.

Demolished and inoperable cars are scattered everywhere. There are several garages in the yard where cars are being worked on, and in the middle of the yard is a huge crushing machine that flattens the vehicles. Stacks of leveled cars, create partitioned walls throughout the entire yard.

Tage hustles towards the old cars that are lined up to be destroyed. He peers into the window of a 67 Plymouth GTX. No keys. He checks the area then heads to a metal box mounted on the wall of one of the garages. As he reaches his hand forward, the box pops opens. He is relieved, happy to catch a break, even a small subtle one. Anything that doesn't require him to break, smash, tear, rip, beat or bust something or someone open, definitely goes in the plus column. He knows he can't afford any extra time spent doing anything, fully aware that officers are gathering outside.

He spots about ten sets of keys hanging from metal hooks, and he swiftly snatches them all. He rushes back to the car fumbling with the keys, and clumsily drops two sets in the dirt. He thinks about grabbing them, but continues on, with a nagging feeling in his head that he is going to need them. When he reaches the GTX, he flips through the keys, trying them in the driver's side door lock.

Shafts of light steak through the yard from flashlights peering through fences and from officers climbing over. He's running out of time. They are preparing to raid.

He continues to sift through the keys. He tosses the useless ones aside and quickly gets down to the last four sets. Every instinct in his body tells him to go back for the keys he initially dropped. Once again, he finds himself arguing, alone, after he tries another failed set. He grunts loudly as he turns to run to towards the keys in the dirt and sees officers file in through the gate and crest the fence. "It's one or the other," he tells himself, as he skids in the dirt and stands conflicted. The officers take up positions as he bolts back towards the car, gambling with the keys he already has in his hand.

He reaches the car and tries the second to the last set in his possession. The key staggers in and catches. He continues to jiggle until it sinks in to the hilt. He turns the key and it pops the lock open. A sudden sense of elation shoots through his body and he suddenly starts to laugh with an awkward embarrassingly out of place cackle, but he foolishly allows himself the moment. He gives a forceful tug on the door handle and pulls it open, just as officers open fire and pepper the car with bullets. Tage throws himself behind the wheel, shoves the key inside the ignition with his head lowered and turns it as bullets pierce the glass.

The engine thunders. He presses the gas and the muscle car rocks its desire to roll. Tage forcefully jams the car in gear, barely seeing over the dash, and he floors it. The car fishtails, spewing dirt and gravel out from underneath the tires.

Circling the yard, he franticly looks for an exit as bullets plunk into the cars frame. The back and passenger side windows explode, with fragments of glass filling the car. Tage spots the exit and barrels toward it. Two SUVs outside the yard move in, attempting to create a roadblock, but stop is no longer in Tage's vocabulary. He crashes through the exit gate and zips between the two cruisers, relieving one of the vehicles of duty. Apparently they still don't make cars like they used to. He is driving a beast.

Tage's face looks like he's been beaten with a bag of nickels. His clothes are soaked and he is covered in sweat, dirt, and blood.

The fleeting thought of an infection is just that... Fleeting.

As he nurses his side with his hand, only one thought consumes his mind, stopping the massacre of his family, which he knows is imminent. Thoughts of his daughter flood his mind as he tailspins onto Capitol Street.

Two patrol cars give chase with sirens warbling. Blue and red lights reflect beautifully on the wet roads. The buildings hover like giant monsters, witnessing and waiting for the outcome of the high speed pursuit. A smatter of people walks the sidewalks and the streets are void of traffic. Tage blows by so many fire filled trash containers they look like runway lights.

As Tage flies through the empty skeletal city, the wind whistles and howls through every crack, crevice, bullet hole and missing window in the car. He whips and slides his car through turn after turn, with the police hot on his tail. He looks through the rear view mirror and sees more cruisers joining the pursuit and giving chase. Tage swerves through a turn, tires screeching, and drives open throttle through an alley. Barreling around another corner he hits the open road. His only speed now is lightning. He glances in the mirror to see the cars on his tail receding into the background, getting smaller with each passing moment. The GTX wheels down the open road so fast, everything is a blur, which reminds him of the teacup rides he hates with a passion. He hits the city limits heading for the dark and desolate hills that he proudly calls home. "Hold on, Sal. Daddy's on his way."

~

Sal lies in her bed with tears soaking into her pillow. She quietly sobs to herself. Pain far greater than she could ever imagine smothers her. She faces the wall, not wanting to let anyone know of her heartbreak.

Sal knows nothing of her biological father, Damon Warren, a local street artist on the world famous Venice Beach and native of San Francisco. His art is recognized throughout the world. Sal, much like him, is surrounded and inspired by many creative forces. They both see, feel, and experience creative beauty and expression in everything. It's easy to see where, Sal, the fearfully and wonderfully made prodigy, gets her talent and imaginative outlook on life; from him, and from her Creator. If there is still a Venice Beach for tourists to visit in the world today, that's where you will find Damon, still painting and drawing art like one would draw breath. It is this obsession that drove away Sal's biological mother, Temeria, who fought to the death trying to protect Sal.

She will never forget Temeria or her sacrifice.

Sal's heart isn't breaking; it is no longer to be found. All she can think about is her daddy, Tage. It was in this painful moment that she feels she will never find the bounds or limits to her agony. There is no light to be seen.

Brandy snuggles close to Sal as if he understands her pain. She is comforted to know she still has her four legged friend that she can confide in. Brandy has always been an outlet for Sal. Everyone around her recognizes that she does not have the typical mind of a six year old, and because of that, some have a hard time relating to her, but never Brandy. Whether Sal is right or wrong, happy or sad, acts her age or shows glimpses of intelligence that is off the charts, he never treats her any differently.

Erika hears Sal's whimpers and notices her facing the wall.

"Can I get you anything, Sal?" Erika speaks softly.

"My dad— Can you get my daddy?"

Erika turns away; witnessing this little girl's sorrow, makes her heart feel as though it is being ripped out of her chest.

She then sits beside her and gently rubs her back.

"Sal, your dad will always be with you. I know it's hard to understand, but..."

"No, it's not," Sal sadly interrupts, sniffing back the tears in order to articulate her response. "He still lives in my thoughts, my memories, and in my heart, even though I'd much rather not have a heart right now. I get it. Life is like a vapor, here today and gone tomorrow." Erika simply listens, unsure of what to say. "I don't have to grieve as one who has no hope, but it still hurts so badly. I know that I will see him again." Tears pour down her cheeks faster than she can wipe them away. "My daddy wasn't perfect, but he was perfect for me, and I want him back here. I want him right now." She picks herself up and sits with her legs crossed and head down.

"Sweetheart, you don't have to try and make sense out of this. Sometimes things just hurt, and sometimes you feel like your whole world is crashing down on you, and even the things that make sense, don't..." Erika's broken words feel so hollow and misplaced as she speaks them to the six year old that is nodding and understanding everything, even in her sorrow.

Sal's body shakes as she battles with her emotions and fights to compose herself. She wipes her tears with the palms of her hands, taking in and releasing short breaths while staring at the floor, in order to stifle the anguish filling her body.

"Healing does not always come through logic or by figuring out the right answers," Erika says.

After a moment of silence and labored breathing, Sal whispers, "I understand."

"Sweetheart, I don't think you do." Sal's watery eyes slowly rise to meet Erika's.

"What I'm trying to tell you is that it's okay for you to be six years old, and it's okay for a little girl whose name is Sal to cry her heart out, so much so, that she doesn't have a tear left to shed, because she loves her daddy with her whole heart and she is going to miss him."

The dam holding back Sal's tears burst. Sal jumps up and into Erika's arms and weeps like the little girl that she is. Erika holds her tightly, unable to stop her own flow of tears. Her eyes drift to a picture on the floor, the finished picture of Tage's guardian angel.

"Lord, please help this little girl. She needs your comfort. She needs to know that everything will be okay. God please make everything all right. Somehow," she whispers.

~

Tage, focused and intense, whips down a dirt road in the hills, heading for the shack. He spots the convoy of government cruisers snaking their way into the hills on a patch of highway below him. He sees them pull off the highway and onto a path where they slow to a crawl with their lights turned off. He turns off onto another stretch of road just above the convoy's position, and drives the car as far into the wooded area as he can before the trees and brush prevent him from going any further. He jumps out of the car with only his blood soaked pants and shoes, oblivious to the blistering cold.

He races through the woods on foot with tree branches and bushes raking across his arms and face. The pressure in his chest grows as his mind begins to count his losses; His wife, his parents, his friends, and now the possibility of his little girl. He pushes himself forward with determination, knowing that he will stop at nothing, and would do anything to put an end to this. The evil he faces will not be victorious this day; they will not claim the life of his child. He continues to charge forward, unable to formulate anything remotely resembling a plan. At this point, he will take it as a win, if he manages to get to his house before they did. Everything else will stem from him first carrying out that objective.

Jetting through the woods, confidence continues to build within him. He doesn't even know this... this person he has now become, until he takes a disastrous spill to the ground, which slices up his chest. Before he can even process what happened, he quickly springs to his feet, spits the dirt from his mouth, and charges on into the darkness.

Chapter 12

THE convoy slowly creeps into the darkened woods, tires crunching on the gravel and dirt. They edge their way forward in the treacherous terrain. The vehicles pull to a stop, unable to continue. The doors shoot open and the men pile out. Jacob and Stevens coolly exit the lead vehicle. Only the sound of crickets chirping and the moan of the wind through the trees can be heard. The others pour out with expert precision. The teams scurry to the back of the SUVs and gather their weapons and gear. Make no mistake about it, they are preparing for war. The smack of gun magazines loading and rounds being chambered echoes through the trees, banishing any living creatures in the area into terrified silence. MP5s, AR15s, and Sig and Glock handguns are locked, cocked, and ready to rock.

They are well organized and focused on the mission. Boyer, the runt of the group and the newest member of Bravo Team, reaches for a pair of night vision goggles and throws them on. He looks around, seeing the well illuminated figures of those around him, and a couple of small critters slowly crawling to their death on the ground. Boyer senses a strange and unexpected silence. There are no sound of boots stepping, guns loading, or gear snapping in place. He takes off his night vision goggles and sees that everyone is staring at him.

"What?" Boyer asks.

Bravo Leader clears his throat loudly. He shakes his head as he eyes the goggles on his head. Boyer, still confused, but catching on, slowly takes the goggles off and throws them back into the SUV. Jacob and his crew then turn and head off. When they do, Davidson smacks Boyer in the back of the head. "What's the matter with you? You don't use those on a hunt, it's too easy. What's the fun in that?" Bravo team shuffles off and leaves Boyer to lock everything down.

A lookout sits in a trench surrounding one of the many campsites located around the shack. He fights to shake off the sleep which insistently beckons him. The young man is in camouflage clothing and is well hidden at his post with a cover of camouflage netting woven into the shrubs encircling him. He is nearly invisible to the naked eye. The wind whispers softly into his ears and he drifts into a quiet slumber. From over the lookout's shoulder, Alpha Team approaches. The young man, unaware of their presence, doesn't move a muscle as they sweep the area. They inch closer and closer to his post.

The lookout's breathing is slow, deep, and rhythmic. His head dips and he catches the slight bellow of his own snore. He snorts and shakes himself awake. He starts to doze off again, but hears the rustling of careful steps nearby, which shoots a chill down his spine. Instantly wide awake and heart racing, his eyes angle up to see Jacob and his team merely inches from where he is sitting, heading in the direction of his campsite; the one he is supposed to be guarding.

He begins to shudder, fear taking over his body. He fights to still himself, to quiet the twitching of leaves and branches beneath his quivering body. Mitchell hears the crack of a branch and stares in the direction of the lookout. The young man's heart beats like the wings of a hummingbird. Fear paralyzes him.

After what seems like an eternity, Mitchell and the others continue moving. The officers slowly begin to pass by the lookout that has one hand on the edge of the trench to steady himself. Stevens' boot steps solid on the lookout's hand as he passes. The lookout remains still and quiet, forcing back the cry of pain from his pinky finger being snapped by the heel of Stevens' boot. After the officers pass, the young man releases the stalled breath he has been holding, which he exhales with a whimper. He pulls out an old .22 revolver and slightly raises it into the air. He prepares to pull the trigger; his right finger slowly squeezing the trigger, his left index finger plugging his left ear. He struggles within himself as he slowly pulls the trigger and the hammer of the gun falls back. He knows that this warning will cost him his life.

The pressure is almost unbearable for him, and the cold harsh reality of not wanting the pull of the trigger to be the last thing he ever does, causes him to ease up. The hammer of the gun slowly slinks back to its resting place. When the officers are a safe distance away, the lookout climbs carefully out of the trench and tries to quickly and quietly make his way around the death squad invading his territory.

A group of about twenty people, mostly Christians, camp just beyond the lookout's position. An old tarnished flower power VW

251

bus has been pushed into the woods and hidden amid the foliage of the surrounding trees and bushes. Poorly constructed tents, makeshift sleeping quarters and lean-tos are strewn among the grounds surrounding the bus.

The people sleeping here are from an underground fellowship in San Diego, CA. Hollie and Gina became close friends with the owner of the bus, Dan, a quiet, stocky, white elderly man who speaks with a slight lisp, who is the closest thing anyone has out there to a pastor. They first met him at a small group meeting he was leading nearly two years ago and Hollie initially thought he had the intelligence of a box of sporks. Dan had asked everyone to think long and hard about this question, "If you were to die today, where would you spend eternity? Heaven or hell?" And he just stood there flipping through his tattered Bible as people shouted out why they believed they would go to heaven... and with the annoyance of a broken record, all he kept saying as he dripped sweat before the crowd, turning the wrinkled and frayed pages, "I can't find it. I can't find it in here." People openly shouted that they thought, they hoped, or they believed they would make heaven their home; some cried out that they were raised in Christian homes, raised in church, that they were good people, some even baptized and sprinkled as a child by a priest or pastor." Dan did nothing more than stand their turning page after page saying, "I can't find it in here."

Hollie wanted to leave. He even tried to get up a couple of times, only to be yanked back in place by Gina, who was just a comment shy of smacking him. Hollie thought Dan was a joke and was even a little embarrassed for him. Some continued to proclaim that they loved God, regularly attended services even now, and gave of their time and money to the church, that they knew scripture and knew all about Jesus and God and that they would make heaven based on that. But the atmosphere in that place immediately changed, like a shifting of the evening tide, when Dan, meek and mild mannered old Dan, looked straight into the eyes of those gathered, while still flicking through pages and said, "I can't find any of that in here… None of it…" He shook his head. "Not one thing that was said can I find in the Bible as a basis for making heaven your home… Because it's not in here."

A deafening hush settled over the crowd, and all that could be heard was the crinkle of pages as Dan continued to sift through them, pinching them with his fingers and sliding to the next page with the flick of his wrist. "There is nothing in the Bible that says because you're a good person you will make heaven your home, but what it does say is that our goodness, yours and mine, our righteousness is like filthy rags. The Bible says there is no one who is righteous. Not one single solitary person."

Nobody dared move a muscle as Dan continued. "Compared to someone else, we can all walk away with a measure of goodness, but if we measured ourselves against the holiness of God, which is God's standard, we all fall short. There is nothing in this Bible that says because I think, or hope I will make heaven based on my denomination, spiritual lineage, godly parents, regular attendance at church, how much time or money I give, or because I was baptized, sprinkled, or spit on as a child. It's not anywhere in this Bible."

All eyes, whether they wanted to be or not, were glued on Dan, hanging on his every word, including Hollie's, who hadn't blinked since he actually began to speak.

"You may say you love God, but so did the people who crashed those planes into the Twin Towers; wrong god, wrong kind of love.

You may know all there is to know about God and about Jesus, but take it from me, from my experience... I was a Christian before the rapture of the church and I was still here after the rapture of the church... Trust me, knowing about Jesus is not enough; you have to know Him; have a personal relationship with Him. Friends, this is not religion, it's relationship."

Mouths hung open. Eyes were wide like Frisbees, and people had forgotten how to breathe.

"What this Bible does say is that Jesus is the Way, the Truth, and the Life and that no one comes to the Father, no one makes heaven their home, except through Him. Period."

All across the room, you could see the wheels turning in everyone's heads, the understanding of why loved ones and friends were gone, and why they themselves remained.

"God loved you before the foundation of the world, and He loves you right now. Jesus loves you, and He wants to have a relationship with you. We can't change the past, but Jesus died on the cross for all of our mistakes, our failures, and our sin, so that we can have a different future in Him; today and for all eternity. As long as you still have breath in your lungs, you can make things right with God by coming to Him. God, because He loves you, is still sending out lifeboats for each and every one of us called, forgiveness. Take it... Take it... If you want to give your life to Him and ask Him to come into your heart, I want you to come join me so I can pray with you." Dan hadn't even finished speaking and Hollie, whose eyes were flooded with tears, took Gina by the hand and they both made their way to him, followed by many others in the group.

Pastor Dan was the farthest thing from a pastor before the vanishings. He was a good man who loved people, and spent much of his time in church, volunteering. He was one of those rare people who would use his vacation time from work to attend his Church's Mission to Mexico trips twice a year. He heard the messages preached from the pulpit, could quote chapter and verse with the best of them, and pretty much knew all there was to know about Jesus. But he learned the hard way that knowing about Him and knowing Him are two completely different things. He came to know Christ moments after what he knew to be the rapture of the church spoken of in the Bible, when most of the people in his life and in his family had disappeared nearly seven years ago. He remembered every word spoken by his Pastor and without a question or iota of doubt, he knew what had happened, and even more importantly for those left behind, what was to come. Pastor Dan, was not schooled, licensed, ordained, or endorsed by any association or denomination, but he was a minister to those who found comfort in this man that loved people, and the words he spoke about Christ. Pastor Dan reluctantly agreed to lead, and those around him eagerly followed him as he followed Christ to the best of his knowledge and ability.

The Church in San Diego wasn't a church anymore, just a pile of bricks, burned boards, and ashes; remnants of the building and the charred bones of the people trapped inside and burned alive under orders of Alexander Demetri, who made a rare appearance to watch and listen to the screams of the dying men, women, and children, with a euphoric smile of approval. Any gathering of people for religious purposes outside of those established by Alexander Demetri always results in death.

Unbelievers, those followers of Christ, driven by an insatiable desire to know and experience truth, congregated in secret meeting places to avoid arrest and execution. Pastor Dan and his group

255

continued helping people in Mexico, which later turned into a rescue effort. There was overwhelming poverty caused by the massive earthquakes after the vanishings. Food was scarce and violence was high; especially with the gangs left over from the drug cartels that were now working with the Mexican police and Border Patrols. And of course, every government agency was under Demetri's control.

Any churches left standing are systematically destroyed along with anyone unlucky enough to be caught inside. Squatters, desperate for shelter and refuge, even know better than to seek shelter within a church facility. There was only one church and one god, Demetri and all will worship him or be killed.

Pastor Dan and his group would rescue Mexicans suffering persecution directed by the government. Thousands of people were thrown into internment camps to await execution. The fellowship was working with citizens that were in an underground movement attempting to free prisoners. It was through this effort that he met Carmen. She was born in the United States, but her father, mother and little brother still lived across the border.

Pastor Dan and Carmen married, and continued with the rescuing efforts, eventually bringing Carmen's family into the country. Because of their involvement with illegal practices they both had a bounty on their head. The last they heard the bounty was up to twenty five thousand dollars each, dead or alive. Demetri wanted to make a public example of them. He knew if he did that he would discourage groups like theirs from forming. Besides that, he rather enjoyed killing Christian leaders. There was a certain sadistic satisfaction in watching them die. If he couldn't be there in person everything would be filmed and he would watch the recordings over and over again, savoring every cry, every scream for help, every prayer that was howled out in agony that went unanswered; it was music to his sick demonic ears.

Sometimes Demetri would insist on being a part of the extraction process, which is what he called the torture of Unbelievers for the purpose of gaining information used to stop further religious activity. He's watched the films with demented satisfaction of Unbelievers' fingers and toes being ripped off one-by-one, arms and legs being shredded by meat grinders, eyeballs scooped out of their sockets, bones being broken from the smallest to the largest, extremities being twisted until the skin snaps, tongues sliced, genitalia severed, all the while being disappointed because no useful intelligence was gathered and he felt that more could have been done. Many of his men conducting the extractions were summarily executed because of their perceived incompetence.

Pastor Dan's rescuing mission surfaced on the government's radar, Dan and his wife decided that they would move their operation from San Diego to Oregon to join with other members of their group who were already there. They started a covert relief effort on property previously owned by Pastor Dan's family. They would leave San Diego, come to the valley and stay on Hollie's property for a few days. Then after a time of rest, they would continue on to their destination.

Jacob and his group spot the glowing embers of a smoldering campfire a short distance away. They fan out and slowly, stealthily, make their way toward the flames. The barrels of their sweeping guns gently reflect the haze of red from the bloodthirsty moon that lingers in the night and sags like an overripe plum. The travelers sleep soundly in their tents, on sleeping pallets, and in lean-tos, with only the sound of the wind through the trees and the low grinding snores of peaceful contentment induced slumber.

They are all tucked away in their thick, tattered blankets, unaware of the pending danger. All are drained of energy, exhausted from their long journey. Everything seems quiet and peaceful as they continue sleeping. Pastor Dan and his wife sleep inside the VW with the doors open. He is closest to the door laying lengthwise in the van, with his arms firmly around his wife who is facing him.

The lookout stands huddled behind a tree along the edge of the campsite a few yards from the closest tent, watching in horror as officers begin to move in and spread out. Unwilling to step out from the shadows, he picks up pebbles from the ground and tosses them at the nearest tent. "Hey! Wake up." He quietly tries to scream. He continues throwing the rocks, but no one stirs. Jacob and his men move about, quietly weaving through the grounds. The young man is racked by guilt knowing that if he had not fallen asleep, if he had only remained vigilant, that his family, his friends, his Pastor, who had trusted him, would not be where they are now. A short lived thought crosses his mind to shout, to scream, to shoot, to do something, even if that meant that his life will be taken, but instead he whispers a prayer to God asking Him to give his friends peace.

The young man collapses to the ground, chest heaving, his body jerking with uncontrollable spasms of sorrow as his mind is tormented by the shrieks of remorse. Jacob stands before Pastor Dan and his wife and is the first to engage his red laser sights. The other Officers quickly follow suit, scanning through the sleeping group and honing in on their target of choice. The young watchman closes his eyes, just as Pastor Dan opens his eyes. Pastor Dan turns quietly as to not disturb his wife and he sees Jacob and the red laser sight pointed directly at him. Pastor Dan lays back down, tightens his grip on his wife, who smiles lovingly and he sings. "I'm overwhelmed, by Your love for me." His wife's smile gets bigger. "I'm overwhelmed by the grace which covers me." Jacob throws his fist up in the air to signal his team not to fire, and he listens. "I'm overwhelmed, just in knowing Jesus died for me. He did it all for me. I'm overwhelmed." For the first time in Jacob's professional career, he didn't know what to think. He has been in this position countless times before, and has personally executed more people than he cares to remember. But there is something strangely different about this moment for him. He feels drawn and conflicted. He tries to make sense of what he is experiencing within himself, but he can't understand it, and because he can't understand it, his defense mechanism tells him to eliminate it, as quickly as possible.

Jacob opens fire on Pastor Dan and Carmen, and the rest of his crew follows suit. Bullets tear holes in tarps, comforters and blankets, and find lodging inside the unsuspecting flesh of those dreaming of a new life. Bodies, both young and old, jerk rhythmically to the muffled thuds of suppressed gunfire. The lookout peeks out from his hiding place. He is unable to resist the temptation to see what's taking place; like rubberneckers on the highway who can't resist taking in a crash site. His heart sinks as tears streak down his face. He collapses back behind the tree, hating himself for acting on the primitive and unexplainable urge to witness the execution.

~

Tai sits alone, stationed as the lookout for the main camp. His heart skips as he catches a flash of movement, but then, whatever he thought he saw was gone. His eyes sweep the area, but he can't fix on anything. He's packin' now, so he swings his gun, nervously darting it back and forth. Again he spots someone, something approaching, and he takes aim, but just as quickly as the figure appears, it vanishes.

"Tai?" A voice calls out.

Tai backs away, scared, eyes as wide as serving platters.

He tries to respond, but fear causes his mutinous voice to jump ship.

"Tai? It's me, Tage."

"Whoa. Whoa. Whoa." Tai thinks that his mind... and his eyes... and his ears... are playing tricks on him.

"Oh, crap", he manages to squelch out, backing away, trying to maintain control of his quivering body and his splintered mind. He is so wound up and his finger so tight on the trigger, that the next blade of grass that bends at him wrong is takin' three to the chest. Tai finds his voice and speaks into the darkness. "Hello?"

Again Tai hears a voice through the rustling of bush and the whoosh of the wind blowing steadily through the trees.

"It's me, Tage. Don't shoot."

Tai retreats a few steps, his movements becoming more erratic.

"It's a ghost. Tage is dead." He says to himself, panicked beyond all comprehension. "This is so not happening right now."

"Tai?" Tage says sternly.

"Okay, that's it." Tai has had enough. He turns and breaks into a run.

Before Tai can pick up any speed, Tage sideswipes him and takes him down to the ground so hard that the wind is hammered out of him.

Tai takes one look at his ghastly appearance and loses it, flopping around on the ground like an air deprived fish, screaming, "I see dead people... I see dead people."

Tage forces his hand over his mouth, and motions for him to shut up.

"Hey, it's me, Tage. What are you talking about? I'm not dead. There's no time to explain. Cops are here right now, and they're on the hunt. We have to warn the others."

Tai continue to stare at Tage's ghastly appearance, still unsure of what to believe.

"Now, I'm going to take my hand away, okay. Don't yell." Tai nods, still deathly afraid. Tage hesitates, slow to remove his hand, because he's not yet convinced Tai is not going to scream at the top of his lungs like a little girl.

Tage slowly takes his hand away and Tai takes in a deep breath.

"We thought you was dead, bruh," he says eagerly.

"By all accounts, I should be."

"By all accounts, you look like you are. Dang boy, you stink. That's nasty right there. You look like I feel right now. Can you get off me, please?"

They are both slow to rise to their feet. Looking at Tage, Tai shakes his head, a slow and steady grin rises on his face. Tai moves in for a hug, but reconsiders.

"How is everything here?" Tage questions.

"Cool, bruh. We heard on the news that all of you were killed."

"Well, it's certainly not for their lack of trying. Come on, we gotta move."

"What's going on?"

"I'll explain on the way. Come on."

They hurry in the direction of the shack, their heads on a swivel, scanning the area with watchful eyes.

Tage breaks into a run. "You gotta run slow okay, I just ate... and my legs are shorter than yours." Tage disregards the request. He runs as fast as his battered body will carry him and Tai struggles to keep pace.

261

Bravo Team makes its way through the woods, cutting swiftly and silently through the brush. They slip into the shadows as a group of travelers venture into an open field headed towards a grove of trees. A gust of wind is interrupted by the slice of a bullet that lodges quietly in the neck of a man in the back of the pack. He falls silently to the ground, unable to voice an alarm. The others are completely unaware and continue moving quickly. Another almost inaudible crack sends a bullet slicing through the air and drops a woman whose yelp goes unheard. Not until the fourth victim falls dead did the group take notice and scatter, mad dashing for their terrified lives, screaming and yelling. From their perspective they see nothing but the cover and safety of the trees, but no matter which direction they turn and run, someone is picked off. A mother carrying her baby is shot in the back. She falls on top of her crying infant who she cradles in her arms. The baby wails as he feels the weight of his mother upon his frail little body. She tries to comfort her child, whispering words of love and affirmation. A man races toward them to help, and a sniper's bullet hits him in the back of the head. The shooting gallery is over in a matter of seconds. Once all the victims are down, the stealth unit abandons their cover. Faint moans resonate, but the haunting squeals of the fallen baby boy, overshadows them. Cold and calculated, the officers put a bullet through anything moving or moaning. Boyer marches straight for the mother and child. He thumps a round in her and then permanently silences the wailing baby.

Hollie sits alone inside the shack, reading by candlelight. His reading glasses hang on the tip of his nose. He holds in his hand, a torn out page from the Bible. He tilts his head down and moves the page back and forth until he could make out the words clearly.

He quietly reads aloud, "1 John 2:6, those who say they live in God should live their lives as Jesus did."

He puts the page down and drops his head.

"Help me to do this God. Help me to live the way You would want me to live... I wish..." His voice trails off as he fiddles with the page in his hand. "I just want to know You more. Teach me, Lord, and help us all to get it right this time. I've spent every chance You've ever given me, and You have always given me one more try. I can't understand Your forgiveness, but I'm thankful for it. Thank You for being a God of second chances."

Brandy suddenly snaps to attention, his whine quickly escalates into loud barks. Hollie jumps out of his chair, startled. "What is it, Brandy?"

Gina rises, instantly alert. Hollie grabs his shotgun just as they hear pounding on the door. Tai quickly moves to the window and begins banging on it. Gina nods the okay for Hollie to open the door.

"Brandy, get back. Hush. Good boy," Gina says.

Obediently, Brandy retreats.

"What's going on, Tai?" Hollie says curtly.

"The police are here, in the woods." He responds with a tremor in his voice.

"What happened? What did you see?" Hollie demands.

"I saw him." Tai turns and looks behind him. Hollie follows his gaze to see Tage, who is scrubbing off what he can of the dried blood on him with a jug of water and a rag. Tage heads to the door. His side gives him a jolt that almost doubles him over. Hollie approaches him as Tage checks to see if the patch job is still holding.

"The radio said you were dead. We thought you were dead, man." Hollie is grinning ear-to-ear.

263

"What would you do without me, my friend?" Tage says with a smile as he yanks Hollie into his arms and embraces him with joy.

Knowing there's no time for sentiment, he rushes Hollie and Tai inside. Gina rushes towards Tage who defensively throws up his hands, knowing what's coming. She forcefully hugs him, totally disregarding his cries of pain. "Don't you ever do that to us again, you hear me?" Gina says as she punches him.

"Trust me. I don't plan on it." Tage says holding his arm and scratching his irritated forearms.

"Look at you. You look terrible," Gina says.

Hollie yells out. "Everybody up. We're leaving."

Gina sets out to awake the others, but the commotion has already stirred everyone. Audrey and Antonio already have their bug out bags in hand.

Audrey keeps her distance from Tage and simply looks him over with bittersweet emotion. She has to force her legs to walk towards him.

Tage moves slowly, his head hanging in guilt.

Audrey hugs him, not wanting to let him go, not wanting to hear what she already knows. They look each other in the eyes.

"What about Walter... and Frank?" She asks, hoping, and at the same time knowing in her heart what the answer will be. Tage shakes his head. "I'm sorry. They didn't make it."

Hollie screams out. "Okay, come on you guys. Get everything you need. Tai, see if there's anyone else in the area." Gina moves through the cabin like a whirlwind, Brandy excitedly runs alongside her. Tai rushes out the door as Tage breaks away from Audrey to find Sal, who is still asleep in a room with her face to the wall. He carefully kneels down beside her, speaking softly. "Sal?"

Upon hearing his voice, she immediately stirs.

"Hey, little one. Wake up," says Tage.

Sal's eyes slowly flutter open. She doesn't want to wake. The pain knows where to find her. When she dreams, everything is the way it should be, and that's where her heart wants to remain. Sadness fills her eyes as she stares at the wall.

"How's my beautiful Psalm?" Sal stares unblinking at the wall.

"Please don't call me that."

"Why not?"

"Only my Daddy calls me that," she responds

"Turn around," Tage says, his eyes beginning to leak like a faucet. Sal hesitates, not wanting her only wish to not come true, to not be there.

"Psalm, it's okay. Turn around, sweetheart."

She begins to turn with her eyes full of tears.

"It's me, sweetheart. Daddy's here." She turns, staring wide-eyed, frozen in doubt, in stunned silence; the only movement she could manage is the steady flow of tears from her eyes. Tage lifts his right hand towards her with his palm facing Sal's.

Her lip quivers as she stares at his hand. He inches his hand closer to her and motions for her to join him. Sal slowly raises her hand and places it on his palm; her hand now filling more of his hand than when their hands first met. Together they sweep their hands in the air drawing the shape of a heart, both too broken and overcome with emotion to speak the words, "I love you with my whole heart." But the moment requires no words. Sal then rushes into his arms and gives him a suffocating hug. She doesn't care in the slightest how bad he looks, how dirty he is or how bad he smells. "Daddy, I missed you. I was so scared. I thought I'd lost you." Tage's world seems complete at this moment. "You can't get rid of me that easy. You, my beautiful daughter, mean more to me than anything in the world."

The crack of gunfire can be heard nearby. The sounds of small arms fire and shotgun blasts echo in the valley, but just as quickly as it begins, the gunfire goes silent.

Tage, holding Sal in his arms, rushes to the door to join the others already gathered.

"So, what are we up against, Tage?" Asks Hollie.

"There were three vehicles, could be up to a dozen officers out there." He tells them.

Hollie begins with, "If we're gonna leave we'd better—"

Antonio interrupts. "What do you mean, if? We have no choice. We have to leave, like now."

"And what about Sean? We'll never make it with him. He's too weak to travel."

"I'll stay with him. We can try to hide somewhere," says Nevaeh.

Antonio spouts off. "Fine, let them stay. You guys said it yourselves, he probably won't make it anyway... Besides, maybe they can help him."

Tage jumps into the discussion, "What makes you think the people out there are here to help us?"

"Honestly," says Antonio, "I don't know what to think anymore."

"Well, let me clear up any confusion for you or anyone else that might be unclear. The police are here to slaughter us."

Hollie attempts to bring calm. "Wait. Hold on a minute. Everybody just hold on. Frank used to tell us all the time that talk is cheap. You can pray good, quote all kinds of scripture and whatnot, but what matters is how you live your life. There's a lot I don't know,

266

but I do know that God wouldn't have us leaving that kid behind."

Hollie grabs Gina's hand. "We're staying." Gina nods in agreement with his decision. "Count me in. I'm not going anywhere," Tage says confidently. "Me too," chimes in Erika.

"Well, I'm sorry, but I think it's suicide. We've got to get as far away from this place as we can, " says Antonio.

Tage shakes his head. "Antonio, you're not going to make it, you heard how close those gunshots were. They will be on top of us in a matter of minutes."

"Then I'd better get going then."

"We should stick together, " says Hollie.

"Only if you're coming with me."

Antonio is anxious to move out, but takes a moment to shake hands with Hollie and Tage.

"Go with God, my friend," Hollie says.

Antonio nods and heads for the door.

"Wait," Audrey says to Antonio. "I'm going too, if that's okay with you."

Antonio nods, looking noticeably relieved to have the company. "I'm going to move fast, so you'll have to keep up." Audrey nods. "I just don't have the fight in me anymore," she tells everyone.

"We'd better get moving, Audrey. Let's go."

Tension is high, and sorrow set in like the hardening of modeling clay. There is obviously no time for long drawn out goodbyes, but Tage needs to get something off his chest. He pulls Audrey aside. Audrey puts her bag down and she looks at him, shaking. "I'm sorry I broke my promise." Tage says regretfully, deathly afraid of the words she would speak.

"It's okay." When she speaks, her lips quiver. "I know you would have done everything you could."

Tage looks away, wondering. He questions whether he could have done anything differently; something that would have brought Walter back home safely to his wife.

"How did Walter die?" She says absently, her stinging eyes staring down at the wedding ring on her aged hand. Tage is ashamed. How could he do that to Walter? How could he think such thoughts about the old man that just wouldn't die. He was a friend. He was family.

"I thought that Walter." Tage hesitates. "I thought that Walter had given away—" Audrey raises her eyes and grins as she lifts his lowered chin. "Hey, listen to me. There are many things that I thought about Walter at one point or another, but the things that matter to me are the things that I know about him." Her words are a soothing ointment to a wound that can't be mended by human hands.

Tage pulls himself together. "He was a man of integrity. He died making a stand for what he believed. He loved God. He loved you... He really loved all of us. That much I knew. He was a great man."

Audrey places her hand on Tage's face. "He still is... And so are you. Don't let your past ruin your future."

Audrey kisses him on the cheek and walks off, leaving her bag behind and Tage pondering her words.

Tage is conflicted, unable to shake the feeling that he is somehow responsible for Walter's death. Maybe he should have insisted that he stay behind. Maybe they could have found another way around the monitoring system that would not have involved him. Audrey turns and looks back warmly at Tage. She and Antonio head out the door together and they disappear into the shadowy woods.

Tage lowers his eyes and sees Audrey's bag. He considers running it out to her, but then sadly he realizes she left it because she will not be needing it any longer.

The remainder of the group gathers near the door, running scenarios, anxiously looking over their shoulders and out windows. They decide that with Sean in tow, their only option is to make a stand. To somehow weather the storm and make it safely to the cave, which would buy them some time. There, they can come up with a long term plan. Tai enters carrying several handguns. He hands one to Tage, who has to wipe fresh blood from the handle. "Couldn't hurt, right?" Tai says, scanning the room. "Where's Antonio and Audrey?"

"They're gonna try and make a run for it," Hollie says. "You have to decide for yourself what you want to do, Tai."

Tai scoffs as he looks around; everyone should already know what his answer is. "You know me. I'm staying with you guys, dawg," he exclaims.

Nevaeh looks at her gun, unsure. "I've never shot a gun before," she says, sheepishly. Tai shows her the basics of using a firearm. He points to the tip of her gun. "Point this end at whatever you want to kill," he says. "Squeeze the trigger to get what you want."

Tage look at the guns with little assurance. "These guns can only do so much. They had them out there, now we have them. That should tell you something. This fight is gonna have to get ugly."

Antonio and Audrey quickly make their way through the woods, heading for the outskirts of the campsite. They are hoping to join the group camped on the perimeter of the property with Pastor Dan. Antonio's lead widens and he turns only to goad Aubrey into moving faster. He threatens to leave her if she continues to fall behind. "Come on. Let's go. Let's go." He snaps impatiently.

Antonio turns back only to trip over something that causes him to stumble forward. Unable to get his feet underneath himself he falls to the ground, coming to a grinding halt face to face with the contorted face of a Hispanic heavy set woman with dark brown hair, freshly killed, blood still oozing out of her gaping mouth. He stares into her unforgettable hazel eyes. She stepped into eternity paralyzed with fear. Her expression says it all. He is frozen in the dreadful moment where his body refuses to take in a breath or exhale. The sound of Audrey's approaching footsteps brings him back.

Antonio backs away painfully and fearfully slow; as if he is face-to-face with a cobra that's got him dead to rights. He rises and turns, breathing fast and heavy, and sees that it is not something, but someone that tangled his legs; the dirty hand belonging to the mangled body of a small boy that couldn't be more than five years old. The child lies amid the rock piles, his arm outstretched as though he is reaching out to him for help. A baseball and glove rests beside his body wanting to play.

Without sharing a word, Antonio and Audrey slowly back away. But when they turn, they now find themselves in the presence of Jacob and his men who stand only a few yards in front of them. The blood drains from Antonio's face and he goes pale. Audrey has a sudden rush of anger that overtakes her. She's disgusted by what she sees. Jacob casually approaches with an insolent smile and Antonio's body goes limp. He drops his gun without even the slightest order or instruction to do so.

"On your knees," Jacob says.

The pair exchange looks.

"Bow!" Jacob snarls.

Antonio drops swiftly to his knees, but Audrey remains standing.

"Maybe you didn't hear me, woman. Down on your knees, now." Jacob demands.

"I heard you just fine. I'm old, not deaf."

The officers snicker in the background.

"I will do no such thing. I will not bow to you or anyone else."

There's a tinge of amusement in Jacob's face looking over this scrappy old lady, until she picks up a rock and throws it at him, narrowly missing his head. The other entertained officers anxiously wait to see what Jacob's next move will be.

"I suggest that you make your peace with God."

"Not that it's any of your concern, but I already have, loser." She holds her hand up in the shape of an "L" above her forehead.

"Then I guess we're done here." In a flash Jacob draws his gun, fires off a round into Audrey's head, and holsters his weapon before Audrey realizes what happened. She continues standing, staring transfixed, straight into Jacob's eyes. Her gaze slowly lifts towards the heavens and a smile traipses across her face. She falls gracefully backwards, appearing as though the wind itself is lowering her slowly and delicately to the ground.

Antonio's mortified body shakes violently, as he fixes his eyes on Audrey's dead body next to him. All he can think to do is scurry away, to gain at least some distance between him and death. He cries out with the only words that manage to form on his lips.

"Oh God, please don't kill me." Antonio pleads, unable to even look up and face his adversaries.

"I'm looking for a girl. Her name is Sal. Do you know her?" Jacob says without emotion.

"What? What do you want her for?" Antonio manages to squeak out as he cowers. Stevens quickly puts a bullet in his leg.

271

"Do you know her?" Jacob demands.

"Yes, she lives in a shack about a half mile down this path. I'll do anything you want. Just don't kill me, please." Antonio begs, to the pleasure of those standing before him.

Jacob decides to play Antonio's game.

"Will you denounce your God?" Jacob asks. "Yes. Yes. I will. I do. I denounce G-G-God. I pledge my life and faith... Everything to Alexander Demetri. I just want to live," Antonio says.

Jacob then asks that Antonio give him his hands.

Without hesitation, Antonio stretches out his arms, his head hanging low in utter submission. "For whoever wants to save his life will lose it, but whoever loses his life for me will find it." Jacob says, to Antonio's confusion.

Stevens marches forward as Antonio is offering himself to Jacob and traps both of Antonio's arms underneath his left arm. A glint of silver can be seen in Stevens' right hand, the double-edged blade of his knife. He digs the blade deep into Antonio's wrist and cuts down the length of his arm. Antonio screeches, face twisted, tongue wagging, and mouth wide as Stevens digs ruthlessly into his other arm, sawing deep into his flesh. Antonio tries to fight, tries to remove his arms, tries to break free of Stevens' hold, but his resistance is hardly even noticeable.

After Stevens finishes carving into Antonio, who continues to scream loudly, he releases his arms, which fall into his bloody lap.

"The world is better off without you." Jacob announces.

Antonio stares unblinking at his arms which freely spring forth his life force. Jacob and his crew turn to leave him to his spineless fate.

Antonio falls to his side, perishing. He struggles to form words, desperately trying to speak.

"Je—sus, please forgi—"

Thwap!

A bullet fired from Jacob's gun rips into Antonio's brain, killing him instantly.

"You're not getting off that easy," Jacob utters. He then strides off into the darkness with the gun still hanging by his side.

The forest is silent, as if the trees are giving reverence to the dead. The bodies of Pastor Dan's group are spread out everywhere. Their blood cries out for justice, but no yet hears.

The moon shines through the leaves of the trees and the wind begins to whistle.

Figures emerge from the shadows of the trees. Bravo Team covertly inches toward the shack, which can be seen in the distance. They pay little attention to the shovels, axes and pitch forks leaning on the trunks of the trees in the area.

Edging forward they continue to sweep the grounds. They stay in formation, but spread out to cover more of the property with precision.

The sound of heavy breathing can be heard blending in with the whispers of the wind. Tai conceals himself in the trees above. He lies on his back with his gun clutched tightly to his pounding chest. He prays that the thunderous beating of his heart and the chill of his breath against the cold night air will not give away his position. His body shivers from the cold and from fear, but mostly from fear. He tries to still himself, "breathe, Tai. Just, breathe." He murmurs to himself as he wipes his sweaty hands on his stained cargo pants. He thinks back to his childhood; the tropical weather, the beaches, the blue water and the closeness of his family. He smacks his

lips thinking about how well his father cooked a Kahlua pig underground. He dreams of dipping his fingers in poi and popping the
top off a can of Spam, his favorite dish. He wishes... to be there
again.

He knows that soon he will be seeing his family, who had vanished along with the others, and the thought hurls him anxiously
back to reality.

His eyes scan the trees in search of his friends. To the south he
spots Tage, out of sight, but slightly lower than his position in the
trees. To the east he sees Erika concealed in the branches of a tree
nearest the shack. She is hardly breathing, but her heart is thumping
like the bass in a Pinto with a stereo that cost three times as much
as the car.

Gina discreetly peers out of an open window inside the shack.
She brushes the hair out of her face then gnaws on her fingers in
search of a nail to bite. The filthy glass has been removed and is
no longer in place. Gina tries to speak quietly to Brandy who sits
whimpering by her side. She tries, to great extent, to get Brandy to
leave, to run, to be free, but he refused. There is no other place in
all of creation he would rather be than by her side.

Gina stops cold when she spots a member of Bravo Team approaching. Hollie is posted outside of the shack to the east of Gina.
He looks anxiously but with determination at Nevaeh, Sean, and
Sal, who hide among the downed trees. Tage makes ready his gun,
closely watching Bravo Leader and Boyer pass underneath him. Erika gives Gina a reassuring nod, and then gets a bead on Bravo
Leader with her gun. Hollie tracks Boyer with his shotgun as he
converges alongside Bravo Leader. Gina, greatly distressed, makes
one final attempt to get Brandy to move away, she urges, nay, begs
for him to leave her side, but to no avail.

Gina stoops down, leaving only her gun pointed out of the window, and then...

Silence.

Gina closes her eyes and draws a long breath through her nose. Her eyes suddenly shoot open and her finger pulls hard and fast on the trigger.

Bravo team crouches, instantly get a bead on the incoming fire, and lays down a hail of gunfire.

Alpha Team casually makes their way through the woods, unhurried, certain that lives will soon come to an abrupt end.

Bravo Team concentrates their fire on the shack, shredding the weathered planks of wood with suppressed gunfire. Gina drops down, covers her head, and scurries to the back of the shack, dragging Brandy, who is yapping madly at the masses of bullets shredding his home.

Hollie rushes out from the fallen trees, heading straight for Boyer. Tage opens fire on Gomez, hitting him in the back of both legs, taking him down. Erika shoots at Bravo Leader, who instinctively ducks, rolls out of her sight-line, and returns fire with expert precision.

"They're in the trees," shouts Bravo Leader.

Tai opens fire on Davidson, pelting him in the back. He unloads round after round, which thump against his heavily armored ballistic vest. Davidson lurches forward and wheels around, unharmed. "That ain't right," Tai says to himself. He then aims for the legs and Davidson takes a hit in his right thigh. He returns fire and a bullet thuds into Tai's chest, throwing him back into the trees.

Boyer continues to spray the shack with bullets, advancing as he shoots. Gina crawls out a back window and falls to the ground. She

quickly jumps to her feet and looks back into the window screaming for Brandy. Brandy takes a running start to jump through, but
a bullet rips through one of his legs and he tumbles. Gina tries to
climb back into the window, calling out to Brandy who limps towards her, yelping. Gina sees the spray of bullets coming toward
her, but reaches in far enough to grab Brandy's leash. "I'm sorry,
boy," she says as she yanks on the leash and flings herself back out
the window. Brandy howls with pain, awkwardly jumping through
the window as a line of bullets narrowly miss him. Gina wraps
her arms around him. With tears in her eyes, she kisses him. Gina
quickly looks around and together they limp away from the house.

Hollie moves to within point-blank range of Boyer and levels
the shotgun right between his helmet and the top of his flak jacket.
He pulls the trigger.

Boom!

A barrage of buckshot is unloaded into his neck, killing him
instantly.

Jacob and his team, realize that something must be wrong, because of the continued gunfire. They double time it through the
woods in the direction of the fray.

Tage jumps down to the ground and grabs a pick ax positioned
at the base of the tree. He takes a huge leap towards Gomez and
plants the ax deep into his back. Gomez' body ceases all activity
for a moment, frozen instantly with shock. His body twitches hard,
then gains momentary functionality. He tries to reach back with his
arms, spinning around in circles like a dog chasing his tail, trying to
remove the ax. He slowly stops turning, collapses to the ground,
and with a single massive contraction, he dies.

Davidson, still standing and unfazed by the bullet in his thigh, continues shooting at Tai, who is slouched against the tree, attempting to return fire. He is bleeding profusely from a sucking chest wound and the left side of his body goes completely limp.

"Oh, this sucks," Tai says to himself as he continues shooting. He starts making music with his mouth, as Davidson repositions himself. He sways to the music in his head. "Oh, that my jam right there," Tai says with an unexpected smile. Davidson opens fire and riddles him with bullets. Tai slumps back into the branches of the tree, dead.

Bravo Leader shoots at Erika, splintering the trees around her. She falls hard to the ground and her gun topples several feet away. She can't believe that for the second time today, she's lost her gun. She scurries to retrieve it, but Bravo Leader's gunfire forces her back behind the tree.

Tage races towards Davidson. Without missing a beat, he grabs a sledgehammer leaning against another tree. Tage winds it back and is about to bash in his skull when suddenly, Stevens opens fire on him. Tage drops the sledgehammer and takes cover behind a tree. He pulls his pistol and fires two shots at Stevens, hitting nothing. Stevens casually makes his way towards Tage, smiling. Tage spots an ax propped against another tree near Davidson's position. Tage quickly surveys the area, seeing no options or escape, and then he looks up. Stevens advances on Tage, gun leading, anxious to pull the trigger.

Bravo Leader moves in for the kill on Erika, slowly circling the tree. Gina Suddenly fires on Bravo Leader. Bravo Leader takes an ineffective hit to his vest. He crouches and shoots. Multiple shots rip through Gina's stomach. Hollie sees his wife fall to her knees.

"Gina!" He screams.

Bravo Leader gets a bead on her and prepares to finish her. Before he can pull the trigger, Brandy comes barreling toward him and latches his powerful jaws on his hand.

Davidson limps forward with Stevens, providing cover, waiting for Tage to be flushed out. Stevens steps behind the tree, eager to blast Tage and sees...

Nothing.

Stevens spins around, scanning the area, then glances up into the trees. He sees Tage jump from one branch to another.

"In the trees. Six O'clock," Stevens shouts to Davidson as he aims up into the trees and shoots. Davidson, who has his back towards the area being sprayed, spins around. He follows Steven's gaze and begins to shoot in the same vicinity.

Tage, now on the ground, wheels around the base of the tree and charges for Davidson with a rusty pitchfork in his hand. Davidson is still shooting up into the trees when Tage thrusts the pitchfork into his body just underneath his flak jacket. The stab is so strong that Davidson is lifted off his feet like a bale of hay. Stevens negotiates the trees to get a better angle on Tage, but he circles it only to see...

Davidson, motionless, with a pitchfork protruding from his body.

Brandy continues to scrap with Bravo Leader, tearing viciously into his now bleeding hand. Bravo leader removes a large blade from his belt, and thrust the dagger into Brandy's body. Brandy howls with pain, snarling and ripping at anything he can sink his teeth into. Hollie charges toward Bravo Leader, ready to blast. Erika snatches up her gun and advances on him from the opposite direction. She is unable to shoot, with Hollie now in the line of fire. They both close the distance, but not before seeing Brandy succumb to the relentless stabs of Bravo Leader's knife. Brandy's lifeless body is thrown to the ground. Bravo Leader immediately gets himself back in the game and targets Erika as the closest threat. Hollie trains his shotgun on him, knowing he only needs a few more strides and he would be within reach. He anticipates the pull of the trigger, never wanting anything as badly as he does now. Just as Hollie's finger twitches for the pull, gunfire rips into his back. Hollie's gun goes flying and he falls to the ground. Hollie's adrenaline-filled body quickly rights itself. He stands, wheels around and staggers aimlessly, blinking hard, unsure of where he is and what he is doing.

Mitchell prepares to shoot Hollie again, but he is forced to take cover when Tage starts popping off rounds at him. Hollie snatches up a nearby sledgehammer. He is unable to carry it, so he drags it towards Bravo Leader, who is shooting at Erika. Erika huddles, waiting for the slightest pause in the discharge of Bravo Leader's weapon, and she returns fire. She aims low and clips Bravo Leader's left leg. Bravo Leader continues to shoot and Erika covers her head. Hollie summons his strength. His grunting grows into a roar as he raises the sledgehammer high above his head.

Bravo Leader turns in time to see the weighty hammer barreling down on him. Hollie crushes him, caving in his entire body, and then he pounds his unmoving body again just to be on the safe side. Hollie stumbles away looking lost; spinning around, eyes darting back and forth, wheeling in different directions, he searches for Gina.

Jacob watches from the shadows, caring more about finding Sal than the safety of his own men.

Hollie narrows in on Gina. He stumbles to his wife's side and collapses. They exchange familiar looks of undying love. They are lost in each other. Nothing else matters.

Erika spots Bell approaching to finish off Hollie and Gina. She shoots at him, but misses. She fires off rounds until the chamber of her gun flies back, empty. Bell ducks behind a lean-to with a clear shot of Hollie and Gina. He raises his rifle and takes aim. Erika picks up a metal rod leaning against the base of a tree and charges. Bell, who spots Tage out of the corner of his eye, coming up fast with an ax in his hand. He turns to shoot at Tage, who is no longer moving forward, but standing still, watching...

Bell's eyes suddenly fix on the ax hurling towards him.

Bell uses his rifle to take the brunt of the blow, but the impact thrusts him backwards. Erika then comes up behind him and drives the metal rod into his lower back and through his midsection. Bell grabs the rod protruding out from his stomach. He screams as he attempts to pull it through.

Weakened, he falls to his knees, flops backward, and dies with his body propped up by the rod.

Tage slowly approaches Hollie, who is kneeling beside Gina. Erika sits beside a tree, weeping.

"We're okay. Go check on the others," Hollie says quietly.

Tage remains still, unable to move, unwilling to leave. He places his hand on Hollie's shoulder.

"Tage, go check on Sal and the others." Tears stream down Hollie and Gina's faces. Hollie reaches up and squeezes Tage's hand, letting him know that it was okay.

Reluctantly, Tage slowly backs away, leaving Hollie and Gina alone.

"Can you move, mom?" Hollie asks Gina.

"Yeah, I think so." She brokenly responds.

Gina tries to upright herself. Her shirt is drenched with blood. She collapses as she tries to stand, but Hollie helps her to her feet. He then unexpectedly sweeps her up and into his arms.

"What are you doing? You're going to hurt yourself." They chuckle painfully at the irony of her words.

Hollie carries her towards the shack, laboring for each step. His legs begin to wobble as he takes his first step onto the porch.

"I have always regretted not doing this on our wedding day."

Slowly he makes it to the threshold of the door.

"I love you, Gina," he says in a strangled hushed voice.

"And I love, my baby daddy," Gina says with her eyes drifting closed.

They share their final laugh together as Hollie kisses her forehead and carries her inside the bullet riddled shack. The door slowly closes behind them.

Chapter 13

S<small>TEVENS</small> emerges from the shadows and slowly approaches Nevaeh, who has a handgun leveled on him. Stevens eyes her devilishly as she stands beside Sean, who is lying next to her helplessly. Sal clings to her leg. Nevaeh is terrified. Her eyes are filled with tears, and her arms shake uncontrollably under the weight of the gun. Her legs feel as though they are going to give way.

Stevens continues to move forward. "It's okay, put the gun down. I'm here to help you," he says in a soft low tone. Sal cries out for Nevaeh to not let him get any closer. Nevaeh tries to force herself to pull the trigger. She knows death is coming, but she can't commit.

"I know. I know. Not everybody can do what you're thinking about doing," Stevens says, as he moves to within arms-reach of Nevaeh.

"He's going to hurt us. Please, Nevaeh. Do something."

Stevens strides forward and calmly reaches out for Nevaeh's gun.

Her whole body trembles in fear. Stevens slowly places his hands upon the gun, with Nevaeh's finger still on the trigger.

Sal suddenly bolts.

Jacob, who had been stalking Sal from the shadows, takes off after her.

Mitchell searches for Erika, who remains hidden in a lean-to with an axe by her side. Sal races through the brush knowing exactly when to turn, leap, or crawl to get to her destination.

The thorny bushes catch on her tie-dye nightgown that hangs out of her camouflaged jacket. Jacob charges through the darkness, with every tree limb and branch reaching for him, unable to slow his unyielding pursuit.

Sal senses that someone is pursuing her, each step and every breath resulting in an involuntary squeal brought on by sheer terror. She drops down on all fours and scurries into a hollowed out tree. She places her hands over her mouth to restrain her instincts to cry out and to try and stifle her heavy breathing.

Jacob scours the area. He stares into the dark shadows surrounding him, listening, feeling, and knowing. Sal sees Jacob's boots turning in circles as he takes in his surroundings. After a few moments, he walks off and continues his search. Sal lets out a sigh of relief, though she can hear noises circling around her.

Sal hears the break of a stem behind her and she gasps. She swings her head and sees nothing but the deepest of blacks...

Out from nowhere a pair of hands snatch her and pull her kicking and screaming into her greatest fears.

Jacob lifts her up and immediately silences her cries with a strangling grip around her throat. He holds Sal up above his head, staring straight into her terrified eyes, finding immense pleasure in restricting the flow of air into her young body. As Sal's legs dangle, her fists try frantically to knock away the hands clutching her narrow throat. Her eyes red and bulging, begin to roll.

Jacob thinks about how easy it would be for him to snap her neck right now; the delight of crushing her windpipe or ripping out her throat as she calls for her daddy sends a most welcome chill down his spine. He resists satisfying his own selfish desires because he considers himself a man of honor, an officer bound by duty, and will unquestionably follow the orders of his superiors. He tosses Sal over his shoulders and sets out in the direction of his car.

Stevens encases his hands around Nevaeh's. He pushes the gun upward, twisting it in her hand to where the barrel is pointing at her face. Nevaeh's eyes go wide.

"It's okay. Shhh. I'm going to show you how it's done. I'm going to show you how to end someone's life."

Nevaeh cries out for help, she begs for him to stop. Sean lies their powerless, his shouts barely reaching the volume of a whisper. He tries to rise, but his body refuses to respond to what his brain is telling him. "Help. Help us! Somebody please." Sean's hands reaches towards Stevens as he forces the muzzle of the gun under Nevaeh's chin.

"Please, don't do this," says Nevaeh.

"I'm not going to do it, baby. You are."

He presses Nevaeh's finger down on the trigger. She uses all the strength she can muster to stop him. "No, please. Oh God. Stop." She cries out as the hammer of the gun slowly pulls back.

"Stop. Stop it. Somebody help!" Sean croaks out

"Oh God... Please..." Nevaeh's last word lingers long into the air. She shuts her eyes. She knows what's coming...

... And it all happens in a flash.

The crack of a single gunshot echoes.

Nevaeh's head flies back and Stevens' body jolts. A look of shock registers on his face.

Nevaeh's body begins to collapse, her hands still wrapped around the gun, smothered by Stevens' hands. Her body tingles all over and she feels lightheaded. Nevaeh's gun goes off and a round discharges up into the air. Stevens releases Nevaeh's hand and staggers forward. A single hole near his neck, just above his ballistic vest, trails blood.

In a fit of rage, Stevens lifts his automatic rifle and fires at will, aiming at nothing in particular; dust rises, bark flies, and leaves fall.

Several shots ring out from the shadows and bullets pierce unprotected areas of Stevens' body as he stares into the darkness. Tage steps out from the shadows, his face without expression and void of emotion. His eyes fix on Stevens as he steps toward him, his gun hanging by his side. Stevens doubles over coughing up blood; no pain, anguish or suffering shows on his face, only a look of astonishment as he stares at Tage in utter disbelief. With one final sneer, Stevens falls down on his face, lifeless.

Tage walks towards Nevaeh and Sean, looking around for Sal as he approaches. He hears someone running up behind them and he turns. Mitchell charges forward, spraying with his rifle. Tage fires a single shot that goes wide and he's empty. No more bullets, no more mags. He turns to find cover and suddenly finds himself staring straight down the muzzle of a gun pointed right between his eyes. He instantly drops to the ground as shots ring out. Nevaeh shoots at Mitchell with her eyes closed and most of her hair hanging in front of her face. Mitchell catches a bullet in his arm; literally blind luck, but it fails to slow his advance.

Without thinking, Tage grabs Stevens' assault rifle, sets his sights on Mitchell and pulls the trigger. Surprised and unprepared for the recoil, bullets from the rifle fly everywhere. He didn't believe the gun would shoot, but he had to do something, anything, even if only to say that he went down fighting.

Mitchell is unscathed by the barrage. He dives for cover behind a tree. Tage, fed up with the cat-and-mouse, marches straight in Mitchell's direction. As Mitchell attempts to peer around the tree, Tage comes up from behind him and annihilates him at point blank range.

Tage, drained, starts back toward Nevaeh and Sean. He suddenly stops dead in his tracks as a dark realization sets in. His mind spins like a tornado. His eyes angle down to the rifle in his hand. He stares at the gun like death itself. He releases it from his hand and it drops to the ground.

Nevaeh stares at Tage, confused by his odd behavior.

"Are you okay?" She asks suspiciously.

She wonders if this is the same man that everyone spoke so highly of. She doesn't really know anything about him, but she does remember the talk about him being dead.

Tage responds to her question with silence and a look of uncertainty. He looks at her, but doesn't see her or anything else, only a blur of distorted images, resulting in his blind like stare into nothing.

Nevaeh calls out again, "Tage?" Which causes him to focus momentarily. He races over to Mitchell's body and grabs his gun. He raises it in the air and pulls the trigger. It fires. He then snatches the sidearm out of Mitchell's holster, points the gun carelessly to the side, and he squeezes the trigger. The kick of the high caliber handgun jolts his arm. He turns towards Nevaeh, fuming.

Tage marches towards her, and she backs away from him terrified, unable to make any sense of his strange behavior. He extends the rear of the pistol towards her. "Take it."

She shakes her head, not knowing who or what she's dealing with.

"Take the gun," he barks as he shoves it into her hand. "Shoot it."

Nevaeh has a hard time getting her shaking hands to cooperate.

"Please, shoot it." Tage tries to say calmly.

She points the gun away, and slowly tugs on the trigger, cringing as she anticipates the recoil.

"Shoot it!" Tage screams.

Nevaeh burst into tears, "I am. I'm trying, it won't move." Tage angrily snatches the gun out of her hand and forces her to grip the assault rifle. "This one. Try this one."

He helps her to situate the gun and tries to get her to pull the trigger.

The firing mechanism doesn't budge.

Tage screams out, red faced, veins popping out of his neck, yelling into the air at the top of his lungs. He checks his hands and examines his wrist. He tears open his shirt and scans his body, but sees nothing out of the ordinary.

Nevaeh backs away, fearful, taking up a position by Sean, who is now leaning on one side. Tage continues his erratic behavior. He begins to pace, bewildered and panicked.

"You have the mark!" Nevaeh says.

The words stop Tage by the throat.

"You brought them here," she continues.

"No. I didn't." Tage yells in defiance, but his eyes give away his uncertainty. Almost trance like he locks eyes with Nevaeh. His mind slips in and out of reality.

"I saw what you just did. You can't shoot those guns without the mark."

There is no response to the truthfulness of her statement or observation. Nothing he can say that will make any sense.

Heaviness drapes over him and a haunting darkness spreads the feeling of death throughout his body. His dream of saving his daughter is and always was an hopeless nightmare.

"Where's my daughter?"

Nevaeh hesitates, unsure as to whether she would be putting Sal in danger by saying anything.

Tage glares at her, his eyes demanding a response. "Nevaeh, where is my daughter?" Before she can even respond, he rushes her and grabs her by her arms. "I'm not going to hurt you. I'm not one of them."

Erika runs up to them with an ax in her hand. "Tage?" She yells, but her words fall upon deaf ears.

"Tell me where she is," Tage says sternly. Nevaeh shakes her head, afraid, frightened by the hardened look in his eyes. Tage knows he has no time for reason.

"Where is Sal? Where is my daughter?" He savagely roars, while squeezing her flimsy arms.

Only a sliver of space separates his face from hers.

"She was here with me, and then she took off into the woods."

That's all he needed to know. In a flash he races off into the menacing woods.

Erika quickly approaches Nevaeh, "What happened?"

"I couldn't… I couldn't protect her, and she ran off. It's all my fault," Nevaeh says, racked with guilt.

"It's okay. We'll find her," Erika says.

"No. He's going to hurt her."

"What? Who, Tage?"

"Yes, he's one of them.

"What do you mean?" Erika inquires.

"He's taken the mark. He was using their guns. We saw him."

Erika is startled, confused by her words. She turns to Sean, who confirms with a nod of his head.

"Well, I know Tage. There has to be an explanation for what you think you saw." Erika speaks as though she is trying to convince herself that he hasn't turned.

"Come on. Let's get out of here before anyone else finds us. I will get you guys someplace safe and then I will find Sal."

The two women work on getting Sean to his feet and they head off in the opposite direction of Tage. Erika looks back, wondering, hoping that there is a reason, and that Sal is safe.

Jacob hurries through the woods with Sal over his shoulder. She fights his grip with all of her might. She lashes out and bites him. Jacob flings her into the air and she lands hard on the ground at his feet.

"I want my daddy," she moans, crying.

"That makes two of us. I've got a bone to pick with your dad and you're going to watch me take it out. If you bite me again, little girl, I will kill you. Do you understand that? Do you want to end up like your mother?" He maliciously asks.

Unable to hurt her physically, he wants to scar her emotionally.

"I know where my mother is. She is in heaven with Jesus and my Grammy and Grandpa. So yes, I do want to end up like her."

Jacob growls loudly. The character of this child enrages him.

Sal lets out a piercing scream when he yanks her up into the air and throws her back over his shoulder like a sack of potatoes.

Tage already knows where they are headed, and after hearing his daughter, he picks up his already relentless pace.

Jacob, the lone survivor of the assault team, arrives back at the company of vehicles with Sal still over his shoulder. He opens the passenger side of his SUV, tosses Sal into the seat, and then quickly runs to the driver's side. Jacob thrusts himself behind the wheel, fumbling with the keys.

"Seat belts," says Sal. "What?" Jacob asks, unsure of what he just heard.

"Seat belts." She repeats, as she snaps her restraints together with a click. "So we can be safe."

Jacob blows her off and starts the engine. He jams the car into gear and floors it, fish tailing as he goes. He navigates through the trees in route to the highway. The SUV kicks up dirt and rocks, dipping and rising as they traverse the uneven and dangerous terrain.

Jacob continues driving like a madman as Sal holds on for dear life. She screams for him to slow down, but her tortured cries and expressions only fuel him to drive harder and faster.

Jacob spots the path leading to the highway. The darkness is starting to give way and the moon is shining brighter. The shafts of light appearing through the trees almost give the appearance of an approaching day.

Tage spots the throw of light from the swiftly moving SUV. He charges up a creek bed and sees the SUV barreling in his direction. He races on foot into the path of the oncoming vehicle.

Jacob, spots a most welcome sight. "I don't believe it." He continues to drive like a maniac towards Tage. He accelerates, trying to get over the bumpy terrain.

"You want your daddy, Sal?" Jacob teases.

"Yes, I want my daddy," she replies with an honest heart.

"You want to see what his insides look like splattered all over the windshield?" He looks at her with a sickening grin, and turns his attention back to the road, staring intently straight ahead.

Sal stretches upward as far as she can and she catches a glimpse of Tage.

"Daddy!" She shrieks.

She notices that he is standing directly in their path, so she reaches for the steering wheel and gives it a forceful yank, causing the car to swerve wildly. Jacob turns into the skid to regain control of the car, and responds to her deed by viciously slapping her. Sal grips her face, weeping loudly.

"Daddy," she cries.

Tage stands directly in the path of the oncoming SUV, eyes fixed, gun at the ready, as the vehicle careens towards him with dust flying.

He trains the assault rifle on Jacob and opens fire. Bullets chip away at the windshield, but fail to penetrate the reinforced glass. Jacob doesn't even flinch at the hail of gunfire. Tage then aims at the engine block; bullets clang and spark, and ricochet off the hood without effect. Tage knows he's running out of time and ammunition. Whatever he's going to do, he must do quickly. The vehicle rises and falls as it continues to slam into potholes in route to its collision with Tage. Jacob's eyes are fixed on Tage as hatred motivates his fury.

"Good bye, Tage." He declares.

Sal pushes herself up to see out of the windshield. She cries for her dad and screams for him to move out of the way.

The SUV barrels forward and Tage takes aim at the tires. The vehicle hits a massive bump and rises into the air. Tage unloads the weapon and shreds one of the tires while the vehicle is airborne. It lands at an angle, trips over the flattened tire and slams down onto its side.

Tage immediately begins to question his actions. He can't believe what he's seeing. He can't believe that he shot at the vehicle with his precious daughter inside. The thought of what could happen to Sal grips him. The sliding vehicle continues grinding towards Tage. He can't even imagine the pain and suffering that would be inflicted on her if Jacob is not stopped.

Tage's jumbled thoughts are cast aside with the vehicle now nearly on top of him. He narrowly misses being hit, by diving out of its path. The front bumper of the SUV takes a dip and the vehicle commences to do somersaults in the air, flipping end over end. Tage's heart stops beating, his blood stops flowing, his limbs quit working. All has fallen still and silent; the only thing moving in heaven and on earth is the tumbling vehicle he is forced to stand by and helplessly watch. Inside the vehicle is a spinning blur; fragments of plastic and metal fly in every direction. With each flip, and every twist of the car, comes the heart wrenching sound of the grinding and crushing of metal. The reinforced windows dislodge, but don't shatter.

The smell of gas and exhaust fumes permeate the air. Jacob's body is tossed about while Sal remains strapped in. She screams, desperately trying to bury herself within her tiny arms. Jacob violently continues to twirl inside the cab, but manages to pull out his gun. He tries to take aim on Sal and he opens fire.

Pop. Pop.

Tage, racing after the fleeing car, sees the muzzle flashes illuminate the inside of the car.

Sal's screaming suddenly ceases. The SUV cartwheels to the edge of the embankment and goes over.

It tumbles down a hill and comes to rest upside down at the bottom of a rocky ditch.

A massive cloud of dust hovers over the wrecked vehicle.

Tage races to the embankment. He looks over the edge horrified by what he sees. The mangled wreck catches on fire as he runs, falls, throwing himself down the side of the hill.

"Sal! Sal!" He yells, his voice strained and raspy.

The wind sweeps through the blaze and the crackling flames roar like a furnace.

As he approaches the car, his eyes first narrow on Jacob, who is partially ejected from the wreckage, caked in dirt and bleeding profusely. His body is contorted, twisted like a hot pretzel, and he lies motionless like a limp rag doll. The inside of the vehicle is filled with smoke. Tage's voice is raw and damaged, but he screams and cries out for Sal for all he's worth. "Where are you, sweetheart?"

He peers through the open rear doors of the SUV. He spots Sal's listless body hanging upside down from her seatbelt. He quickly works his way around burning debris and makes it to the passenger side door. He suddenly gets weak when he sees Sal, still strapped into her seatbelt, but unmoving. She has cuts and scratches on her head, face, and on one of her arms where her jacket has been ripped back. Her legs hang with scratches, scrapes and abrasions on her knees. There's a pool of blood on the right side of her night gown and her nose is bleeding. He kneels down and reaches into the cab. The flames continue to grow as gas leaks from the SUV.

"Sal, honey. Wake up, okay," he pleads as he works at undoing the seatbelt. His arm is being seared by hot metal. He can hear his skin sizzle, but he doesn't flinch. He's consumed only with saving the life of his little girl; the only thing that matters to him in this world, the only good thing that life has to offer him now.

The choking smoke thickens around the vehicle. Jacob begins to cough. He looks around unaware, and struggles to free himself. A stream of fuel is running down his pant leg.

Tage manages to undo Sal's seatbelt; she falls into his awaiting arms and he carefully pulls her out of the vehicle. Jacob spots Tage heading back up the hill with Sal. Jacob stretches out his busted arm to retrieve his handgun lying on the ground. He braces his arm against his body, and muscles through his suffering, to take aim on Tage. The hammer pulls back. He completes the pull of the trigger.

Pop! Pop! The shots go wide. Tage ducks down, but continues to climb. He throws an angry glance at Jacob and marches upward, carefully holding his daughter.

Jacob's arms shakes uncontrollably as he tries to force the trigger back. He growls and yells with extreme guttural cries as his legs are consumed by the blistering heat. He drops the gun and attempts to scurry away from the vehicle.

Tage gently lays Sal on the ground, his tears flowing unashamedly. He places two of his dirty and trembling fingers on the side of her neck and checks for a pulse. Nothing.

"Oh God, please," he prays as he lowers his ear to her mouth in hopes of hearing even the faintest of breaths. Still nothing.

His body begins to shake uncontrollably as he places the side of his head on her chest. Desperate. Hopeful.

Tage checks out the pool of blood and finds a bullet hole in her shirt and discovers that she has only been grazed. He positions himself above her to do CPR, but he can't bring himself to press on her chest.

"I can't do this. What do I do?" He speaks to no one in particular as he cries resentfully. He picks up Sal and holds her in his arms. He brushes the hair away from her face and wipes the blood. Weeping, he places his hand in hers and tries to draw a heart in the air to tell her, "I love you with my whole heart." But her hand simply flops back to her unmoving body.

"Oh, God... And you want me to follow You? They followed You." He yells into the heavens. "They loved You. You've taken everything from me." His body is racked with unbearable agony as he holds Sal tightly in his arms. "I have nothing left to give..." Tage turns his attention back to Sal. "I'm sorry, baby. Daddy is so sorry." He looks up into the night sky. Tears mixing with snot from his nose made its way into the corner of his mouth.

"What do You want from me?" He shouts to God, with a heart as lifeless as the grave.

Jacob's lower body cooks against metal, as flames nearly consume the car. "Help me. Somebody help me," he screams.

Tage, with his eyes tightly shut, holds onto Sal agonizing over his loss. Faintly he hears Jacob's cries for help.

"God, I'm sorry. I'm sorry. Jesus, forgive me." Tage's eyes suddenly shoot open. His anguish turns to anger. "No!" He snarls, looking up into the sky, rocking his slain child back and forth. "I can't. I can't." He continues holding fast to Sal, screaming into the night.

He wails. He laments... He yields.

"God, I'm so sorry. I need you. Jesus, I need you." He stares at her with sorrowful eyes and kisses her forehead. He slowly lays Sal down on the ground and struggles to get his wobbly legs underneath himself. He wipes his fallen tears and snot on the sleeve of his shirt.

He forces himself, makes himself walk away.

Tage staggers towards the embankment. He looks over the edge and sees the SUV consumed by flames and Jacob screaming as he desperately tries to claw himself away from the burning wreckage. Tage stumbles down the side of the hill. Jacob's body begs to be delivered from the blistering flames licking at his lower body. He howls into the night air with a high pitched wail seldom heard from a man. With his tongue pulled back into his throat, his cries sound like a pair of feral cats brawling in an alley. His head cranes down as if he has passed out, only to be jolted back to the searing agony; like he had been strapped to a malfunctioning electric chair that can shock with the best of them but has forgotten how to kill.

Jacob spots Tage trudging down the hill; certain, even grateful that he is coming to kill him. Tage works his way around the flames, which shoot out unexpectedly as puddles of fuel ignite. When Tage reaches Jacob, he sees that his pant legs have been burned off and his legs are charred black, his legs are almost cooked down to the bone.

Tage grabs him and drags him up the hill, to the sound of Jacob's shrill cries. As they hit the crest of the hill, Tage looks down and sees Sal's body lying lifelessly on ground. The SUV explodes with brutal, bone shattering force, and the two men fall to the ground. Tage lays face down in the dirt with no reason to get up, no reason to move.

He suddenly hears the faint whisper of "Dad," but he refuses to move; unwilling and unable to believe. After hearing the beautiful sound for a second time he lifts his head and his eyes, ever so gently as to not startle or scare away whatever is happening to him. His eyes set upon Sal, still lying on her back, straining to reach for him. "Dad?" Sal calls out quietly. "Dad, are you okay?"

Overjoyed, Tage's eyes widen as a flourish of warmth rushes through his body.

Jacob watches. Still. Quiet.

Tage scrambles to her and lifts her into his arms. "Are you hurt, Daddy?" Sal says, worried.

"Daddy is fine. Daddy is wonderful. Are you okay?" Tage responds.

"You saved me, Daddy?" Sal proudly declares.

"No, Psalm. I didn't know how to save you. God did." Tage insisted.

"You saved me because you were willing to let me go." She tells him. Tage hugs Sal, delicately holding her with all the love he can gather. "Thank You, Lord. Thank You." Tage gratefully speaks out.

Sal looks at Tage with a smile filled with mixed emotions.

"Mommy wanted me to tell you she misses you." Tage stares into Sal's eyes. "And she will see us when our work is done."

"Is that right?" Tage asks.

Sal nods her head, smiling, "She looked so beautiful. She was with Temeria... and she said you did honor her, by the way your raised me."

Tage lifts her into his arms, unable to formulate words.

Tage turns towards Jacob and they lock eyes. Tage is without expression. Jacob is unable to understand any of what he had just witnessed. A fleeting moment of regret flashes across his face, then he lowers his head and breathes his last.

Tage and Sal trade looks and a smile. He resists the urge to think about what might have been. He sighs deeply, grits his teeth, and takes one painful step after another into the darkness.

Epilogue

THE pale sun finally decides to show itself, peeking over the horizon. A third of it is blacked out, refusing to give forth light. Tage, Sal, Erika, Nevaeh, and Sean gather in front of a large freshly dug grave surrounded by trees. A single paper cross lies on the newly packed dirt. Written on it are the names Hollie, Gina, Tai, and Brandy. There is also a drawing of a heart on the cross and inside the heart is written, "I love you with my whole heart." They would have buried Brad too, but his body was nowhere to be found.

The group scatters leaves and brush upon the grave to conceal it. Afterward, they join hands and pray. The sun is warm and inviting. Sal feels that God is letting them know how special they are to Him. Somehow, they know they have a purpose during this time of great sorrow, and will help others find the Truth.

The group distances themselves from the cabin and watch from high in the hills as the shack and the surrounding area buzzes with law enforcement, government officials, and news reporters.

The first three officers on site enter the shack to clear the building, and after a few minutes inside, shots suddenly rings out, followed by blood curdling screams and body parts being hurled out on of the windows. The Officers didn't know what hit them, but the group knew, once they saw Brad, or what used to be him, stagger out the front door; his skin has an eerie greenish white tint, and his darting eyes are yellow. His upper body looks as though he took several bullets to his chest and back, but there is no blood pouring from his wounds. In his mouth is one of the officer's arms, dangling like a bloody piece of chicken. He grunts and growls at nothing and takes off into the woods. The group struggles to make sense out of what they are seeing, but Sal reminds them about what the Bible says in Revelation 9:6 "During those days men will seek death, but will not find it; they will long to die, but death will elude them." Brad, who attempted to kill himself, for the sake of his brother, has become one of the flesh eating living dead.

Tage's father used to tell him that the way you end one season in your life will determine how you will begin the next. He ponders the thought as he looks at Sal, Erika, Nevaeh, and Sean. He realizes that today is a new beginning of sorts for all of them.

The shack is destroyed, and all evidence of life out in the foothills is erased. Anyone who is found dead, dying, or alive is burned.

A purple butterfly lands on Sal's shoulder, to everyone's surprise. It flaps its wings, gently hopping along the length of her arm, and then flutters off. Nevaeh and Sal, walking hand-in-hand, turn and walk off in the same direction the butterfly flew, down a weed covered hill, with the occasional flower, and a river of blood racing alongside them. Tage and Erika follow behind them carrying Sean on a makeshift stretcher.

Tage, Sal and the others don't know what the future holds, but they know the One who holds the future. No matter what happens, they are determined to fight the good fight of faith and teach people the truth about Jesus Christ and about Alexander Demetri, but right now, Tage needed to see a certain someone about his watch.

Acknowledgments

Unbelievers is a story. It is a work of fiction based on Scripture and my overactive imagination. Within the pages of this story, many of the characters, some mentioned by name, others by description, are based on real life friends and family members whom I love so dearly; those who have impacted my life in one way or another. As a writer, and with their permission, I chose to honor them in this way. Thank you, friends and family. I am blessed by your presence in my life.

To Kristi L. Smith, my wife, my best friend, and my partner in crime... I'm just curious as to how a nerd like me, landed a beauty like you? Must be a God thing because you are way out of my league. You are amazing and I love you.

To my kids, Alexis, Jaylin, Jordan, Alayna, Aleigha, and JOSIAH... Everything I do, with God's help and direction, is for you. My family is more precious to me than anything else in the world. You are all special in your own ways and I love you more than life itself. Never stop chasing after your God dream.

To my mother, Donisha Worsham... I'm married with six kids and still can't manage without your wisdom and guidance. I love you mom. Thank you for being you, thank you for being an incredible woman of God.

Frances Portillo... Where would the Smith family be without you? You edited this book under the gun and have worked with us on many projects over many years. Thank you. The best is yet to come.

I would also like to say a special thank you to my sister in Christ, dear friend and fellow Author, Linda Piercy, whose invaluable insight added a whole new dimension and dynamic to this book.

Onward and upward,

Trevor L. Smith
3 John 1:2

Author's Bio

Trevor L. Smith is a minister, produced screenwriter, award-winning film-maker, and motivational speaker. Smith graduated from New Life Bible College in Marysville, CA in 1997, has pastored for nearly 15 years, and has dedicated his life to challenging people to use their God given gifts, talents, and abilities to make an eternal difference in the world through media and art.

Trevor L. Smith lives in the Sacramento area with his wife, Kristi, and their six kids, Alexis, Jaylin, Jordan, Alayna, Aleigha and JOSIAH!

Smith also conducts writing and filmmaking camps and workshops through his Disruptive Media Academy. If you are interested in having Trevor L. Smith speak at your school, church, camp, or function, or you would like to attend or host a writing or filmmaking workshop, contact us at info@usherance.com

Copyright/Publisher Info

Usherance, Sacramento, CA
First Edition: December 2012
Cover Design: Trevor L. Smith

www.usherance.com
Editor: Frances Portillo
ISBN 978-0-9888383-0-7

Like us on Facebook:
www.facebook.com/usherance

Follow Usherance on Twitter
www.twitter.com/usherance

Follow Trevor L. Smith on Twitter:
www.twitter.com/iTrevorSmith

Interested in learning screenwriting or filmmaking?
Visit our non-profit media school, Disruptive Media Academy (www.disruptivema.org) or www.usherance.com to check out THE UNSTOPPABLE FILMMAKER book or to inquire about our classes and workshops.

Sacramento, CA

UNBELIEVERS

Trevor L. Smith

Questions about Christ, or what it means to be a Christian?
The Unbelievers novel is a *story*; a work of fiction. It is a dark depiction of a future time period that is described in the Bible regarding the rapture of the church and the great tribulation..

"For then there will be great tribulation, such as has not been since the beginning of the world until this time, no, nor ever shall be."
Matthew. 24:21

With all the craziness going on in the world today, and because of some of the unimaginable events described within the pages of this book, the author wants to tell you, and tell you again that God is head over heels in love with you. His son Jesus Christ came into the world to bring us peace, hope, life, and light. Not darkness. God's grace, mercy and forgiveness is available to all of us through faith in Jesus Christ. If you are reading this book and you find yourself wanting to begin a relationship with Jesus, or you have questions about what it means to be a Christian, feel free to contact us, we would love to connect with you.

Onward and upward,
Team Usherance
info@usherance.com